The White School

By

Patrick O'Cahir

Argus Enterprises International
New Jersey***North Carolina

The White School © 2013. All rights re-
served by Patrick O'Cahir

A-Argus Better Book Publishers, LLC

For information:
A-Argus Better Book Publishers, LLC
9001 Ridge Hill Street
Kernersville, North Carolina 27285
www.a-argusbooks.com

ISBN:978-0-6157614-7-3
ISBN: 0-6157614-7-X

Book Cover designed by Dubya

Printed in the United States of America

Dedication

To my wife Kim. Only she knows why.

Table of Contents

Elijah

Now I see why white people don't like to do stuff that get them in trouble. They got too much to lose. I mean they got trips to Bermuda, to Florida to see Disney, and just like, you know, out to eat three times a week. And I mean real restaurants, not church covered dish stuff. My friends ain't, I mean don't, got nothing like that. That's why all them get in trouble every weekend. For some of them that's the only time their momma even talk to them- when they be picking their sorry butts up from the police station.

I am black. My name is Elijah, like the prophet from the Bible. I ain't religious but my momma is. So she named me Elijah. I don't care much about the name cause all my friends think it is one of them African names like Kaneisha or Tykwan. Most of them don't know what my name means cause their momma be sleeping in on Sunday during church time. And that's because on Saturday night their momma been out drinking and messing with every fool that smile at them. Man, for what my momma is, she ain't no shame to me and my brother. She a good woman, could lose a few pounds, but she a good woman. She don't bring no embarrassment (or no fools) to our house. Ain't no one knocking on the door on Tuesday with flowers looking for a zippy repeat of Saturday night. No, not with my momma.

My daddy is gone so she love Jesus instead and believe that the Bible is what God meant for us to do. Now me, I ain't too sure about the Bible. But I ain't gonna tell momma that cause she will talk all day and night until I agree with her. But what do I know? I used to think I knew a lot. I had everything figured out-especially white people. Just like everyone else at Carver Middle School. They all say that white people be racist against black people. Everyone says that. Me too. Then I switched schools. Now I ain't too sure what I know. You see, white people ain't just white. They different in a whole lot a ways.

When I first came to East Edgewood Middle School I felt like I landed on a different planet. I'm serious. Everyone (except a few kids) kept quiet in the halls, and sat still in class. Didn't no one yell out or make wise cracks like at Carver. I remember telling momma that first day how out of place I felt I was at "The White School". You see East Edgewood Middle School is mostly white kids. Rich white kids. I mean Hummer and BMW rich. They bus us blacks, oh, I mean African-Americans, in because our school didn't make its goals last year under the No Child Left Behind Act. So that means we gets to choose to go to another school in our zone. Well, East Edgewood Middle School is that other school. And my momma says it's got the highest scores in the county so me and my brother have to go there. Momma says-then we do. So we got to learn like white kids learn. I did learn, but not all of it came from any book. Like I said, when I first got to East Edgewood I thought like, well...different than I do now.

Some of the white girls would smile at me- but most looked away. Most of the guys were cool. In my first week I heard the "N" word in the hall. Naturally, I dropped my books and bowed up. Nothing happened. Now if I hear it I just ignore 'em. Ain't no use to fight an ignorant person. That's what Mr. Bridges say anyhow. He is white, but he ain't. At first I thought he was just another redneck Assistant Principal. I mean the gut, the gray hair combed over the bald spot, and his face always be red (don't ask about his neck cause his chin sit on his collar and you can't see it); you know classic redneck Assistant Principal. I mean he was like the epitome (that means the top of something) of what I thought white people that hated black people looked like. Except for one small problem. He helped me figure out what racism really was. He is the...well, he did not deserve what Raquan done to him, I mean Raquan paid for it- besides I don't want to talk about that right now.

Like I said, some of these white girls smile at me. A couple of the teachers even kind of like me. Most don't. I mean us blacks, or should I say African-American students, bring these teachers test scores down. Like if it wasn't for us then East Edgewood Middle School would have higher scores. But they get beat every year by Atlantic Heights Middle since they let us in. Atlantic Heights don't get people transferred in- even I know that. It's too far from our neighborhood. Teachers here be constantly telling us about the scores, kind of clandestine like (that means secretly) so that we feel bad but can't say they said something. If we did our parents would call and give them a whole bunch of rough talk about racism and civil rights and stuff. These white teachers be too smart to let that happen. So there ain't nothing you can do-except tell Mr. Bridges. And even then it's just…well at least Bridges try to treat people right.

White people don't know what it be like. I mean when we get off the bus and come into the cafeteria the teachers on duty step closer to each other and hold their hand over their mouth. Most of the fools from the 'hood are too busy acting ghetto to see it. But I see it. I know what they be saying. White people don't know how obvious they can be. Glances out the side of their head. I know what those glances mean. What are they doing here? It still bother me but it don't. Like when we go to the mall and get followed by security.

Security don't follow the white kids. Sometimes the wiggers get followed but they just fools so I ain't gonna talk about them. Heck, we just going to the mall. Maybe trying to meet some girls, have some fun, hang out with my homies (that means friends), a few jokes, that's all. We don't want to steal some old lady's pocketbook or nothing. We ain't all thieves. Well, some brothers are. I ain't gonna lie about that. Some of my friends steal just to steal. They give us all a bad name. Most of us just want what white people want. A little fun on a Friday. That's it. There ain't nothing sinister (that means evil) about us. We are just kids out to be kids. But because our skin is a little dark, and we get a little loud (in the 'hood you got to be heard), security always follow us. I seen a group of white boys and they were just as loud but security didn't hassle them or ask them where they was going. But three black kids? Oooh, jeesh. You woulda thought that they was carrying AK-47's or something. Tell me that I am different then them white boys, and tell me how, and I might start to believe you. But… ah, to hell with it. It ain't gonna do no good. Some white people done made their minds up and that's it. But I digress (that means to go back to something else). Let me tell you about East Edgewood Middle School, which is what I started telling you about.

In East Edgewood Middle School the kids want to learn. I mean for real. They really want to learn. At Carver Middle School, all the kids did was bother the teachers. I even seen them give the cock-eyed janitor a wedgie one morning. That was funny though cause he was still picking at it when I seen him at lunch. In the hallway at Carver, people would scream and yell and drop their books on the floor. Some teachers put up with it but most left as soon as they could. Heck, Mr. Albemarle, this young guy from this T.E.A.C.H. America program, man, he lasted only three weeks. We knew we had him when he started crying on like the third day of school. From there he was only wasting time. One day he finally flipped out. Hollering at everyone in class and calling on the intercom for help from the office. The principal (and security) escorted him out. He was going on about "I tried to help you people" and "No wonder they can't read." When he popped out, "To hell with all you niggers!", security slapped him in the face. Our security guard was a big guy from our neighborhood, played a year of college football is what they say. But he hit Albemarle square in the face and Albemarle spun right around like a fool. But Albermarle ain't the only one that quit. Man, every year we would have all of these new teachers. It was different at East Edgewood. Most of them teachers had been there for like, their whole life. Mr. Bridges was new; I heard he taught at one of the West End schools. Yeah, maybe that's where learned about us black folk. I remember the first time I got sent to Mr. Bridges.

Like I said, I thought Mr. Bridges was just another old white guy that didn't like African-Americans. He looked like the kind on television that you just knew had no time for black kids. This was the first time that East Edgewood had us bused in so it was new for everyone. One day I get written up on a referral for being rude to my math teacher, Ms. Taschenburger. She didn't like me from jump. She went on and on how high her test scores were last year and she would always look at me and Sherise. Sherise momma is church friends with my momma. We both knew what ol' fat ass Taschenberger was thinking. Anyway, she wrote me up for back talking and being defiant. She always asking me why I didn't do my homework. So finally, I done got sick of her and told her to leave me alone. So she wrote me up. Later on, when I was in gym class, Mr. Bridges called me to his office and I was ready to go off on him too. I had been at the school for a week and I wanted to go back home. They didn't want me here and I didn't want to be here. I was never a good student anyway. But I could fit in at Carver and didn't bother the teachers that much- so they passed me on. But here, I didn't fit in-they knew it and I knew it. That whole first week I could hear momma talk on the phone at night about racism at the school. Man, I was fixing to blow. So, I get to the office and Mr. Bridges asks me what happened.

He asked me what happened.

I had been to the principal in my last school and he just start accusing and threatening as soon as you walk in. No one ever asked me what happened. But Bridges did. It made me kind of like settle down; just a little. So I told him all she care about is her test scores. And Bridges said, "No kidding? What was your first clue?" I smiled and he did his little eye thing. He kind of smiles but only with his eyes, his mouth don't move, if that make any sense. Seriously, his mouth don't move, but his eyes smile. Momma thinks I imagine it. So I stopped talking and he said that he had to assign me to lunch detention. That's it? Lunch detention? I took it and left. Back in the locker room, when I was changing, I realized he was the first white man, I mean like old white man, I had ever talked to. All the people at my last school were either black or real young. I was in the eighth grade, fifteen years old, and I had never spoken with a real white man before. Jeesh… right?

I thought about Bridges on the bus ride home. I mean the ride was an hour and a half long so what else do I do? The white kids be home in fifteen minutes cause their mommas pick them up. We got to ride all the way to… ah, who cares. Anyway, I was talking about Bridges. He was different than anyone I ever met. I about fell down when my momma met me in the front yard and told me that school had called. Didn't no one ever call from Carver so I didn't know what to expect.

"A Mr. Bridges said that you were written up for being rude to your math teacher." Before I could sell my story she said, "But he said that you were very respectful in his office and…" Then she had tears in her eyes like in church when she felt the Spirit. She grabbed the rail as she walked up the rickety front steps. "…and then he said that you seemed like a fine young man with a lot of potential, a natural leader. He said you were well spoken."

Momma broke down and hugged me right there on the stairs like we was in church but this time it was just me and her and I felt uncomfortable. That night when her friends came over to sit on the porch she bragged about me going to the White School and that they called today saying I was a natural leader. (She left out the part that I had lunch detention.) Mr. Bridges was the first person that had ever called my momma with something nice to say about me. Ten years in school (I got held back in second grade) and this was the only time that someone from any school ever said something nice about me. I went to sleep thinking about my "potential". I wasn't too sure what it meant. That's another part of learning at The White School. They teach you all these new words. At my old school all the teachers did was try to talk black- and that didn't cut it coming from some of the white teachers. Anyway, I know what potential means now. It means what you might do if you try hard enough.

A couple of weeks goes by and I see Bridges at the buses and in the halls. He would be correcting the white kids and people; ya know telling them to get to class and stuff. One day I be dumping my lunch tray and I had to walk right in front of him cause he was standing behind the garbage cans. I didn't think he remembered me but I gave him my nod as I walked by. He said, "Hey Elijah. How's things in Ms. Taschenberger's class?" I about fell out. He knew my name? He remembered me from that one time? I wanted to thank him for making my momma so happy but all I said was "Awright." He smiled with his eyes (I swear he does that) and I dumped my tray. I was so surprised that he remembered my name that I forgot to put my chocolate milk carton in the recycling bin- I just threw it in the trash. There be over a thousand kids in this school and about forty of us from Carver Middle, and he remembered my name. Jeesh… right?

A couple of weeks after that Sherise and I be talking at the end of Ms. Taschenburger's class and the old stank hag start yelling at me again. I mean everyone be talking, putting their stuff away, and she say, "Elijah, sit still and be quiet please." It just hit me wrong. I look around and all the other kids was talking away and she gonna talk about "Elijah be quiet please." Sherise laughed at me so I had to do something. I slammed my desk back and left the room. Taschenberger wrote me up but I didn't even know until Mr. Bridges called me to his office the next day.

"So what happened in Taschenburger's class yesterday?" So I tells him the story and he says, "I hear you okay, but I am going to back the teacher. Three days lunch detention." I thought, man, I hate this school. It's always the black kids in lunch detention. Every now and then one of the wiggers get in there but it's usually black people. I grabbed my referral and pushed up to leave. Then he spoke.

"Let's hear it."

I stopped and looked at him. What did he want to hear? It was like he read my mind but wanted to be sure so he tried me.

"I want to hear how they treat you here." I sat back down and looked around, then said it.

"These people are racist. They don't want us here. Especially Taschenburger."

Bridges sat back in his chair and folded his hands behind his head.

"So?"

I looked at him. What? So? Usually white people tell you how nobody is racist and then try to explain how they ain't racist and try real hard to be your friend. I spoke before I knew I was talking.

"So it ain't right."

"No, it isn't."

I stared straight through him. He didn't flinch, blink or redden his face. He just sat there. Then he tried me again.

"So what are you going to do about it?" I was like…surprised. I stood up. He looked up at me, never leaving my eyes.

"What? I'm telling you. I… some of these…" Then I got mad, but more like confused.. I was expecting him to say how everyone is treated the same. Or that they don't care if a student is "…black, white or yellow!" And then I should just shut my mouth. I mean that's all I heard in school. But I knew the way things was. I knew the truth. But here was this white guy, I mean an old white guy, with gray hair combed over and a big gut, telling me that I had been right all along- that these teachers were racist! I couldn't move my lips. I must've looked quite the fool standing there with my big mouth open. Mr. Bridges smiled with his eyes and said it again.

"So what are you going to do about it?"

"Me? What am I gonna...? What about… Me? What can I do?"

"Deal with it. Elijah, I would love to sit here and tell you that there is no racism here. I could go on and on how the students and teachers here are not racist and if anyone says anything racist then they will get suspended. That it doesn't matter if you are black, red or yellow. I could sell you that line and send you on your way." Mr. Bridges got up and looked out the window. "But I would be lying to you."

Bridges leaned down onto his desk. He looked me straight in the eye. It still makes me feel uncomfortable to look someone in the eye. In the neighborhood that means you are about to fight. But this time I looked him right back. His eyes weren't smiling.

"There are people in this school that are racist. They look at someone's skin color and judge them. The best thing you can do is learn to deal with those people. I mean I will address any name calling and stuff like that- but the other things, young man, you have to deal with yourself."

Young man? He could tell by the way I stopped moving that he had hit home.

"But…"

"Do you want the truth?"

"No, lie to me like all white people do."

Bridges didn't even blink. I mean I hit him in the white belly of his pretend world; and the man didn't even blink.

"You will see racism in your life. Your whole life." He stepped backward as if to release himself from some mold, and then walked over and sat in the other student chair next to me. His big eyes attached to mine. I dared not look away.

"Yeppir, you are most likely going to find racism on every avenue you walk down. But I will tell you this. Not all of it is obvious, and not all of it is from white people."

I was ready to run out the door. I had heard my whole life that only white folk were racist; that blacks were the "racee" of white prejudice. It didn't even make sense what he was saying. My mouth moved before I knew it.

"How can black people be prejudice? They the ones that are being put down. Have been since slavery."

"It's not just the white people are putting black people down. I mean for a couple of hundred years white society kept its foot on the neck of the black man. But, I don't know, in the last thirty years, whites have tried to make it right. I have never personally done anything to black people. Maybe my grandfather did. Who knows? But I just want you to know that racism; real racism comes from people that take your skin color into account before they get to know you."

I was so mad I was ready to pop him. How could he say this? Everybody know that it's the white people... I spoke.

"Black people are racist?"

"How do you define racism?" He threw me off with that. Racism is when white people pick on black people and don't let them get jobs and...

"Racism is when you judge, or prejudge someone based on the color of their skin. Have you ever heard anyone call you any racists names here in school?"

"When I first got here I heard the "N" word a couple of times."

"A couple of times?"

I nodded. He leaned forward again, his fingers and knuckles turning white from his weight . Most white people shy away when you talk about racism. I felt weird.

"Do you ever hear the "N" word in your neighborhood?"

I thought for a minute. Only every day, all day. That's all I ever hear in the 'hood. Nigger this and nigger that. Come here, nigger. Go away, nigger. Look at that nigger. Old fools, young knuckleheads, cute girls, old fat women, heck everyone uses the "N" word in the 'hood. That's what it's all about. Right?

"Racism is when one person, or group of people, judge another group based solely on the color of their skin, or their heritage. Did you ever hear anyone at school use any term here at school to describe a whole group?"

I closed my mouth. He was right. I heard more racism in the 'hood than I heard at school. By a long shot. That's all I hear in the 'hood, about how white people keep us down, white people are all racist, white people don't want us around…"

"Elijah?"

I could not speak. Finally words escaped through my open lips.

"Are you trying to say that white people ain't racist?"

"No, I am trying to say what I am saying. Look at racism for what it is and see it as an obstacle to overcome. It is not insurmountable. Don't let anyone ever tell you different. You are responsible for you. You will hear people blame others for their position in life, but I ask, no I'm telling you to take responsibility for what happens to you." I thought for a minute, and then I got up and left. On the bus ride home my head was buzzing again. I tuned out all the fools and their ruckus. Like I was in my own world thinking about what Bridges said.

Over the next couple of months I got into a few more problems with Taschenberger. But for some reason she didn't write me up. In June, I graduated. Momma showed up in one of her Sunday dresses and a feathery hat. It would have embarrassed me before but not now. She was so proud of me. Her and Sherise's momma yelled out when they called our names. Most everyone else was quiet when their child's name was called, but that's alright. Sherise and me just smiled at each other. We even went out to eat at this expensive place (they had napkins made of cloth) after the ceremony. Me and momma and my little brother Daniel. Some of the white kids from my class was there with their parents. I nodded at them and they waved. I kept my tie on for the whole meal. And I ate with my best manners, but Daniel spilled some water. Momma laughed.

Now I am looking forward to going to high school. Yeah, it's another White School, but that's okay. I need to take care of Elijah. Bridges says I should start checking out colleges now, ya know, shop early. I'm still black, but I like being called an African-American now. So you can keep the "N" word to yourself. I don't have any time for it. I still see some things the same, but not everything though. I also know that ol' smiling eyes Bridges was right. What I do with my life is up to me. I can blame white people but then I am no better than the redneck racist that blames black people. I got to take care of Elijah. I know I live in a racist society.

I just ain't too sure who the racists are anymore.

Momma and Me

The mottled Buick slowly inched out of the cracked driveway. The back bumper, already low, scraped lightly along the road. The brake lights brightened the trash piled in front of the abandoned house across the street. Helen McDaniel hit the brake and the car yanked to a stop. She released the pedal slowly, grimacing as the slow grinding against the asphalt reminded her of yet more degradation to her battered vehicle. The light of the dashboard cast a green glow onto her dark face. Her eyes took on an eerie glow when she grimaced bug-eyed at her daughter Hallee. As Helen lifted her foot gingerly, the car continued to inch backward, then leveled, and the grinding stopped. All was silent, until Hallee screamed.

"Watch out!" Helen hit the brake again causing the car to rock back and forth on the worn suspension system. She overthrew the gearshift into park.

"What?" she hollered.

"You almost hit that pile of trash."

"Let me drive. I been seeing that trash for two months. I know exactly where it is without even looking."

Helen jiggled the gearshift until the transmission caught in drive. The car slid forward through the Projects. She looked away from the men on the corner passing a brown-bagged bottle back and forth. Her daughter, Hallee McDaniel, a first year eighth grader at East Edgewood Middle, folded her arms to start the dialogue that had been the forefront of their daily ride to The White School.

"I hate getting up this early. The car is dragging again, there's hoodlums drinking on the corner, and we almost smashed into a pile of garbage. Plus, we are going to go broke with the gas it take to get there. Who gonna pay that bill? Why can't I just go back to Carver?"

"Don't get started on that again. Carver failed last year. The teachers failed, the students failed, everybody failed. A dang bunch of failing goin' on, that all. You were'nt getting any education..."

"Yes I was. We all got an education. There was good teachers. This just another way to give them an excuse to shut down the school. They been trying for years. Carver and I did just fine."

"Just fine is not going to get you into college, little girl. East Edgewood is the best school in the county. You know what I say about education."

The little girl crossed her arms and mocked her mother, shaking her head from side to side.

"That's why white people are successful. Because of education. They educate themselves. It has nothing to do with your skin color, little girl. It got to do with education."

"That's alright. You make fun of yo' momma. But when you get 'cepted into college, the first one in our family, you'll understand what I'm saying. Who was the last kid from Carver Middle School that went to college? Never mind, who was the last kid from the West End that went to college?"

The little girl bounced up in her seat and turned to face her mother, almost choking herself on her seatbelt.

"Oh, oh, I know. Bobby Washington. He went to Appalachian State to play football."

The young lady sat back in her seat and folded her arms. She had finally bested her mother. Finally made a point that Momma could not dispute. What Hallee really wanted was to be around her friends, kids she had grown up with, started school with, done hair with, talked about boys with - she was not concerned about the gas or the car. But her mother usually always had th last word. And suddenly, a glimmer of hope. She had left her mother speechless. The car sputtered as it left the off ramp and entered the highway. A tractor trailer blew its horn at the slow-moving vehicle. Mother and daughter stared forward as the truck passed by.

"Football?"

Disappointment fell upon Hallee like a bucket of water on the gray dying embers of a tiny campfire; victory slipped through her folded arms. She knew what momma was going to say. She pulled her arms tighter and readied for the onslaught.

"Football. When does football season start? I'll buy you some of them cleats so as you don't slip and slide as you run fo' a touchdown."

They rode in silence as the cars passed them, some hit their horns, and others shook their heads. Momma's car only went so fast. It was really embarrassing on the highway. Hallee looked back over her shoulder. She could see the lights of The West End. "The ghetto" as the white kids called it. But Hallee never thought of herself as living in a ghetto; not the real ghetto. The real ghetto was a place somewhere in New York City where the buildings were all abandoned and people walked around with guns in their hands selling crack to prostitutes. Every now and then the police would come and beat everyone up and yell "nigger" a lot. That's what she used to think of when she thought of the ghetto. Four weeks at The White School had changed all that.

Only three of her friends from her old school had been chosen in the lottery. The parents were told the lottery was indiscriminate, that students were picked "randomly" by computer. But none of the kids that had failed any classes at Carver got into The White School. Only students like Hallee that had A's and B's were chosen to go to The White School. That did not seem to be "random" to Hallee. But Hallee could not verbalize to her mother what was really bothering her. It wasn't the drive every day, because she could take the bus. It wasn't being away from her friends, as she could see them after school and all weekend. And it wasn't that the classes were harder; she just studied a lot more.

It was the white girls.

Actually, it was the rich white girls. She just didn't feel good enough around them. They weren't openly rude to her, they would do stuff like ask her where she bought her clothes. And then snicker. They didn't ignore her, although some were kind of snobby. She just didn't feel comfortable around them.

They had everything, she had nothing.

They went to Europe in the summer; she went to the Community Center. They shopped at the mall in stores like Saks and Macy's, she shopped at Wal-Mart. They could shower, brush their hair, and be out the door in minutes. If Hallee washed her hair it would take an hour to get it back the way she liked it.

They had everything, she had nothing.

Her mother's voice startled her as she sat recirculating her self-pity.

"Is anyone saying anything to you…you know, racial stuff?"

Hallee sat in silence. This is the same discussion they had once a week. She knew that if she told her mother about hearing someone whisper "nigger" every now and then, her momma would march up to the School Board with her big rehearsed speech about racism.

"No, momma. It's nothing like that. I just don't feel comfortable around all those rich white kids."

"They ain't no better than you. Don't ever let them tell you that."

"Momma, they don't have to. I hear it every day in the neighborhood when I come home. That is all I hear. The kids all be talking about The White School, the parents ask me about The White School, everybody wants to know how things are at The White School. It's like if I went to school on a different planet."

"You will let me know if they start with the racial stuff. Child, I will be up and in that school in a jiffy."

"Momma, it ain't gonna make no difference. Black people always going to be in the ghetto. It's been…"

"Child…"

Hallee knew that she had raised her momma's ire. She knew what she was going to hear. And she knew she had better not interrupt her mother while she was hearing it.

"…I used to listen to my momma tell me about Martin Luther King Jr. She met him, you know. I remember…"

Hallee heaved a sigh, loosened her arms and sat back in her seat. *Oh, God, not the Martin Luther King story.* Hallee stopped listening as her mother told the story. She would tune in from time to time to find a point to argue.

"… how momma used to tell me as a child. She told us that Dr. King said that one day little black children and little white children would go to school together. And it happening. You doing that. See? We living King's dream, don't you see?"

"Living his dream? Momma how long ago was that? Fifty years ago? Black people still live like... Ain't nothing changed. Black people will always live in the ghetto. White people don't want us with them. We different than them. They let some of us in, if we look white, and talk white, and dress white, and act white.

Then they can hold us up and say, 'Oh, look everybody, we helping the poor little black girl, isn't we wonderful?"

Her momma put both hands on the wheel. She steadied herself, and then she did that thing with her lip that she does when she's about to let loose. She talked in slow measured words. Like when she catches Hallee talking in church.

"You don't know how far we have come as a people. My momma had to go to a school that was blacks only..."

"Oh, you mean, uh, like Carver?"

Helen McDaniel drew a breath and continued like a freight train rambling past a squeaking mouse she continued.

"Child, it weren't that long ago when it was against the law for black people to even leave our neighborhood. Against the law! You could be arrested. It was against the law for black people to sit in the same restaurant as white people. It was against the law for black people to vote. Dr. King changed all that. So we may get dirty looks by some ignorant white trash as we sit in that restaurant, or go to that school, or leave our neighborhood. But we ain't getting arrested; they ain't turning them dogs loose to bite our asses, or be shooting us with them big water hoses... or beating us with clubs and sending us to jail. We got a long way to go. A long way to go..."

Her mother's eyes welled up with tears. Her lip quivered as she leaned forward and, although she was driving, she put her chin on the steering wheel. Then she leaned back and wiped her eyes. Hallee felt foolish, like when the church deacon preached about kids not being appreciative.

"They used to hang black men from trees…with ropes. I know you seen the pictures. They would beat blacks to death with sticks and clubs. To death! I once saw a bunch of white boys beat up a retarded black child for bumping into one of them. I'll never forget that. He was just trying to get by. Didn't no one help him. My sister grabbed me when I stepped up. We just watched…stood there and watched. I wasn't but seven or eight years old."

Hallee looked out the window. She hated when her momma cried. She felt better when her momma yelled at her, or sent her to her room. But she hated when momma cried. And she hated the people (it was usually white people) that made her momma cry. She saw the truck that they had cut off pull up aside them. Hallee wondered how he got behind them. He must have stopped somewhere. The man held up his middle finger. She could not hear but it was unmistakable what he said. Hallee could actually tell when people were say- ing the "N" word without hearing it. She turned back to her momma and she was wiping her eyes. Hallee stared at the road ahead.

"But we prevailed, we believed and we overcame. Nine black kids were the first to go to a white school in Arkansas back in the fifties. It was so bad that they had to call in the Army to protect them. The Army. One lit- tle girl had acid thrown in her eyes. Do ya hear me? Ac- id. The others were spat on and called names. They still went every day. And what about them shooting Dr. King? And Medgar Evers. They shot Evers right in his driveway in front of his children. In front of his children. They didn't find his killer for thirty years. And what about those young men up in Greensboro? Just boys, really. They sat at the white counter… and…"

Hallee's mother broke down and wiped her eyes. It took a few seconds but then she steeled her jaw. "… and what about Rosa Parks? Do you think she was uncomfortable? She refused to move out her seat and they arrested her. Sent her to jail. Ya know what jail was like for black folk back then? And not to forget the other people that had their houses burned down, their dignity…"

Momma broke down into sobs. Hallee looked at the trucker that had flipped the finger. He was doing it again and mouthing the "N" word so Hallee looked away. Hallee's mother had caught her breath.

"So now, my spoiled little baby, the product of all of these injustices, the benefactor of all this pain, is allowed to go to a school and learn something so she can be a success in this white world. And she's complaining. My momma, and my grandmomma would have jumped at the chance. She once told me she cannot remember a time when she saw white people that they did not hear the "N" word. Nigger. There I said it. That was her world. And now you just want to stay in the damned ghetto because you don't want to have to stand up and do your part. You don't want to be uncomfortable. And then what will you leave for your children?"

Hallee lowered her eyes. She knew that black people had always been put down, heck she learned that in second grade when big, fat, pasty skinned Ms. Magnuson read stories of the Civil Rights movement to all the kids at Lincoln Elementary School. Even then Hallee knew that she was different than white people. In an elementary school full of black children, being read to by a white teacher, Hallee knew that blacks were different. And she knew that white people didn't like them. That's the message she got from Ms. Magnuson and her stories. So all she could think about was being uncomfortable. In fifth grade her friend May May had a book with the pictures of the men that had been hung by the neck from trees. Or the one guy that the whites had dragged behind their truck. In the picture the white people were standing there with their children.

They were smiling.

She had heard Dr. King's speech for the first time when she was in the third grade but she didn't understand what it meant. She just stared back at the white teachers that were staring at them as they listened. Hallee had heard all of her mother's speeches, but like all children, decided to file it under 'Parental Banter'. She had seen the pictures, and read the stories, yet Hallee did not see that these were just average black people that were standing up for themselves. Against the odds. Like in her new school. Hallee never thought that she could be one of those people.

Until now.

Driving down the highway, with all the white people in their new cars honking at her, all the white girls in their designer clothes waiting at school to insult her, all the white teachers with their condescending looks waiting to say something about test scores, and all the people in her neighborhood waiting for some positive word from the front lines – she got it. It just clicked. Hallee turned to her mother and smiled.

"We better hurry up, Momma. I don't want to be late."

The Cafeteria Ladies

The shadowy kitchen pulled in the faint light cast off by the small bathroom bulb. The silver tables reflected what they could. The black oven stood barely visible. The heavy woman, who everyone called Miss Janet, moved slowly between the stainless steel cutting table and what she knew was the oven. Miss Janet breathed in the weak odor of pine disinfectant as she noticed a buildup of wax around the circular metal leg of the stainless steel tables. *I will have Phyllis scrub that today.* Miss Janet had to square up her books today; everything had to balance. Miss Janet saw everything in black and white, and never wanted to be in the red. And the biggest problem she had every month was balancing the books of those people on the free lunch program. She had never been a proponent of the free lunch program. She just could not understand how those people could not give their child a bologna sandwich, an apple and a soft drink in a brown bag - yet they strutted around with big, gaudy fake fingernails; at least forty dollars worth.

Forty dollars.

For that much money those people could buy lunch for their child for a month. That would be two dollars a day times five days times four weeks. Yes, forty dollars would cover it. No, free lunch was a choice that those people made. But what bothered her the most, what put 'a bee in her bonnet' (to quote her mother) was that those people could not even turn in their paperwork to get free lunch (and also free breakfast). Fill out the form, show that you have a need, turn the form back in. Your child is now given a number on the computer; they type it in and get free breakfast and lunch without paying even a dime. It was not à la carte (although that's what most of them would try just about every day). Most of the little thieves would put chips or extra cookies on their tray and act like they didn't know it was extra. Free lunch students were entitled to an entrée, a salad and milk. No chips or cookies or anything else that was not on the free lunch menu. A lot of them stole what they wanted. The others would argue. It was a constant fight. *Put the cookies back! You don't have money in your account, no chips! You can have an apple.* And then their parents would call and tell the administration how Miss Janet had embarrassed their child, had denied their child "their right to eat". But today was collection day.

Mr. Bridges always joked that they should take three of the largest boys and have them stand there while Miss Janet asked the students to pay their lunch bill. Just like in the old gangster movies. But that was before the free lunch kids got here. Bridges was a good administrator, he always supported Miss Janet. Bridges always stayed on the kids to pay their bills, but this year she had seen him (more than once) give the children money for lunch. Miss Janet was sure they never paid him back.

The sound of the walk-in freezer, its characteristic metal handle clicking, turned Miss Janet's head. It was Donna, her cook. Donna was always the first of the girls in every morning. Donna was meticulous about her food and took temperature readings every ten minutes (instead of the required thirty). Donna had been with Miss Janet for fifteen years now. They had started together at Pineville Elementary School as servers. Miss Janet had helped Donna through her husband's cancer and was like a grandmother to Donna's boys. For years Janet and Donna discussed how things have changed since they were in school. "Kids today…" kind of stuff. But the arrival of the 'No Child Left Behind', students had sent their discussions to a fever pitch level. Barely a day would go by when one of them did not relate an incident about "those kids". In the last two years their free lunch count went from three percent to twenty percent.

Miss Janet respected Donna's desire to keep the lights off in the morning and had learned to work in the dark. The pair smiled and worked without speaking. Phyllis the serving girl appeared and flicked the lights on. Donna showed her irritation by squinting at Phyllis. *Time to get to work*. Miss Janet went into her office and retrieved her list.

The list.

The list had twelve names on it. All but one were free lunch students. The odd one out was a student that Miss Janet had let purchase a lunch on credit (which was rare for her). The student was a good kid, from a good family, and Miss Janet knew that they were having financial problems. *If these free lunch kids can get away with it; once in a while one of ours can get a break too.* Miss Janet hated to give a student lunch that did not pay. Most were given peanut butter and jelly sandwiches, milk, and an apple of Miss Janet's choosing. She always kept the old apples for such children. Federal law says she could not let them go hungry. A peanut butter jelly sandwich would satisfy the Feds and their incessant handouts to those people. The silence and darkness meant relaxation time ended when Phyllis illuminated the kitchen. Miss Janet broke the silence. It was time to work.

"Phyllis, I noticed there was some sort of wax, or food build-up around the leg of the cutting table. That's the first place the inspectors check, you know."

"It will be gone before breakfast."

Phyllis was a born cleaner, her house was immaculate. Phyllis loved a clean kitchen. When students left a mess in the cafeteria, Phyllis would be furious. On more than one occasion she had told Miss Janet that there were no messes before "those kids" got here.

The girls readied themselves for the day. Donna pulled meat from the freezer so it could thaw for lunch. She mixed up powdered eggs and warmed the bagels. Phyllis brought the orange juice out in crates and unlocked the milk container. The night custodians had been helping themselves to the milk again. Miss Janet held up her list.

"I have a dozen kids that owe money. I wish the administration would do something with these kids. And, surprises, surprise, eleven of them are on the free lunch program. I don't understand those people."

Phyllis cocked her head back as she struggled with the crate of orange juice. The crate pinched her finger and she yanked her hand back. The orange juice crate fell the last three inches into the cooler. She shook her finger in the air as if to fling off the pain.

"Damn. Damn! Who owes money?"

"Those kids. The free lunch crowd. Eleven of them."

"Why do they have to pay if they are on free lunch?"

Phyllis shook her finger a few more times and then put it in her mouth.

"They did not turn their papers in on time. They charged lunches they were not entitled to. So we put it on their account. The government doesn't pay us until the paperwork is complete. So it puts us in the…"

"Sounds about right. Oh. I will tell you. Those kids trash the school. They make a mess at breakfast; they're allowed to be rude to us. Am I right, Donna? Donna, huh? Am I right?"

"You know how I feel about them. I am glad I never see the messes."

"You need to leave the kitchen once in awhile."

The trio laughed and went about their work. Donna spoke loudly as she trudged back to the oven.

"Although, I do agree with the rude part. They come pushing and shoving and demanding to pick their piece of pizza; demanding certain sandwiches…Give me this, give me that... The other kids take what you give 'em. And they're paying for it."

"You see? I'm not the only one that notices it."

Miss Janet took an interest in Phyllis's finger. She looked down her nose through bifocal glasses.

"The skin isn't broken. Does it hurt?"

"I'll be fine. I just get so distracted when I think about those friggin' kids. Why do they have to come here? They were doing just fine... Actually, we were doing just fine without them here. I don't care how they were doing any more than they care about me."

"Well, they are here, and they owe me money."

"Good luck getting it."

Donna walked over and looked at Phyllis's finger. Her face registered concern and she pursed her lips.

"Hmmm... You know what bothers me the most about those kids? Is when they complain."

"When don't they?"

"No, I mean when they complain about the food. My parents never had much, ya know, so's I understand what it's like to eat peanut butter sandwiches while the other kids are having ham and cheese. I know the feeling. But what gets my goat is when they complain about the food. It's free. They don't have to take it."

"I agree with you, Donna. One time. Just one time I want to tell them, 'Have your mother make your lunch if you don't like it.' But, hey, I need the job."

"Yeah, me too. Hey, maybe I could take up stripping…"

The girls laughed. Miss Janet smirked and nodded at Phyllis's finger.

"You know it's been ninety three days without an accident. Phyllis… do you want to report this?"

Phyllis shook her head. Miss Janet drew a deep breath.

"Then I agree with you. So many times I just wanted to tell them the same thing. Could you imagine if their mother made lunch and one of those big fake fingernails fell into their sandwich."

Phyllis had just put her finger in her mouth. She laughed as she spit it out and the girls heaved and guffawed together.

"But she's probably too busy complaining about white people to make a sandwich…"

"… or find a job."

"We can't solve that problem. Blacks have been like that since my grandpa's day. I just want my money so the books will balance."

"Yes ma'am, they have. But what does the administration say? I know…"

"Mr. Bridges talks to them, but I feel that he favors them sometime."

Phyllis turned her head quickly.

"You had better be careful; Bridges usually gets his coffee around this time. He will be in any minute."

A disembodied voice emanated from behind the food warming tower.

"Already here… and already got it."

Donna and Phyllis scurried to the freezer open mouthed, big eyed and clenching their teeth in surprise when they met up. Their faces betrayed them as guilty of running their mouths. Both stepped into the cold walk-in freezer. Miss Janet felt obligated to talk to Mr. Bridges. He was stirring his coffee as she came around the large warming tower. She looked down, and then decided to go on the offensive.

"Sorry you had to hear that. It's just that we are so frustrated with those kids."

"Those kids?"

"The 'No Child Left Behind' group that came here from Carver Middle. They are rude, very rude, they push the serving table, complain about the food, they're loud, and just about every other word either begins with 'F' or 'N'. The girls are frustrated."

"How do you think they feel?"

Miss Janet shrugged her shoulders and appeared genuinely confused by the question. Their point of view had not been a part of her opinion of them. She opened her mouth but no sound came out. Bridges spoke.

"If you had to get free lunch, how would you feel?"

Miss Janet remained mute.

"If you had to ride a bus for an hour and a half, on an empty stomach, how would you feel?"

Miss Janet made a face somewhere between exasperation and a goldfish gasping for breath.

"Do you know why some of these kids don't have their forms? It's because they haven't seen their parents in weeks, or they are constantly moving from one place to another. One weekend at their grandmothers, a couple of nights with their aunt or just staying with friends down the street. It is hard to keep track of anything, never mind one sheet of paper, under those circumstances."

"I get that. But shouldn't we hold them just as responsible as the rest of the kids? Isn't that what you always say? Prepare them for society?"

"You got me there. I do say that - don't I? I just think it is hard to teach a kid anything on an empty stomach. Anyway, I hear you. Actually, I overheard you."

Miss Janet and Mr. Bridges laughed and the tension drifted away like steam from an open pot. Bridges turned to leave. Miss Janet spoke to the back of Bridges' head.

"I still have to balance the books. I have a dozen kids that owe money."

"I know. I know about the books. But Janet, think about what it must be like to be these kids. Their whole world has changed since they got here. You don't think they feel out of place?"

"Sure they do. So why not just stay at Carver Middle?"

Still stirring his coffee, Mr. Bridges slowly made his way to the door. He stopped, spun around on one heel, and then walked straight at Miss Janet. The portly woman backed up.

"Sadly enough the ones we get have the most involved parents. Think about it. They went to the district office and filled out the papers to transfer their child. That took initiative. They wake their kids up early, and then send them to a school that's over thirty miles away."

"These are the good ones?"

"That's a heck of a way to put it. But yes. Let me say it another way. These are the children of a culture that is steeped in hopelessness, anger, and frustration. For generations they have been told they are worthless, subhuman. That their lives mean nothing. Their grand-parents were not even allowed to drink out of the same water fountains as our grandparents. Most of these 'No Child Left Behind' boys have a better chance of ending up in jail than college. Their culture has embraced their isolation and attempted to identify themselves with it."

"Then why don't they change their culture?"

"Good idea. Maybe we can help. How about we start today? With the group that volunteered to come here from Carver?"

A call from the walkie-talkie requesting Mr. Bridges to the office ended the conversation. Donna and Phyllis (who had been listening to the entire exchange through the half-open door of the walk-in cooler) emerged with still clenched teeth and prepared for breakfast. The kids came, the black kids were loud, but this time cafeteria ladies did not chastise them. And, for some reason, they quieted down. After breakfast, Miss Janet felt herself getting nervous. This was usually her big day. She typically had the front office secretary call the indebted students over the public address system. Miss Janet was a believer in doing something special like that. Maybe a little bit of shame would do these kids some good. Maybe next quarter there would be no overcharges. The whole school knew the students were being called to the cafeteria to pay off their debt. They had to stand up and shuffle past their classmates.

It was a walk of shame.

Miss Janet entered the front office. Mr. Bridges was talking to Betty Petty, the front office secretary. Betty stopped nodding and looked at Miss Janet.

"Do you want to call your over chargers now?"

"Yes."

Miss Janet fidgeted with her paper. Betty enthusiastically reached for the public address microphone. Miss Janet stepped forward and softly circled Betty's wrist.

"Let's do it a little differently this time. How about we call them individually over the classroom phone...uh, privately, and then have them report to Mr. Bridges office so we don't embarrass them."

Mr. Bridges smiled.

Betty Petty frowned.

The Perfect Lawn

Rudy Taschenberger was mowing his lawn when he heard her car crunch the gravel in the driveway. After twenty years of marriage he could tell what kind of mood she was in just by the way she stopped the car. When it rocked back and forth after jerking to a stop, like it did today, Rudy had learned it was better to work on the lawn until the sun went down. The driver side flew open and his wife emerged; she grabbed the stack of papers that she took home daily, and stormed into the house. Just like she did everyday for twenty years. He waved and as she hip checked the car door shut. A crow flew overhead and the movement caught Rudy's eye as his wife burst into the house. *Ahhh, to be that free.*

Rudy scrutinized his next door neighbor's lawn. It was getting a little ragged on the edges. *Bob must have missed it with the weed-wacker last week. Probably too busy with that pretty young wife of his.* The crow landed on the telephone pole across the street. Its cawing sound beckoned Randy to look up. *It's laughing at me.*

Rudy had already mowed and carefully observed the blurred orange line spinning a straight edge on his bluegrass lawn. Through his fogged goggles he surveyed his yard as his nostrils flared and he inhaled the fresh cut grass. If he quickened his pace he could get to his bushes before dark. The blur of a screen door signified it was time for dinner. She was going to let him have it tonight. The crow called and Rudy twisted around for one last look. *Can a crow smirk?* If so, this one was smirking at him. Then suddenly, obscenely, the beak snapped to the right. For a second the black bird hung on the pole. Then it fell. Soundlessly, it glanced off the telephone pole and slammed onto the ground. The Benson twins ran up to it, laughing and high fiving each other to the sky. The crow opened its beak one last time as Jimmy Benson cocked his pellet gun and snapped his head back and forth looking for his next victim. *Murderous little bastard.*

Rudy reached down and caressed the velvety softness of his purple tulips. *They need water.* The Benson twins were kicking the crow as Rudy dawdled outside as much as he could. Instantaneously, he knew that she would be out to chastise him. This would give her control. That was the last thing Rudy wanted. He had nothing in this marriage- no sex life, no children, and no hope. After all she had taken, he refused to let her have...

"Rudy, are you coming or not? Dinner's getting cold." The door slammed before he could respond. Marriage was like that. At least Rudy Taschenberger's marriage was like that. Whoever could come up with the most limiting statement would win for the night. Dinner getting cold was a major coup. Rudy put away his lawn sanctuary tools and trudged haltingly up the stairs like a condemned man ascending the gallows. Taking a breath, he entered the ring. His opponent's immaculate kitchen challenged his pristine lawn. She swung first by overly slamming the dishes, pushing them around the sink as she clenched her jaw. A whiff of pot roast lightened his mood. *God praise the crock pot.* For whatever she wasn't, she could do a slow cooker better than most wives. And Rudy had the extra fifty pounds to attest to that. He poured his own drink, as he usually did, and then he picked up his plate from the counter. He held it in front of her so she could give him his portion and grimaced when he saw that his piece was smaller than usual. *Eat slow tonight.* After a few minutes of accustomed silence she took another jab. *Here we go,* thought Rudy, as he settled in for round one.

"I have had it. I have had enough of this school. I have had enough of No Child Left Behind. I have had enough of these African children."

Not the black kids again.

"Ever since they came to my school they have been nothing but trouble. T-R-O-U-B-L-E. Trouble with a capitol "T".

Rudy knew better than to say something other than to act as if he was interested in her ranting. In truth, Rudy wanted to tell her to shut the hell up, something he wanted to say for the last twenty years. His mouth slowly opened as his Cremaster muscle pulled them in tight for the night.

"Oh, really. The African kids. Are they exchange students?"

"Don't get cute. And Mr. Bridges... I have had it with him kow-towing to these kids, and kow-towing to their parents. Can you believe he called me a racist to-day?"

He knew her propensity to embellish when she was upset. It became even more pronounced when someone had caught her doing something she should not.

"Bridges? He actually said that to you?"

"Oh, don't be such a fool. He is far too sneaky to say what he means. But I know he thinks I'm a racist. He literally insinuated it, in not so many words."

"Literally?" Rudy sat in silence. *Fool? Yes, you miserable bitch. I am a fool. I have been a fool for twenty fucking years. I should've left you and your saddle ass after you pulled that stunt on the honey-moon.*

"Well, what did he say actually say. dear?"

"That kid Elijah. You know comes to my class just to irritate me. He's always talking, he's never prepared, God forbid he does his homework. And pray tell, he is going to bring down my test scores."

God forbid your test scores come down.

"Well, did you write him up? You have some food on your lip."

"Are you purposely acting like ass tonight Mister?" She wiped her lip and missed the string of meat. It hung for a second, quivering with her voice. Then it fell. Rudy watched it hit her plate and get scooped up in the next forkful.

"No, I..."

"Of course I wrote him up. The last time he got assigned to lunch detention. This time Mr. Bridges called me down and let me know, and I quote, Elijah felt that I was picking on him. And, get this -that I did not like blacks."

Rudy picked at the roast. It was good. He liked the carrots and the potatoes that had stayed above water and dried out a little bit. They were brown and crunchy. He found a piece of celery. He sucked it between his teeth and tongue. It was the little pleasures in life. A piece of celery, no manhood. Food cooked to perfection while his non-orgasmic, sexless wife droned on and on about the black kids. He did not want to swallow the piece. It tasted too good with the loose gravy and the salty meat flavor. He thought of the crow, gasping for its last breath. He opened his mouth.

"I'll, well, I'll…"

"Are you even listening to me?

"Yes, you were…"

"Oh my God. It is like talking to the wall when I talk to you. How can I ever get the idea that you would understand something that I have said."

"Honey, it appears you're taking your day out on me."

"What? I would expect you to understand."

"Why don't you just transfer?"

Rudy got up from the table and poured himself a full glass of wine. He needed something to take the edge off.

"Why should I have to leave? I have been at this school for twelve years. Just because somebody decides that little darkie is not getting an education at Carver Middle school, they send their sorry black asses here."

"Well, black schools have historically been substandard. Maybe it's about time we leveled the playing field. And give old darkie a fighting chance."

"Are you saying I'm a racist also? I have done so much for those people over the years. Do you remember that I used to teach at Carver? I did my time. It did no good then, and it will do no good now. It is their culture to be stupid."

"Uh, you taught summer school thirteen years ago. Their culture? How can you say that?"

Mary glared at her husband. Their marriage had been one of acquiescence. They had never had children, after three years they stopped trying. Mary had immersed herself in her teaching, and Rudy absorbed his time at the bank. (Although once a month he visited a hooker).They made good money, lived in a good house in a good neighborhood, and from the outside the Taschenburgers appeared to be good, God-fearing, tax-paying Americans. But Mary's experience at Carver middle school thirteen years ago left her jaded toward black people.

That whole summer she came home in tears. They tore down her bulletin boards, ruined her group activities, and interrupted her class each minute. One day she stayed a little later than usual and a strange man, who was later arrested for murder, was milling around her car. Mary was trapped and called her husband to come get her. By the time Rudy arrived thirty minutes later the man was gone. The next year Mary got a job at East Edgewood Middle school.

The White School.

With a receptive audience, Mary very quickly became known as the teacher with the highest test scores in the county. "Give me kids that want to learn (and also that wear Gucci and vacation in Europe) and I will give you high test scores." That was until the ghosts of Carver returned.

"I just don't see why they don't stay where they stayed for decades. Things were fine. They were happy, we were happy, everything worked out."

Rudy had had enough. He had been hearing about the Carver kids for months now. This cold, lifeless marriage was starting to bother him. As he approached middle age he thought of all the things that he could have done with his life. He was not too old to have children. He could start another family. It had never been determined whether it was him or his wife that was infertile. *Maybe God decided that she was just too damned mean to have children.* Why should he have to spend the rest of his life listening to this woman complain about blacks? Integration was here to stay. Finally. It was well over fifty years ago when the Supreme Court decided to integrate the schools with 'all due haste.' And now the descendents of slaves were finally being allowed a chance at a decent education. And this miserable being that he had endured for the last twenty years wanted to stop that education.

He thought about sticking his fork in her eye. His hand tightened around the handle as he looked at the tines. *God, would she scream.* If he jammed it deep enough, maybe, just maybe this hateful pig would expire. *Gee, your Honor, I have no idea how that fork got buried in my wife's eye. Can I go now?*

"Why not read about their culture and try to understand how black kids think?"

"I understand black kids just fine. They think about basketball, they think about rap, and they think about drugs and sex. They love having children out of wedlock. They think about robbing people, stealing stuff and lying every chance they get. I understand black kids just fine. And that is none of my doing, Mister. I did not teach them these fine qualities. Their mothers did."

Mary put her hands on her hips and shook her head side to side mocking the way the black children spoke. Before Rudy could respond she continued on her tirade.

"You know you're part of the problem? People like you are the problem. All I hear from these black kids, and their parents, are excuses as to why they can't succeed. They blame the white people, they blame society, they blame the drugs, and they blame everyone but themselves. You want to stop black people from living in the ghetto? Make an announcement in every ghetto in the United States. 'Hey, all y'all, stop blaming white people and start taking responsibility.' That's what is needed to change darky's culture. Make an announcement."

Rudy sat for a minute; he had heard the same from his father years ago during the Watts riots of the sixties, the Civil Rights movement. He remembers the old man telling him that everyone is exactly where they want to be. It was back when watching the news was an event. You planned your day around it. Home from work, a beer, meat and potatoes dinner, the evening news, another beer, bedtime. Rudy's life was similar, with allowances for modern technology. He had substituted wine for beer due to an acid reflux condition he developed in the first year of his marriage. And bedtime for him did not include a squeaky mattress and muffled sounds that came from his parents' bedroom. (Unless you count his wife tossing and turning all night while complaining about the black kids in her sleep.) Rudy found himself speaking again. Maybe just to punctuate the dreariness, or to push his mundane existence to a tolerable level. And maybe the wine now absent from the glass and crossing his bloodstream had released the demons of frustration.

"How do you not see what has been done to black people over the last two hundred years? They started out as slaves in this country. Talk about the American dream? Everyone that stood up was either beaten into submission or killed. Education? It was against the law to teach a slave how to read. That is why they don't value education. And what education? That of the white society that has kept them down? The white society that holds its foot upon the neck of the males of their society? They read white history. They learn white English..."

She pushed her plate at him. It skittered off the table, dumping its contents on his lap before becoming airborne and splitting in two on the floor. Rudy clenched his fork. *Just one. Just one good fork jammed right in that that fat face of hers.* He would love to watch her fat ass fall from that chair. He could almost imagine her looking up in shock with the other good eye. He released his grip. The police don't come when you pummel them with words.

"Don't you preach to me, Mr. Unemployed Banker. It is my money that has kept this house afloat for the last six months. Six months of your whining. How all they are hiring are young guys out of college. How dare you? The food you're eating comes from my money. That shirt -I bought it. Then for once I have a bad day because some bucket beggars are ruining my school I don't need you to... That's exactly it. I don't need you."

She got up from the table.

Rudy did the dishes, wiped the table and swept the floor, and wrapped up what was left of the dinner. He would have this for lunch tomorrow. The rest of the evening went as usual. Rudy watched the news on CNN, switched to the McNeil Lehrer hour, read the financial page, and went downstairs. Mary went about her nightly ritual of cold cream, curlers and her long flannel nightgown.

As usual he pretended to fall asleep in the easy chair. She looked at him and harrumphed before returning to the cold marital bed. As soon as his wife was asleep Rudy dialed her number. Fifteen minutes later he was on his way to his monthly tryst.

Tonight he was going to get all three hundred dollars worth.

A Broken Down Bus

Darius Scott said the bus broke down because we were black. I don't know about that. But I do know my grandma died yesterday; and I sat in the bus parking lot at school while she went to heaven. I wish I could have been there.

I don't want to get ahead of my story. My name is Sherise Jackson. My grandma had been sick for a long time with cancer. She did chemo and everything. Last weekend was real bad for Grandma. Momma almost kept me from school this week. I wish she did. But my new school don't let kids to be absent and Momma said like she always do.

"You know how them white peoples is. They just looking for a reason to send you back to Carver. You better get on to school, girl. Grandma has been through some rough times before."

Momma knows that I don't get home until after five thirty. East Edgewood Middle School was a far ride from my house, far away from my school. My real school. My home school, Carver Middle, is what is they call a failing school. We did better last year. But the school still got an "F". That means that all of us that got "A"s, well we really got "F"'s compared to the white kids. So we get to go to another school. East Edgewood - The White School. Only problem is that The White School was an hour and a half rickety-old-smelly-bus-ride away. Longer when the bus breaks down. And Darius says, the bus breaks down because we are black.

All the girls love Darius. He funny, kind of tall, gives the teachers at The White School a rough time. He has the longest dread locks I ever seen. I remember he started growing them in the third grade. His friends call him Doctor Dread, some of the girls use that name too. I like Darius, I mean I like his name better as Darius. He talk a lot about a lot of stuff, his dread locks swinging and his hands flying, but he might be right. About the bus, I mean. It is an old wobbly bus. All the other buses, the white kid's buses, are new and shiny. Some even have air conditioning. Ours has heat, I mean if Miss Lakeitha let you sit up in the front. Then you can feel the heat a little bit. You freeze your black ass off in the back. Anyway, I mean the white kids should ride the old bus cause they don't have to go as far as we do. But they don't. We do.

Our bus is full of black kids from the same neighborhood. We the ones who got lucky, they picked our number in the lottery, and so go to The White School. But they pick us up at what my grandma call oh-dark-thirty. She full of old fashioned sayings. But anyway, that's five thirty on my watch, which means I got to get up at four forty five to work on my hair. And I always said goodbye to my grandma as she be poking around the coffee pot, because one day, like yesterday, I might never see her again. The day my bus broke down. And

Darius say that happened because we black. It seemed like any other day at The White School.

We all had the windows open and Ms. Lakeitha, our bus driver, she went to turn the key and it made it a sound like someone wrapped a scarf around a puppy's head and then stepped on its foot. Everyone screamed. Ms. Lakeitha yelled to be quiet, and Darius jumped up and said, "Yeah, all you niggers shut up." Ms. Lakeitha stared at Darius and he sat down. She don't play, even Darius know that. She turned the key again and this time there weren't no sound at all. Ms. Lakeitha shook her head and said something about 'ain't nothing ever going to change'. Then she picked up the radio thing. And we all knew to be quiet when she called on the radio to get the bus fixed. At first the man on the other didn't answer and then she got that tone that black women get and asked again.

Suddenly a voice said that a mechanic would be there in ten minutes. Ms. Lakeitha said, "Sure he would." But we didn't know if she pushed the button when she said that or not. She struggled to reach two worn-out basketballs under the well. Everyone groaned.

"Ain't no use in 'plaining. Just go play, children." So Darius grabbed the first ball and jumped off the bus. All the other buses had left so the parking lot was empty. There was two old rusty baskets and we had played with them every time the bus died. It was fun the first time the bus broke down. It happened on the second day of school. All the white kids buses was leaving and someone on the other bus yelled, "The nigger bus is stuck." But no one said nothing cause we was shocked that they be calling us niggers on the second day of school. But they did. Anyway, Ms. Lakeitha just said to ignore that so we did. Even Darius did. We were all nervous about being at The White School for two days so we ran off and played and jumped around like we was at home. And there weren't no white people around so we could be ourselves. The school was empty, and it was just getting to be cool outside, with the leaves pretty, turning yellow. The boys played basketball and the girls just sat around and watched them. Darius was good. He be hitting about every shot. Then Darius pulled this skinny light-skinned kid's pants down. He tried to get Darius but tripped. We laughed and pointed like we hadn't ever seen anything so funny in our whole lives. It was comical, like grandma would say.

Then a police car came. As usual, we looked at each other.

And then another one. They took the basketball from the boys and asked Ms. Lakeitha to come and talk to them. Ms. Lakeitha threw her hands up and one policeman stepped back and put his hand on his pistol. Ms. Lakeitha shook her head and walked to us, waving with her hand to the bus.

"Back on the bus."

We all stood there and I knew that Darius was dying to say something but he kept still. Not because of the police, but because he knew that Ms. Lakeitha would 'skin his black ass'. It was in everyone's eyes. For the first time in my life I felt like a nigger. I mean I felt closer to my friends, and like we were in it together and all that. But I started to think that maybe white people were right. Maybe I was just another nigger. Maybe we were all just niggers and belonged back at the failing school. Ms. Lakeitha walked right through us as we dragged and we followed her to the bus. Out of the corner of my eye I saw something move. Some of the white teachers were looking out of the front office window. Darius pointed at them but Ms. Lakeitha shook her head no.

We got back on the bus like we was stepping into church. Everyone sat down quietly. A couple of girls did each other's hair. Some put on their ear phones. Pretty soon the boys in the back started arm wrestling and tapping each other on the head when the other one wasn't looking- you know, boy stuff. The police pulled away but parked down the street where they could keep an eye on us. We spoke about how dumb boys were. We spoke about ways to do hair. We spoke about how hungry we was. But no one spoke 'bout The White School, or the white teachers (who were still in the window). No one.

Around an hour later, when the mechanic finished twisting his wrenches and making his faces, Ms. Lakeitha said, "Sit down, time to go home." Everybody clapped. The mechanic asked when Ms. Lakeitha stopped driving for Carver Middle. Ms. Lakeitha looked in the mirror and told him that she still drove the kids from Carver, just to a different school. And then the mechanic apologized that she had to drive so far.

"Must be after seven o'clock before you get home."

"It going to take me a lot longer to get to the mountain top."

We live in Charlotte, and there ain't no mountain there. If I'm not mistaken the mountains take all day to get to. Then Darius yelled out, "This bus broke down because were black.", and everyone got quiet.

We drove home. Most everyone's momma was at their bus stop, and they was crying and carrying on plenty. Some of the kids whose momma never showed up walked close with the other kids' mommas. It was like they just came home from the war, ya know like them movies I had seen in social studies class about the big war. I mean I didn't do nothing great but I liked feeling like everyone thought I did. Everybody felt good. Then I saw my momma, she just stood there holding my little brothers hand. She had been crying, but now she stood with that face she tried to put on when she was trying to be strong. I knew that something was wrong.

I found out on the walk home that my Grandma was gone. I mean they took her away. Later on I heard Momma tell my auntie how she had found her, and knew. She just held her hand, and my little brother held her other hand. After awhile momma had called the preacher and he got things going. Momma had just stood there holding hands with my little brother right up until she saw me at the bus stop. She had heard the bus broke down from our neighbor.

Darius told everyone all the way home that the bus broke down because we were black.

Across Twenty Years

There was a gap of twenty-two years between them. Mrs. Gray was forty-eight years old. Victoria White was twenty-six. But if education is truly exponential then that is like comparing a new car to a horse and buggy. As always, the natural division of old versus new was inherent. The experienced teacher influencing the novice is also what kept racism alive in the public schools.

Victoria embodied the young energetic teacher full of ideas, strapped with commitment, and destined to change the lives of every student she met. Always at the top of her class, Victoria was determined to stay there. Her students would have the highest test scores in the school. Period. She knew that her test scores would mark her performance. But she also felt the need to help students overcome the cycle of poverty that marked them. Her senior project? Standardized Testing and the African American Male.

It was ironic to Victoria that during team meetings her colleagues talked about working together, sharing ideas, and giving each other their best lessons. They also snickered and complained about blacks. That was only if one of the two black teachers at East Edgewood were not around. But if loud-mouthed Ken Montel, or the soft-spoken Adelaide Raggett just happened to have been reminded that there was a staff meeting there was a behavior change that would make Dr. Jekyll cringe. Then the teachers would go overboard the other way, saying how they helped blacks, or how nice Adelaide's hair looked today. Someone would always make mention of the two black students that were doing well or how they worked at some nameless inner city school countless years ago. In the few months that she had been at East Edgewood Middle, Victoria White had seen more prejudice, more racial profiling, and more unfair treatment – than she had read about in two political science courses at the university. At times she felt that maybe she had been sheltered from racism in high school. Or maybe it was because the so-called professionals that she used to admire were so blatant about their disdain for black students.

Victoria White stood next to Mrs. Gray, a matronly woman; who would not hesitate to tell you that she started teaching in 1985. According to Mrs. Gray, she had seen it all.

"Sweetie, don't let this new stuff bother you. What they label as twenty-first century learning is the same stuff we called cooperative learning. If you stay in this business long enough, you will see that every five years they just rehash the same old crap and give it a new name. It's like the ice cream shop's Flavor of the Week."

What Amelia Gray called Flavor of the Week, Victoria White saw as progressive education. The most effective way to teach based on the latest research. But like a bee that you were afraid to swat at for fear of getting stung, Mrs. Gray droned on.

"Honey, when you have been in education as long as I have, you will know what I'm talking about. Some genius looks up with an old idea, shines it up, repackages it, and gives it a different name. Then he sells it to the ignoramuses on the school board. Then they shove it down our throats and tell us to swallow."

A loud crash snapped both faces in the direction of the gym. It was Eddy, the slightly alcoholic custodian. One of the three broken desks he was taking to the dumpster had fallen off the flat cart. He cursed as his attempt to return it to the cart resulted in the other two dropping off of the other side.

"Oh, for a minute I thought it was the darkies from Carver. Except that they would be much louder. You will know when they get here."

Amelia laughed to herself while Victoria, hoping to keep the discussion on a safe level of intellectual banter, ignored the comment. The last thing she wanted was to hear Mrs. Grays' treatise on the inferiority of the African-American student. It just made her uncomfortable. Victoria steered the conversation back to state testing.

"How else can you assess what a student knows unless you give him a test?"

"That depends what you are testing him for. Are you assessing that he can regurgitate the notes you gave better than the cretin sitting next to him? Are you assessing that the miscreant can someday use the information? Or are you assessing which level of success in life that prodigy will attain?"

This left Victoria in a quandary. Mrs. Gray actually made sense this time. The bigoted know-it-all that was universally avoided by just about everyone that knew her had made a debatable, yet intellectual, comment on standardized testing. Victoria did not know what to say. On one hand she came here to be the whiz kid teacher that produced the highest math scores. This is what she learned for four years at North Carolina State Teachers' College. This is what the latest educational research told her was important. As a freethinking, easily impressionable college student she bought it all. Everything that had been done in education for the last two hundred years was a waste of time. Trial and error by untrained teachers still utilizing medieval methods of instruction. According to her professors all that mattered were test scores. That was the measure of a teacher. Test scores-oh, and helping the inner city black students like in one of the movies they watched in Methods of Education class. It was if Amelia Gray had read her mind.

"All you young kids coming out of college today think about are the test scores. When I left college in 1984 they told us we were to make each child into a well-rounded responsible citizen. It was a nation at risk in those days. So we used hands-on activities, cooperative learning, critical thinking - the list goes on and on.

But today all they care about at the Brainwashing Institutes of America is how to teach to the test."

Victoria slipped into a confused area like a lost motorist that was given directions and did not know whether to count the next fork in the road as the first right turn. In general observation during staff meetings Victoria had characterized Mrs. Gray as a burnt-out teacher holding onto her blurred lesson plans as if they were the Rosetta Stone. If Rosalind Franklin had held onto the X-ray diffraction picture as tightly as Amelia Gray did to her worksheets she may have discovered the double helix long before Watson and Crick stole it from her. She just knew that Mrs. Grays' boring lectures dulled the minds of the students. And only Gray's way, the ancient practice of lecture and drill, could unlock the full potential of any student. Victoria wanted to walk, no she wanted to run, as far as she could from this boisterous vestige of education. She turned to leave.

"Well, okay. Anyway, I had better get going. I have morning duty."

"Where is your morning duty?"

Victoria was walking away as she spoke; hope rising as she saw an avenue of escape. She talked out of the side of her neck when she was about five feet away from Mrs. Gray.

"Cafeteria."

Mrs. Gray shook her head. Her strings of pearls jingled along with the two keys attached her ID badge. It sounded like somebody pouring a handful of pebbles down the gutter.

"I'll come with you. They should not give that duty to first-year teachers. Let me show you how to keep them in line."

With her back to Mrs. Gray, Victoria rolled her eyes. *I almost made it.* She hesitated, and searched her caffeine-deprived mind for the words that could save her. Victoria turned, opened her mouth, but expressed only air as the older woman overtook her. Mrs. Gray was already talking.

"You have to sit them down in their seat; do not give them any freedom. And make an example of a least one of them. Especially the black kids."

Shocked, Victoria's mouth stayed open and her eyes grew wide. Amelia Gray picked up on her mood.

"Sweetheart, don't give me that 'we're all equal speech' either. I started out just like you. Actually I started out teaching at Congress Middle School. Inner-city. Eighty-seven percent minority. I was going to change the world. Oh, yes I was. I was going to reach those little niglets. But I found out—just like you will—you cannot help those people."

Victoria's pace slowed. *Niglets?* She pained for a way out. *Restroom? Stop at her mailbox? Pretend to make a phone call?* She was not as upset at what Mrs. Gray said, although it was very rude, but that the old hag felt comfortable enough around Victoria to have said it at all. In her short time at East Edgewood Victoria was starting to realize that it would be harder to reach a lot of her African-American students than she had planned. Okay, no big deal. But unreachable had not entered her mind. She had commiserated with her friends during happy hour at Buzzbees Bar and Grill about the black students. But these were friends, she could trust them. And no one would use the words like Amelia Gray had spewed forth. Victoria's group all talked about racial differences intellectually; and danced lightly around their own feelings towards blacks. Each one bellowed to the group that they, of course, were not prejudiced. Her best friend, Dina Blackstone, had even dated a light-skinned black guy in college. Prejudice was "old school" mentality-it was not for the free thinking college educated minds of today's future teachers. Although their parents had enjoyed a black and white society, Victoria's generation was expected to see people in shades of gray, or more descriptively, tinges of brown. Everybody was equal. It was just that some were more equal than others. Her generation accepted all minorities. The dark kid on that Nickelodeon show; or that one on the High School Musical movie, and, boy, was that Eddie Murphy hilarious. As long as he wore glasses, and/or did not aggressively pursue white girls, her generation whittled his ethnicity into acceptance. But here was this artifact, this throwback, this hateful woman -a seasoned teacher who was supposed to be setting the example - labeling and berating African-American students. Victoria's eyes bulged as her white neck flushed unevenly.

"Oh honey, don't be so naive. Us girls have got to stick together in this business. If we don't talk frankly about reality, how could we ever solve anything?"

They had arrived at the cafeteria. The early students sat still, doing their homework or chatting quietly.

Victoria positioned herself at the center of the cafeteria. From here she could see all four corners. Things were calm and quiet.

"Things will be nice and quiet until that bus gets here."

"Yes, they will."

"Oh, so you're seeing it also?"

Victoria spoke too soon. Young and inexperienced, she went into protection mode around people she did not know, more so around the older know-it-all-teachers (like Mrs. Gray). But in her first month of teaching Victoria had softened. A lot of what they had taught her at college did not work. And a lot of what teachers, older teachers like Mrs. Gray, had said bore out to be true. Without thinking Victoria acquiesced.

"I just don't get why they have to be so loud?"

"Me either. It has something to do with living in the ghetto. Some sort of excitement level... Some sort of loudness equals existence, or maybe it's got something to do with them not being given any attention as children. The loudest one gets recognized."

"Do you really think it's that basal?"

"I am not sure. But have you ever driven through the West End at night? I went once, years ago, after a few drinks on a Friday. It was after ten o'clock and I really wanted to see how these kids lived. I drove down Martin Luther King Boulevard; wow, did I panic. It looked like a riot. I mean they were running in the street and all sorts of stuff. But then I noticed that most of them were smiling. Which killed my riot theory. Some were dancing around a car that had its stereo on, and most were drinking. I mean just about everyone had a brown-bagged something in their hand. It was insanity. And there were little ones. I mean like five and six years old. Ten o'clock at night and these little kids were playing in the street. All I could think about was the Rodney King riots."

"Rodney King?"

"He was a degenerate that got beat up by police back in the 1990's. Problem is, back then hardly anyone took video so the cops whaled on him. You wouldn't understand this, but there was life before the internet and You Tube. People did stuff and no one filmed it. Anyway, the cops beat the devil out of King for resisting arrest, evading police, stuff like that. But that part didn't make it into the video. The fact that King kept lunging at police, and trying to attack them, didn't make it into the video or the daily news either. The fact that King had been arrested a multitude of times missed the six o'clock report. The video beating of Rodney King caused riots in Los Angeles. A lot of damage and, here's the funny part, they destroyed their own neighborhood. They are protesting discrimination and yet they burn down their own neighborhood. White people just laughed. In private of course. In public we all had to act like we cared. It was so ironic. Anyway, that's what I thought about when I drove through The West End."

"You should have gone during the day. I did. Actually, they told us in school to visit the neighborhood of the kids we were going to teach…"

"Uh, that means you visited the mansions of East Edgewood? That's where our kids are from."

"No, I did this when I student taught. I did a semester at Kennedy Middle."

"Oh my, Kennedy? I have a new respect for you. How in hell did your tender ass survive Kennedy?"

"It wasn't easy, believe me. I would come home in tears every night. My boyfriend and I broke up, I was a mess. I saw that there was an opening there last August - but I would rather work as a stripper than go through that again."

Ms Gray laughed with Victoria White. The laughter shortened the gap between the old teacher and the young one. Mrs. Gray took a step closer and lowered her voice.

"Sweetheart, with that body, you will make a heck of a lot more money than you will in education!"

"I just don't understand blacks. They fight against the people that are trying to help them. I mean I have put together some good lessons, no… some great lessons. They, they trashed…I mean trashed every one of them. On the first day of school before I even got into my classroom they stole a box of pencils and my flash drive. It was so frustrating I could not even start class because my presentation that I had worked on for weeks was on that flash drive. I taught from the board the entire day."

"Yeah, I hear that. You know you think if you work hard enough and you get to a school like this they would reward you. But then they send those animals to us."

"What I don't get is where they get their attitudes from?"

"Exactly. I mean they get handed everything. Welfare, food stamps, free busing, free lunch, and let's not forget all the free Christmas presents. The yet they still are ungrateful."

"And here we are trying to give them an education so that their children do not have to grow up in the ghetto. And they still give you the hardest time. They don't do their homework, they come late to class, they disrupt everyone - and then their parents call you and tell you that you're prejudiced."

"Well, I don't have that much longer to go before I retire. I really don't know if I would recommend for a young person to get into education today. Like I said - it used to be that you started at one of the crappy schools, like Kennedy, and if you worked hard, did your time, they would move you up to a good school. A school where kids wanted to learn…"

Victoria felt relieved. She had held in her true feelings for years. Now she finally felt like she was a part of the staff. Amelia continued.

"…school where the parents taught their children. The children were prepared for school."

"And don't you love how the black teachers always intervene when you are trying to correct a black student."

"Oh my God. They did that all the time at Kennedy. I had one teacher tell me that I could not relate to the children. When I wrote a kid up she would stop him on the way to the office, take his discipline referral and then let him sit in her class for the rest of the period. I was only a student teacher so I dared not say anything."

A few students filed in from the car line. They quietly took their seats. Some put their heads down while others talked to friends.

The teacher shared moments of agreement. They looked around the quiet, well-ordered group in the cafeteria. The drawings, hung on the wall by Mr. David the art teacher, had been framed by the PTA at a cost of forty dollars each. One of the PTA members owned an art supply company. The art department was grateful that they never had a need for supplies. The walls had been painted the summer, new tables were installed last year, and the stage had been refinished over the summer. The curtains were brand new. Parents had provided the teachers with padded chairs and real office type desks. The floral arrangements in the teachers dining lounge, and the paintings on the walls added an ambience unknown in most schools.

"You know, you can't say all blacks. That would be wrong. Kevin Johnson has gone here for three years. He is an 'A' student, plays basketball, and was in last year's production of Phantom of the Opera."

"He was in 'Phantom of the Opera'? That was a dark play."

The pair laughed again. One, whose lack of experience was overcompensated by her enthusiasm and her cutting-edge style, the other whose ego said her age and lack of enthusiasm was as a result of a school system that did not work. They had bridged their gap today. The polar opposite philosophies, the twenty two years of different experiences, the view that they both had - one looking forward and one looking in the rear view mirror; all of this had been cast aside when they walked upon the common ground of how black behavior disrupted learning. The cratchety burn out and the spry energetic teacher had one thing in common. Neither one could understand why students of African-American heritage simply could not conduct themselves in a fashion that allowed for an education. There were no political parties here, affirmative action groups, or bleeding heart liberals. There stood only two teachers who spoke solely on their experience. That experience was similar. As a matter fact it was the only similar experience they shared.

"You know the funny thing is these kids have not changed in twenty-two years. What you are describing, what you went through at Kennedy, I saw the same thing in my first year, two decades ago."

"Really?"

The young teacher thought for a moment. Could it have really been the same twenty-two years ago? Everything she had heard about Mrs. Gray bore out to be true. She was a bitter, burned-out, opinionated teacher that was set her ways and believed in nothing new- unless she invented it. The kids thought she was boring, the parents knew she was repetitive, and she had been doing the same lessons since Reagan was in office. But it struck Victoria White in a hot moment of cerebral reflection, that with all of the new educational advantages, all of the research, integration of technology, new teaching methods, everything that had come about in the last twenty-two years, blacks had remained the same. But what she could not understand, nor ever would, was why. Why had all of these advances left behind a segment of the population as if they had been stranded on a desert island? Was the ghetto a desert island surrounded by moat of despair? Was there no escape from this island? She was told in college that education was the route to success. Why aren't black people following this route? Just then she stepped back into reality. That bus would be here soon. It was usually the last bus. Victoria understood that some of those students had been on the bus for an hour and a half. That could explain why they were so rambunctious when they came in. That could not explain everything.

"You know, I feel guilty talking about this..."

Mrs. Gray's large frame turned quickly. She put her hands on her hips and furrowed her brow at the younger teacher.

"How are we ever going to solve the problem if we do not first identify it?"

"I thought you taught Language Arts? You sound like a math teacher identifying the problem."

Mrs. Gray laughed and upended her coffee mug, finishing it. She swung the cup around as she moved her hands wildly. It was as if she wanted to jumpstart her words. A drop of coffee flew out of the empty cup and landed on Victoria White's crisp pink shirt. She saw it happen, as did Mrs. Gray, but in the spirit of their newly forged alliance, chose to ignore it. As Mrs. Gray began her tirade she glanced occasionally at the drying coffee on Victoria Whites clean pink shirt.

"Of course we have to identify the problem. We get these kids for a few hours a day. We try to teach them how to act, some math, English, or even history. I mean I bend over backwards trying to tie in lessons during Black history month. You would think that they would listen at least in February. They still don't do their work. The problem with blacks is not the color of their skin, it is their culture. It is a slave culture."

Victoria White glanced at the clock. They would be here any minute. It was almost eight o'clock. Maybe the bus would be late, giving her a reprieve. Regardless, she had to be in her classroom at eight fifteen. There were a few days when, for various reasons, the bus arrived after the last bell. Whoever had duty on those days wasted no time in leaving the cafeteria. Yesterday, just as she turned the corner she heard the gym door slam. She could hear them from the other side of the building laughing, yelling and rapping. Maybe today the bus would be delayed and Mr. Bridges would have to deal with them. Victoria was tired and just wanted to go to her classroom. After ten minutes with Amelia Gray, Victoria just did not have the energy to repeat herself to these kids. She thought she saw the bus pull into the loop. But while she rehearsed her reaction to the yelling and pushing, Amelia Gray continued to talk. She was not listening as Amelia wildly waved her hand, the one without the coffee cup, and said goodbye. Her heart was racing as she awaited the invasion that would pierce the silence of the cafeteria. It was like a surprise attack each morning, an expected, but unstoppable ambush. If that was the bus then any minute those kids would crash through that door pushing, laughing, and screaming. And Victoria would have to raise her voice just to be heard. And then she would have to decide whether or not to pursue the N-word that was said loud enough to hear down in the kitchen. Victoria stared blankly at Mrs. Gray's departing form and then realized the old woman was still talking.

"... And no matter what you do they still blame you for their situation. Good luck!"

"Ahh, yeah...yeah, exactly. I was just thinking about them coming in. Every day this week my stomach has been in knots. I am glad this duty is only for one week."

Almost to the corner Amelia pointed to the door.

"Here they come!"

Mrs. Gray pointed to the left of Victoria Whites' ear. It caused her body to turn and as it did she saw a flurry of activity behind the glass doors. Mrs. Gray spoke loudly to Victoria.

"There's the other part of the issue."

There in the middle of the raucous group was the new black teacher, Ken Montel. He was cutting up and joking as bad as the students were as they stampeded like a pack of buffalo into the silent cafeteria. Without his required tie and collared shirt, one would not be able to tell which was the student and which was the teacher.

Victoria took a deep breath and approached the mob.

Bridges

His father called them colored. His grandfather was less kind and more descriptive. Mr. Bridges lazily watched the three black men in front of the convenience mart as they passed around a bottle of wine. *Seven o'clock in the morning and they're drinking.* Bridges shook his head and sped up. The thought of alcohol, after last night, sickened him. Bridges slowed as he approached a small mob of students traveling along the sidewalk. A tall, blond male passed a cigarette to the kid next to him. *I know that kid.* He raised his foot and the truck slowed down. Bridges peered out the window at the students. The other student cupped the cigarette and whispered "Mr. Bridges" to his blond friend when the Assistant Principal's truck was alongside them. By the time he got out the cigarette would be gone. Bridges pushed the gas pedal.

Bridges turned the red Ford pickup into the school parking lot. Entering the building he kicked the mud off his shoes. Pulling out his master key he slipped in the side door. *Please just let me get to my desk today before something...* Mr. Montel, the new transfer math teacher walked towards him. He detected a subtle look of annoyance on his face. The smell of counterfeit

Drakkar cologne, masked by a strong alcohol carrier, preceded the well-groomed black man. Montel raised his eyebrows as if he forgot something, turned and walked the other way. *Good morning to you too, Mr. Montel. .*

Bridges continued down the hallway past the lockers, two of which were half opened, their multi colored contents hanging like the innards from a gutted deer. Bridges entered his office from the back door. He smiled sardonically when he saw the folders left over from yesterday. His desk (which would be more at home in a Fortune 500 company), although full with folders and papers, was neat and orderly.

"Good morning Mr. Bridges." His secretary, Sandy Gabrielle, smiled as she placed a cup of coffee on his desk.

"Good morning, Sandy. And how are we doing this fine morning?"

"Me? I'm fine. I guess there was a big fight in the West End last night. My husband saw it on the news this morning. Plus, you remember today is a half-day; the kids get out at twelve fifteen. I have a feeling those Carver kids are going to be, as you always say, wrapped tight today. Oh yeah, bus nineteen-oh-five called. Well actually, the bus depot called and said bus nineteen-oh-five needs you to meet them at the bus loop."

"Half day? Oh yeah. That's right. What time does nineteen-oh-five get here?"

"I'm not sure. I think it's one of the first buses."

"Thank you Sandy, I'll get out there. What happened on the bus?"

"Rasheem."

"That's all I need to know."

"Twelve-fifteen will be here before you know it."

Bridges slid into the small restroom next to his office that had 'Administration Only' at eye level. He rubbed the now dried coffee stain from his white sleeve with a wet paper towel. He looked at the little brown tidbits of paper towel and a beige wet spot on his sleeve and shook his head. Over the running water he heard shouting from the front office. He turned off the gold chrome faucet and pushed through the door. It was Mr. Montel going at it again with Sandy. Bridges' stomach had quieted but his head still pounded.

"I don't care what the machine say. There is no way I made a thousand copies this month. Somebody rigged the machine. I bet the white teachers get to make as many copies as they want. You take good care of their numbers, don't ya?" Bridges stepped in as Sandy put her hands on her hips.

"Mr. Montel, the machine counts the copies, we don't. The copies are in black-and-white so therefore it does not pick one color over the other."

"That's right—black-and-white. Black on white – just like this school. The white is already there and someone has to put the black on it or it don't make no sense. Without the black it would just be white paper."

Bridges smiled at the young black man, Montel was deadpan. "Thank you for that analogy, Mr. Montel. Surely there must be something else you can do besides hand out a worksheet."

"Mr. Bridges, are you trying to say that all I do is give worksheets?"

Bridges hesitated. Teachers were filing in and checking their mailboxes. The last thing Bridges wanted was another confrontation with Mr. Montel. He really did not feel like sending him home again today. No substitute would come at this hour. Pick your words.

"How many copies did you need, Mr. Montel?"

Mr. Montel relaxed his shoulders. He stood straighter and smirked victoriously; staring directly at Sandy he spoke.

"Just enough… just enough for my students today."

"Would one hundred and fifty be enough?"

Mr. Montel dropped the master copy on the copier. Bridges nodded. Sandy shook her head in disgust and flipped open the top of the copying machine. A thin woman, whose face appeared to have enough remodeling to put any plastic surgeon's child through college, pulled up her tight jeans as she pushed through the office door.

"I need to see Mr. Bridges."

"Yes ma'am. I'm Bridges."

The woman glanced at Mr. Montel.

"I got a problem with a …a…student bothering my Ashton." She glanced nervously, signaling with her eyes towards Mr. Montel. Bridges extended his hand. He knew that perfume. *Charlie?* It was a welcome relief from Mr. Montel's fake Drakkar concoction.

"Mr. Bridges."

"Sarah Mannheimer."

Sandy spoke from the side of her neck. Her face was illuminated by the green glow of the copying machine light.

"Don't forget bus nineteen-oh-five."

Bridges stopped at his office door, his jaw tensed, and a sudden dull pain entered his chest. It did not eclipse his throbbing headache, but it made him stop. Just a little anxiety, it always goes away. He rubbed his pectoral muscle, below the clavicle and to the left of the sternum. Sandy saw him grimace while massaging his chest.

"Are you okay?"

"Yeah, that… just a little tension…uh, anxiety. It goes away. I'll be alright."

"It's happened before? You definitely need to get that checked out."

"Yeah, I have an appointment with my doctor next month."

"Next month? You shouldn't let that go."

Bridges left for his office and slid behind his desk. He smiled as Ms Mannheimer, and just as he opened his mouth, a loud crash came interrupted him. Holding up one finger, Bridges hustled out the door, his keys jingling rhythmically. He followed the eyes of the teachers in the hallway. The crash came again, this time louder. The teachers pointed as if he were oblivious to the obtrusive sound.

"Around the corner. That black girl just stole a band instrument."

Bridges broke into his patented have run, half fast walk across the open atrium. As he rounded the corner before the band room he saw Sherise Jones zipping up her backpack. The open locker of band instruments had been rifled through.

"What happened here?"

"Always ready to blame black people for something."

"Sherise, I simply asked what happened here."

"I didn't do nothing. I be walking... then I hears..."

"How did those band instruments get on the floor?"

"I just as sooprised as you is- I just walking and bam - it all fall down."

Bridges saw a flute case sticking out of Sherise's oversized purse. He stepped closer. She smelled of mint Lifesavers and baby powder.

"Since when do you play the flute?"

Sherise turned her body to put it between Bridges and the purse. Mr. Montel rounded the corner with his copies in hand.

"Why are you even in here at this time of..."

"She with me for tutoring, Bridges." Mr. Montel approached Sherise and grabbed her by the elbow, directing Sherise to walk with him. Montel looked down, and then drew a breath.

"Hold on a minute, Mr. Montel. Sherise, is that your flute?"

"It done felled into my purse as I walked by."

"Can I have it please?"

Mr. Montel reached behind Sherise and retrieved the flute. He put it on the floor and slid it to Bridges. It stopped a couple feet short of Bridges. Both men looked at the flute case as if it were a prisoner in the halfway across the bridge at Checkpoint Charlie. Montel reconnected with Sherise's arm and directed her back to her escape route. Bridges stood still, then picked up the flute and looked around. Mr. Montel murmured to Sherise and the pair laughed. Bridges pulled his radio from his belt and stepped amongst the instruments.

"Eddie, could you come by the band room, please?"

The radio crackled. A small band of teachers had formed behind Bridges. White teachers. They spoke in hushed voices with mouths agape in disbelief. Kathy Kassman, gym teacher, marched toward Bridges. She was a pretty girl, mid-thirties (or so she said), health-conscious, and an excellent role model for the kids. Teaching physical education was her life. She had been at East Edgewood for thirteen years.

"Mr. Bridges, you know she stole that flute. And I can't believe Montel would cover for her. Sherise was not here for tutoring because Montel had just told me he thought tutoring was a …well, forget it. I just know she wasn't here for tutoring. Those kids get dropped off early, they break into the school, then run roughshod over everything…they roam the halls. I see them every morning… nobody dares say anything to them."

Kassman threw her hands in the air, shaking them like a preacher. Bridges rubbed his pectoral muscle again. The radio crackled.

"This is Eddie here."

"Eddie, would you come by the band room? There's a bunch of instruments that have been knocked out of a pile. They're all over the floor."

"Be a few minutes. I way out at the dumpster."

"Are they going to empty that thing today?"

"Suppo' to ha' done it yed'day."

Bridges returned the walkie-talkie to the back of his belt. Kassman stood awaiting an answer. Bridges put the flute back into the pile.

"I'll look into this."

Kassman threw up her hands. The others shook their heads as they dispersed. Bridges trudged towards the front office. This time he entered through the front door to the office. This was not his usual route, but it was the quickest way to get away from Kassman and her pack. Bridges extended his hand to the two parents sitting in front of Sandy. The male slowly extended his hand, limply shaking Bridges'.

"Good morning, Mr. Bridges. How are you doing this…"

"Uh, Mr. Bridges, you already have a parent waiting…"

"Oh, thanks Sandy." He turned to the frowning parents. "I will be out in a few minutes."

"And don't forget the buses. Nineteen-oh-five?"

Bridges glanced at the clock. He had five minutes before the buses pulled in. Then it would take ten minutes just to hear the bus driver's story about Rasheem. He forced a smile at the parents as they sat looking up at him.

Bridges walked briskly into his office. The clock on the wall ticked loud enough for him to look at it. I have been here less than half an hour. The Charlie perfume reminded him of the tight-jeaned parent. He sat down and, just as she opened her mouth to speak, the radio filled the room with Sandy's voice.

"Mr. Bridges? Beau Brickman just called and said there were two students smoking behind the portable classrooms."

"Was one a …"

Sandy stepped into his doorway, her radio in her hand. Smiling, she spoke into the walkie-talkie in a mocking manner.

"…tall blond kid? Yes, good guess."

"Mr. Bridges, please. One of those black transfers is bullying my son. I am sure you hear that every day, but I demand that something be done. Ashton doesn't even want to come to school, feigns a headache, or a stomach virus, or he just starts crying spontaneously. And his grades are falling- all because of those students. They are wrecking this school."

Bridges retrieved his yellow legal pad. It was full except for a few lines. He readied his pencil at the bottom of the page.

"What is your son's full name?"

"Ashton Mannheimer." Bridges placed his pencil down on the desk beside the pad.

Bridges picked up the pencil and scribbled 'Ashton Mannheimer – bullied by…' and turned his face up.

"And who is he being bullied by?"

"Some black kid name Depravius or Demonstrius, or …"

"Demetrius Blackstone?" She sat up and shot her finger at Bridges.

"Yes, that's him. He keeps pushing my Ashton and taking his pencils off his desk, stuff like that. My husband told him to sock him one, and believe me - you do not want my husband to come down here. Plus, it's not worth it. Not for one of those Carver kids. I mean getting suspended or anything like that." She leaned forward and placed the back of her hand to the side of her mouth. Her eyes darted around the empty room as if someone would hear her.

"Plus, you know how those people are. You can't say a thing to them without...you know… them crying racism." Bridges sat still, his pencil frozen in place above the yellow pad. He opened his mouth, closed it and wrote 'Demetrius Blackstone' next to 'Ashton Mannheimer bullied by-'.

"Ms. Mannheimer, I will address this first thing this morning. I know Demetrius. If this continues I will…'

"Tell him that if this continues that I am filing charges. I'll have him arrested. It needs to stop today."

"I will contact his parents. Please call me if this happens again." Bridges rose. Ms. Mannheimer stood turned on her expensive shoes, and left. Bridges, overwhelmed, looked down at his desk for a long minute. When he raised his head the other two parents sat in front of him.

"Mr. Bridges." He shook the hand of a heavy set female in a business suit. It appeared to be the first time she had worn this particular garb. The man spoke without lifting his eyes.

"We are the parents of Jillian Goodson. She is in Mr. Montel's class. We want to..."

"I'm Jillian's mom. She is a great kid; you won't never see her down here. I promise. She gets good grades. It's just…I don't want this to sound wrong, but we want to switch her out of that Mr. Montel's class."

"Do you mind if I ask why?" The Goodson's looked at each other. Papa Goodson spoke first, looking at Bridges for the first time.

"He favors the black kids." Papa Goodson held up his hand. "I know what you're gonna say, but he does. He calls on them before anyone else. My daughter sits there with her hand up and Montel always passes her by and calls on the blacks. We just want her to get a fair shake, that's all. Just a fair shake."

"I am sure that Mr. Montel is fair. Sometimes perceptions can…"

"We want her out of that class. If you won't do it we can go to the principal."

"Well, Ms. Rubenstein will not be in today. It is a half day, as I am sure you know."

"That's why we didn't think of sending Jillian today. I mean she says that you all don't do nothing during the half days anyhow."

"Uh, yes...we have normal classes during these half days. They are just shortened."

The Goodsons stood up to leave. Bridges was confused.

"Mr. and Mrs. Goodson, please sit down. Let me look into the situation, give me a chance to..."

"To tell you the truth, Mr. Bridges, we just don't think...Well, even my father don't think it's right the way these blacks carry on, like I have seen on the news, protesting and complaining 'bout every damn, er, uh, dang thing they can. Do you really think they are going to give a white kid a fair chance when they are out there yippin' and yappin' bout how unfair they have been treated? Shoot. Black teachers all think its payback time. You didn't have any bullying at this school until they let them, uh, Negroes in here. No sir, I want my daughter out of that class - pronto."

Pronto? "Well, give me a chance to talk to Ms. Rubenstein. Okay? I will call you."

The Goodsons walked away without shaking Bridges' outstretched hand. Sandy walked in and mockingly shook Bridges' hand.

"Hi, Sandy Gabrielle. I work in the front sometimes, that is, unless I am running copies for the black teacher. Glad to meetcha." Bridges smiled. "Bus nineteen-oh-five sent a kid in to get you."

"On my way."

After suspending Rasheem off the bus for throwing an apple out of the window, the rest of the morning went painfully similar to every other day at East Edgewood Middle School. Parent phone calls, hall duty as classes changed, a multitude of corrections to students yelling, pushing and running in the hall. Teacher complaints. Bridges absorbed everything from the hallway being too cold to "My classroom is a sweat box". Bridges addressed as many situations as the shortened day would allow him. Hours later, as the sun beamed high in the sky; Sandy popped her head into his office.

"Buses."

Bridges snatched his walkie-talkie and disappeared through the back door. After cueing a bus driver to move forward, Bridges called for Sandy on the walkie-talkie.

"Ring the bell. They're all here." A few seconds later he heard the distinctive sound of the dismissal bell. The students emptied out like ants from a disturbed hill. He hurried some, told others to stop running. Within ten minutes the buses left like a retreating army. Like one of Pavlov's dogs Bridges clipped his radio to the back of his belt and prepared to run the gauntlet of teachers that would accost him as he made his way back to the office. The first was Mr. Montel.

"Mr. Bridges. I don't appreciate meetings being held about me without my presence."

"What meeting are you referring to?"

"Jillian Goodson. Her parents came to my class this morning and told me that Jillian done been transferred out my class. They wanted her books and all her papers. Why I was not notified about this? And when did we start sending parents to the classes unannounced?"

"No one transferred Jillian out of your class. And you know the codeword if parents come to your class, don't you?"

"Yes, yes, I know your silly codeword. That ain't the point. They said they done met with you. And that you would check it out with the Principal. They…they were rude, and no offense, but as white trash as they come."

Why would I be offended?

"Mr. Montel, I will talk to Ms. Rubenstein about this and get back to you tomorrow."

Bridges continued down the hall. After stopping for three teachers and one child that had missed his bus, he made it to back to the office. Sandy had his coffee ready. Bridges shook his head.

"You would think the teachers would be in a good mood. They only had to work half a day. Hey, thanks on the coffee but I'm going to grab some lunch off campus. You want something?"

"Did you even eat breakfast?"

"Today or yesterday? You sure you don't want anything?"

Sandy shook her head.

"No, I'm good. But I need to go to the mechanic when I get back. I hit a pothole and now my front end is wiggling."

"I didn't notice."

The pair laughed and Bridges became serious.

"Your front wheels could be out of alignment. That could cause uneven wear."

"I know. I used to date a mechanic."

"Did he notice?"

Before she could answer he was out the door.

Sandy could see Bridges through the glass windows of the office. Her gaze was interrupted by the intrusive sound of the phone.

"It never stops." Sandy picked up the phone. "East Edgewood Middle School." She placed the phone on her chest and instinctively pointed open-mouthed toward Bridges as he was getting into his truck. She returned the phone to the side of her head and spoke quickly. The coiled cord pulled it off of her desk and it clunked on the floor. A tinny voice repeated hello three times. Sandy looked back then ran through the front door. She yelled as Bridges left the parking lot.

"It's your wife!"

He was gone.

Patty Ferguson

I do not relate well to black students, although I am, myself, what one would call black. I have listened well in school, and nodded my head as the teachers taught black history, but I just don't relate to it. In a way I resent the way Americans treat me, but it really does not affect what I want out of life.

I was born in Germany. My father is United States Army Major Robert G. Ferguson. He insisted that his children carry the names of regular people. He named me Patricia, and my brother's name is Robert. Thank God, because my mother tried to give me one of those made African names like Squabeitha or something. I am glad my dad wouldn't let her. I like my name. It allows people to not judge until they meet me.

The Germans were nice to us but we lived on base. In the military everyone is pretty much treated equally. There's no ghetto like in America. Base housing is base housing. If your father is an officer, like mine, then you lived in a bigger house. But there was no gangsta language or drooping pants. Everyone was military, we all acted the same. We had to follow the dress code on base, we spoke English and we got along. No one was naïve or color blind, and some black people stayed to themselves, but for the most part everyone stuck together as Americans. I guess I never really saw racism until I came to the States. That was in September grade. Actually, let me digress a bit. I first came to America when I was in fifth grade. I visited my father's family for Thanksgiving. They lived in Charlotte, North Carolina, just west of where I live now. It was the first time I had been exposed to Black Culture. And what a culture shock it was.

I have a huge family in the states. I had never met any of them before that Thanksgiving. I had lived my whole life on Ramstein military base. It was strange being around so many black people but what struck me was the language and the way they dressed. I had seen a couple of movies but nothing prepared me for this eye opener. I had this Uncle Reggie and all he talked about the whole dinner was racism. My cousins were all dressed like extras from some Los Angeles gang movie. And, a if on some cue, every other sentence everyone laughed raucously. And I kept hearing the "N" word. I mean when I went outside with the kids, that's all my older cousins would say. Maybe everyone is super sensitive on base but I never heard that word as much before. It devastated me when my older cousin (who was actually kind of cute) called me one. He looked right at me, and without blinking an eye, called me over.

"Come here little nigger."

I felt like I was in some Tom Sawyer book or something. It was surreal. They kept saying it over and over. Like they were trying to say it until it couldn't be said anymore. It was very uncomfortable. When I went inside one of my father's sisters said something to me but I could not understand a word she said so I went back outside to the "N" word marathon. I remember just wanting to get back to our hotel. Which we did after Aunt Kaneisha called my dad an "Uncle Tom". Dad didn't even get mad. He politely said that it was late and we had better get going. He just stared straight ahead as we drove back to the hotel. After fifteen minutes of silence he spoke. My mom flinched at the intrusion.

"So what do you think about your family?"

It was one of those questions that you really could not answer; so I said something about them being nice. Dad nodded. We spent the rest of the week exploring the mountains and even went to a Race Car Museum in Mooresville. Last year dad had "his twenty in" and retired from the Army. He had saved up a whole bunch of money and my mother wanted to get closer to her family so we moved to East Edgewood.

American education was different.

That's the first thing I noticed was the teachers-well let me be upfront. It's not all teachers; it's the white female teachers. But they make up a majority of the teachers in America. Right? They all seem so uneducated. Not in their subject, but in world affairs. Maybe it was because I had lived in Germany for so long, but I felt that they really did not know what they were talking about when it came to what was really happening in the world. I did my Black History report about American education. Everyone else, all the black kids anyway, were doing theirs on Martin Luther King or Michael

Jordan. One intellectually adept, yet socially isolated classmate (who I made instant friends with) did her report about Frederick Douglass. A couple of others did the civil rights movement and people like Rosa Parks and Medgar Evers. But the funny thing was – all the black kids got "A's" on their paper regardless if it was one paragraph or ten pages.

I have fit right in at East Edgewood. Well, with certain kids that is. I do not relate well at all to the ghetto kids. It's not about being black or white. It's about being you. I never considered myself black. But those white teachers do. It is like I am their token or something.

I am going back to Germany when I graduate. It's somewhat ironic. In America we are taught that the Germans are the racists. They are the one that claimed to be the Master Race and all that stuff. Maybe that was true sixty years ago, but they are past that now. The Germans never called me any names, or treated me any different. They never expected me to act any way, or talk a certain way, or dress a certain way. That's uniquely American. On base I felt that I was accepted for what I accomplished and the way I acted. That is not true about America. And the blacks are just as bad as the whites – worse in some cases.

Concerned Citizens

The silver Hummer pulled into the school, right into the teacher's parking lot. The man with the Italian shoes, Tag Heuer Carrera watch, and pressed white expensive shirt, straightened his van Heuson tie. He was a tall man, used to getting his way. Although he was not a lawyer his business, selling commodities overseas, had him rubbing elbows with attorneys on a weekly basis. More than one time on an out-of-town field trip he downed a few beers with his company's attorneys. He looked out of place amongst the teachers that were passing through the office as school readied to open.

"Mr. Bridges, please."

The secretary looked at him quizzically. She had not even had a chance to ask him if she could help him. His well-manicured fingernails, hundred-dollar haircut, and high-testosterone square jaw told her that he was a man of authority.

"Mr. Bridges is out at the buses."

The man turned without response and disappeared through the door. He knew where the buses were, and he knew Bridges by sight.

"Sir. Sir, you cannot go out there. Please sign in. Sir."

But it was too late. He had heard her but continued walking. He was going to corner Mr. Bridges and that was that. There was going to be no long wait for some perfunctory meeting weeks from now. His point would be made, and his threat would be conveyed.

At the bus loop Mr. Bridges saw the man striding meaningfully toward him. His gait was threatening and did not match his dress. Bridges had seen the man pull into the teacher's parking lot earlier that morning. Bridges quickly scanned his memory from the day before. He thought of the forty or fifty kids that he spoken to, the fifteen phone calls he had returned, and the two dozen or so e-mails he had received (he had of yet responded to only half of them). *Who was this man? Which one, of any, of those various methods of messaging was this man connected to?* Bridges have been doing this a long time. And he knew that parents who came this early were usually trouble. The tall man approached Bridges. Mr. Bridges automatically stuck out as hand.

"Steve Bridges, assistant principal."

"I know who you are. My son has come to the school for the last three years."

"Do I know your son?"

"What? I, er, his name is Richard Mannheimer. But that's not the issue. The issue is bus number twenty seven..."

The tall man did not appear to be used to being questioned. Mr. Bridges had caught him off guard like a heavyweight boxer that just caught one on the chin by a no named fighter. Bridges spoke again.

"We have seventeen buses. Was there an incident on one of them involving your son?"

The man cocked his head and did not attempt to hide his irritation. He took a step to the side of Bridges. Just as Bridges went to speak to him again two buses pulled into the loop. One stopped next to the two men. The driver opened the door and shouted to Bridges the number of students on that bus.

"Forty-eight."

Bridges wrote this down on his clipboard and told the driver to let the kids off. Bridges looked at the tall man.

"It should be just a minute."

The tall man's mouth opened wide and his eyebrows were raised. Mr. Bridges caught this as he walked past him to the next bus. The driver opened his door, yelled out the number of students on the bus, and once again Bridges wrote this down on his clipboard.

"I'm sorry. But all seventeen of these buses will be here with the next ten minutes."

"Oh, I see I caught you at a bad time."

"What happened on your son's bus? I haven't heard of any incidents from last night or this morning. Usually, the drivers will call in. But that's only for serious matters."

Bridges wanted to debate this man; that whatever is supposed to be up was minimal compared to what he dealt with daily. But he wanted to do so without overtly insulting the well dressed tall man. This man, who appeared to be wealthy and used to getting his way, had shaken Bridges up a little. Bridges had learned over the years that this type looked down upon teachers and school officials as if they were public servants there to serve them, and them only. He had developed a technique, which he was employing now, which (Bridges felt) leveled the playing field, and put these people in their place tactfully. Three more buses pulled in to the loop. Bridges waved them forward and walked quickly to the tall man.

"Excuse me, once again. I have to record these buses. I will be right back."

The tall man's cell phone rang, and for a minute he was in a daze. It sounded again, and then again. A student walked by and pointed at the man's pocket.

"I think your cell phone is ringing."

The main came out of his daze and reached into his pocket just as the phone stopped ringing. He looked at the screen. It was his wife. He would call her back.

"Sir, we don't allow cell phone use on our school campus. I appreciate your support on this. We like to have our adults set the example for the children."

This is not at all what the tall man expected. He expected to come in giving worn-out, tired school administrator his directives without dispute. He expected whatever menial protests the administrator put up would be quickly extinguished with his threats of the press and his lawyer. But the tall man never thought the conversation would even get that far. Yet, here he was being treated like a bus boy by this big-bellied man with the red face and thinning hair. He did not even have time to get upset because of the shock. Mr. Bridges returned to the tall man.

"I'm sorry. You were telling me about an incident on your daughter's bus."

"What? No, no… that's not the case. There is no incident. The bus…"

Two more buses pulled into the bus loop and another one appeared down the road.

"Excuse me just one minute."

The tall man turned to see this wagon train of huge yellow buses flashing their lights amidst a sea of students swarming out of them like ants. He walked straight at Mr. Bridges.

"Excuse me, what would be a good time to talk to you about my son's bus."

"Right now, I guess. Unless you want to wait…"

"Sure, I will wait until the buses are unloaded."

"No sir. After the buses are in I have to monitor the cafeteria. From there I rush to the Media Center and read the morning announcements. Then I have a meeting with the principal, but I'm free around nine thirty. How's that for you?"

"Can I just tell you about my son's bus? Will you hold still for a second?"

Mr. Bridges held up one finger and moved forward to bring the next row of buses in so that the others that were quickly piling up on the road could enter the parking lot. He went to the bus and listened as they yelled the number of students on the bus, and Bridges methodically wrote the number on his clipboard. By the time he made his way back to the tall man two more buses had come in. Mr. Bridges shook his head, threw up his hand (the one not holding a clipboard), and made his way back to the front of the buses. The tall man walked briskly towards him as Mr. Bridges worked his way from bus to bus.

The tall man had become very agitated as evidenced by his reddened face. He put his hand on Mr. Bridges shoulder, slightly turning Bridges to him. This man was not accustomed to being ignored.

"They have placed a horde of criminals on my son's bus. I want those criminals off that God damn bus and I am holding you responsible for doing so! Got it? Good day, sir." The tall man started to walk away, thought better of it and returned. "If not, you will be hearing from my lawyer." The man turned again, and stopped abruptly again. He walked angrily up to Bridges and stood inches from his face. Their faces were the same color. "And I will bring Channel Nine News Action Alert here for you to explain to them why you are putting sixty kids on a bus that was made for forty. Good day sir."

Satisfied that he had made his point, and too embarrassed to turn back, the tall man marched to his car. There he discovered a note on his windshield that rudely thanked him for parking in a teachers' parking space. He crushed the note and tossed it to the ground.

Mr. Bridges continued on his day as if he had just heard that lunch was changed from pizza to chicken soup. He listened to voicemails, scanned a dozen e-mails, and had been stopped by PTA members four times. He had been accosted by three women from the Fine Arts Network, and the president of the Athletic Booster club. Over the last three days he had been barraged by parents complaining about the change in the bus constituency. He wondered if the tall man had orchestrated the onslaught. The simple situation was that the transportation department had to consolidate two buses into one. The students from The West End were being accommodated in order to shorten their two hour long bus ride. The closest bus to that part of town was from Edgewood Highlands.

The rich section of town.

In Edgewood Highlands the smallest house was five thousand square feet. Everyone who was anyone lived in Edgewood Highlands. The children went to either private school or to East Edgewood Middle School. It was the wellspring from which the presidents of the Fine Arts Network, the Band Boosters, the Athletic boosters, and the last fifteen presidents of the PTA flowed forth. These parents would have no part of their children riding on any bus with black children. And the barrage this morning made Goodman realize that they were organized.

The tall man kicked at the crumpled note as it blew away and then got into his car. His frustration peaked as he got stuck in the line of parents dropping off their children to school in the morning. By the time he left that line he was fuming. *Tonight.* He would rally all of his neighbors tonight. He reached into his pocket. He tried to retrieve his cell phone, but it was stuck in the tight cloth. He yanked and it pulled free. Pushing one-button, three rings later, his wife answered.

"I called you."

"I know, I was in a meeting with Mr. Bridges, the Assistant Principal."

"Did you get those criminals off our bus? Richard refuses to ride the bus until they are gone."

"Call everybody you know that is tired of the damned blacks. Have them meet at our house tonight at seven. I will get Montano's to cater it. Call Montano's and tell him how many people you expect. We are going to put a stop to this."

"Yes, dear. That is a good plan. I'll get on it after my tennis lesson."

By six thirty the Mannheimer house was full of their neighbors. The guests, angry and in focused conversations, picked at the garlic bread and pasta, the bruschetta and the eggplant. There was plenty of food for everyone and a few minutes before seven o'clock everyone sat down.

"Thank you. Thank you, everyone for coming to my house on such short notice."

The group nodded. Most were still eating and drinking. They sat places the Mannheimer children had never been allowed; on the Victorian couch, the Prince Louis chairs, and the ottoman from Germany. The remaining guests either stood or perched on the various other chairs taken in from the storage room. The huge fireplace allowed ten people to sit along the sill. All in all there were over thirty people in the Mannheimer living room. Richard Mannheimer spoke again.

"We pay more taxes than anyone else at East Edgewood Middle School. I am not asking for special favor, and I'm sure none of you are either. I am asking for consideration. It is our money funneled through the PTA that pays for most of the school projects. Our money that has purchased Smart Boards for ten class-rooms. The courtyard, the flowers, the bushes, includ-ing the maintenance, is paid for by us. For many years they sent one bus to our neighborhood. Our children enjoyed riding on that bus. They may have rode a little longer than most, but the trade-off was they all had their own seat."

The group chuckled.

"They were so well behaved the bus driver could concentrate on the road. Well, that has changed."

The crowd nodded and murmured agreement. A good number were putting down their plates; others were sitting up and listening. They would listen to Richard Mannheimer. He knew everyone in the busi-ness community and had a lot of influence. If anyone could change this bussing fiasco it would be him.

"God help East Edgewood Middle administration if there is a bus accident."

The group applauded and responded randomly amidst the staccato of applause.

"I agree."

"Yes, our precious children are not safe."

"We never had any bus problems before."

"We have paid our dues; we have paid more than our share."

"This is about safety."

"There are just far too many kids on that bus."

In the corner of the room, picking a string off a cheese stick stood Maggie Evers. She lived alone with her daughter Margaret. Her husband, a New York detective, had been shot to death in their Long Island driveway when her daughter was three years old. Grief stricken Maggie sold her Long Island house at the height of the real estate boom and walked away with a tidy $200,000 dollar profit. Unbeknownst to her at the time her husband had taken out three separate life insurance policies totaling over $1.5 million dollars. That was in addition to the state life insurance and her husband's pension. Maggie was a schoolteacher at Lincoln Elementary School. Ninety five percent of her students were on the free lunch program. She obtrusively, and mockingly, cleared her throat. All heads turned to Maggie. She put her cheese stick on her plate and placed it on the cherrywood end table.

"Why don't we say what this is really about?"

Her strong New York accent reached the people before her words could. Richard Mannheimer stepped forward. The bodies between him and Maggie moved to the side like an old-fashioned Western where the hero and the outlaw faced off to draw their six shooters. Richard drew first.

"Maggie, I know you work with the uh, underprivileged children. We all appreciate your sacrifice. This is not about…"

"Racism? Sure it is. What if the bus just picked up twenty more kids, but from our neighborhood? We wouldn't have this many people at your house. However, I must say to Richard, the food is fantastic. We should meet every week."

The crowd chuckled and everyone heaved a sigh of relief. Yet they hoped Maggie would not attempt to get up on her soapbox, especially in Richard Mannheimer's house. That would be social suicide. Maggie lowered her shoulders and appeared to be backing down. Then she drew a deep breath and squared off at Richard. The crowd that had been milling back into the space between the two separated again. It was on.

"Sacrifice? I work with children that no one else wants to acknowledge even exist. With all the money in this room we should be ashamed of ourselves that there are young children going to bed with tater chips still stuck in their teeth and Mountain Dew on their breath. A spread like this could feed the families of every kid in my class for a week. And now these kids, their older brothers and sisters, want to break out of the poverty cycle. And we are conspiring like assassins to stop them. Es tu, Brutus?"

She walked forward into the no man's land between her and Richard. She looked every one of her neighbors in the eye. The women turned away, they were trophy wives. They did not have to work. They went to aerobics, took tennis lessons, vacationed in Europe, and had the occasional affair. They knew they had it good. However, most of the men stared right back. There was no husband present for them to answer to. This was a male dominated gathering. Women did what they were expected to do. Half way between them Maggie stopped and picked up her purse. Her accent preceded her again.

"You can fool yourselves all you want. This is about racism. And you should be ashamed of yourselves."

"Maggie, the bus is overcrowded; our children have to drive an extra thirty minutes. And the new, uh, students on the bus are disruptive and distract the driver. Consequentially the driver takes his eyes off the road. Therefore, our children are endangered. You can scream racism if you want. But it is my job, as a parent, to keep my child safe."

Sarah Ingle stepped forward. She was a friend of Maggie's. Sarah's husband attempted to stop her by placing his hand on her forearm. Sarah pulled away. Sarah had three children; two were in East Edgewood Middle school. The youngest stayed home with her. Since the bus change Sarah had been driving her children to school. She stood in front of Maggie with her eyebrows raised in understanding.

"Maggie, you know I am not racist. If those kids were poor white trash or something like that, I would still be here. This has nothing to do with skin color. It has to do with keeping our children safe. Not just their physical safety while they ride the bus; but their emotional safety. Both of my children have told me about the profanity, inappropriate behavior, and how those kids jump around from seat to seat. One of these kids hit my Winthrop with a book for sitting in his seat. It broke his glasses and cut his eye. Of course we went to school. But the black bus driver did not see it - so therefore it did not happen."

"Maybe they will settle down after a while. They're just kids."

"Maggie, it's been weeks. From what I hear that is how they acted on their other bus."

"I just don't want to be part of this. It just… It just isn't right."

Richard Mannheimer had heard enough. Instinctively he puffed out his chest, and then he bellowed.

"Then you are welcome to leave. The rest of us have worked all day. We have a lot to do. Tonight we have to come up with a plan, not theorize on our personality differences – or weaknesses."

Breath was held. Maggie and Richard stared into each other's eyes. She knew the rules. It was Richard's house, therefore he made the rules. Leaving would allow the conspirators to run unchecked. At least she could temper the damage they were about to cause.

"I am sorry Richard. I was just speaking my mind. Of course I would love to stay. Mainly for the food, I must confess."

The group laughed as Maggie exited through them. They filled in the void while turning their bodies to face Richard. The door slammed and they raised their chins.

"We need to start a phone calling marathon. Who can take notes?"

Sarah Ingle took a pad from her Gucci purse. She held it up. Her husband handed her a Cross pen.

"Ready."

Richard smiled. He was where he usually was. In charge.

"Okay, Bill you call our board member, Cheryl Zumwalt. I have her number. Let her know that it is election year."

Bill nodded, Sarah transcribed.

The rest of the evening was filled with each family member being assigned someone to call, or someone to coerce, or threaten. After a half hour of assignments, Richard stopped.

"It's eight o'clock. Thank you for coming, I know you have to get up early. Let's get to work."

Annie Is Not Black

Every Sunday she would sing in front of the entire congregation. No problem. It never made her nervous; she had done so since kindergarten. Looking out at her neighbors, her friends from school, and her mother as she sang was natural. But today her neighbors and friends were dozens of miles away; and her mother but a silhouette in the back of the darkened theater. And she did not feel natural.

A cluster of girls gossiped behind her. To her left, and above her, the ropes and rows of ceiling curtains gave the backstage area a mazelike appearance. She could get lost back here. Ropes were attached to curtains that looked like huge sails and could be slid on runners to hide crew members when necessary. The stage emptied into dressing rooms, prop rooms, and two rooms for makeup. There was even a huge door, the likes of which she had never seen, that pulled up on suspended rollers. It was for unloading the stage props that were delivered by truck. This stage did not resemble the stage at Carver Middle School. Carver's stage was in the gym, and it did not have any makeup rooms or anything of that sort. Behind the stage was a single door to the cracked parking lot. The only curtain was torn, worn and had not closed (the ropes were too short) since the Liberty Pentecostal church donated it back in the seventies. She looked out over the chairs in an attempt to distinguish the identity of the vague forms of the judges. Behind the five forms a cadre of bodies milled in the aisle; their whispers threaded through the silence leaving only the conspiratorial inflection of their hushed tones to anyone not within the circle. Of the fifteen teens jockeying for the main role, eleven had left the stage already. A skinny sixth grade girl, lit up by the spotlight center stage, was more than two minutes into her song.

Hallee was next.

The other students had predicted the cast already. All of them had been together in many plays, going all the way back to elementary school. Their experience told them who would get which part. Ricky Stranchion, one of the nicer white kids, bumped up to her from behind.

"Oh, I'm sorry. I didn't see you."

Hallee put her hands on her hips and was ready to let this racist jerk, whoever it was, have a piece of her mind. When she saw his face she then lowered her shoulders and exhaled in recognition. It was Ricky Stranchion from gym class. It was not like Ricky to insult blacks. He truly had not seen her.

The earnest nature of his voice decried innocence beneath his years. Ricky Stranchion was an eighth grader, small for his age, and son of Dr. Donald Stranchion. Dr. Stranchion was a generous supporter of the arts, particularly at East Edgewood Middle School. His annual contributions alone could have funded the program at Carver Middle School for ten years. Ricky had been cast in every East Edgewood play, and every musical, since sixth grade. Hallee whispered back.

"Hey Ricky."

"You nervous?"

"A little."

"First time on stage?"

Almost on cue, the music stopped. The hapless sixth grade vocalist on stage continued to sing, but without the mercy of the music, sounded like the combination of a run over yelping coyote in its death throes and the squealing brakes of the tractor trailer truck that hit the wild canine. In mid note the judges thanked her. A polite round of applause masked the snickers, while the darkness concealed the distorted faces of cohesive dismay. The skinny girl left the stage just as Hallee loudly answered Ricky's question, unknowingly projecting her voice across the theater. Even the whispering band of conspirators heard her.

"No, I sing in my church programs. Ever since I was..."

The skinny girl looked back at Hallee as she faded into the darkness. One time, while visiting her cousin's housing project in the Bronx, Hallee had thrown a cup full of ice at rat she that was scampering down the hall. The rat stopped and glared at Hallee. This skinny girl had the same look in her eyes. A metrosexual voice originating at the judges seats entered the darkened theater. Although it encompassed the entire room, it was directed at Hallee.

"We need quiet backstage."

Ricky placed his hand over his mouth, and then whispered.

"Good luck."

The intrusive omnipresent voice summoned Hallee. "Hallee McDaniel."

Her body froze. She remembered her friend Sherise telling her that she will never get into the play; that the rich white people gave money so their no talent child could get a part. Hallee's family, which consisted of her and Momma, had not given a dime. And besides, Sherise had said (and this is what echoed in Hallee's mind), 'Annie ain't black.'

When Hallee conveyed that information to her mother (on the way back from church last Sunday), her mother turned around and threatened to walk straight back to church. Hallee had had enough of the Holy Spirit for one day so she promised her mother she would try out for the play. Momma spent the rest of the walk (interrupted by a stop at Ruby's Do-Nut Shack) reminding Hallee about Dr. King, and Rosa Parks, and all the people that had sacrificed so she could go to the White School.

In the darkness of the stage, Hallee McDaniel had not moved one muscle since hearing her name. Ricky, although not blocking her path, moved further aside. The bright light beckoned to her, it was but a few steps, yet the comfort of darkness became her solace. It was like when she was swimming in the ocean and the air was cool so it felt better to stay in the water. She relished the anonymity, knowing that soon the light would expose her. She could still walk away, never having been seen. Away from the circle of light that would force everyone to make the same face; and breathe in the same thought.

She's black.

Hallee had watched all the others enter the lit circle, all of them singing for three minutes. Some rattled the pipes, most were okay, and a few were pretty good. None were black. Not that it mattered. It was unanimous among those auditioning, at least the ones that Hallee overheard. Chelsea Dufresne would be Annie. It helped when your mother was the chairman of the Fine Arts Network and raised more than eighty thousand dollars for the program. Chelsea's was Juliet in sixth grade, and last year she played Willy in Willy Wonka and the Chocolate Factory. This year Chelsea wanted to be Annie. So did Hallee. Not for a cause, or to stir up trouble, but because this might be the only chance that Hallee had to be in a musical. White people think that people like Hallee are always out to prove something, or to make statement. That may be true for some- but today and when the sun came up tomorrow; all Hallee McDaniel wanted was for a chance to sing in her school's musical. *So why not try out for the lead role and take what they give me?* For a minute Hallee thought of asking if she could sing in the darkness. But that thought was eclipsed by one undeniable belief. *Momma would kill me.*

The silence generated by her hesitation flowed like water past the lighted area, across and down the stage and swirled around the feet of the judges. The judges shifted and fidgeted, one of them cleared his throat. There should be a body appearing in the empty lit spot, and it should be some new kid named Hallee McDaniel. A new kid that hardly anyone knew at East Edgewood

Middle School. And, if she stepped forward, everyone would know that this new kid was black. Hallee stared at the illuminated area from the darkness. Ricky grabbed her arm and she flinched at the intrusion.

"Go! You're up."

Other whispers flew up like doves from the brush as the level of backstage silence rose. "Who is Hallee McDaniel?" "Where is she?" "Looks like Hallee isn't here." Heads moved side to side in the dimness of the theater. Helen McDaniel held her breath, closed her eyes and then prayed to Jesus. Just as the metrosexual voice boomed again, Hallee twisted her hips to walk off the stage. Except for one thing. Her feet would not move. She thought of Dr. King, and Rosa Parks and all the others that had sacrificed – and then it hit her.

None of them had done it alone.

They had gone on protests together, on sit-ins together, been hit by the water hoses and bit by the dogs together, no one went alone. This was not what any of them would do. This was one little foolish girl that was about to embarrass herself for trying out for the role of Annie in a stupid middle school musical. And Annie isn't black. This wasn't a speech in Washington, or a march through Selma. Even Dr. King said that they would pray together, go to jail together, and stand up for freedom together. Together. Not alone on a stage full of white girls. As soon as she believed what she was thinking, she knew how Momma would counter her argument. She could almost hear Momma quoting Dr. King. 'One day little black girls and little white girls would go to school together. And that people would judge one another not based on the color of their skin, but on the content of her character.' Hallee knew the quotes. Or of them. And she knew how her Momma would paraphrase the quotes to fit the situation (like Momma always did). That they should judge you not on the color of your skin for this role, but the beautiful voice that the Lord gave you. It would be a slap in the face of Jesus for you to hide that voice. And she knew that her mother would win - especially after she brought Jesus into the argument in that high voice that still scared Hallee. But more important and more immediate than any of that- a familiar shape had stood up and was slowly walking toward the stage.

Momma was coming for her.

Suddenly her thigh twitched and then shuddered movement down to her foot. Her mind insisted that her foot cease its movement, but it did not heed. The other foot, seeing the mutiny, pulled Hallee closer to the circle, and then waited for its partner to reciprocate. Soon the rebellious pair coordinated a progression of steps and carried Hallee right into the halo of light. She stood blinded and exposed. Hallee saw only the light and felt the halting of her mother in the aisle. The gentle creak of a chair signaled that Momma had sat back down. Hallee drew a long breath. Then the voice came.

"Ah, honey. This audition is for the role of Annie. We have the other auditions, and uh, the orientation for stage crew tomorrow."

Hallee felt her shoulder turn ever so slightly. She was used to being told what to do by adults, and she usually obeyed. Her autonomic need to fit in and conform lifted up her foot. But the other foot would not comply. Hallee could sense her Momma getting ready to speak. Hallee turned back and looked past the spot light.

"I know."

There was a murmur from the judges, an overt lip smacking from someone in the group of parents, and even a muffled snicker from the skinny girl with the scornful rat look. Hallee was out in the open, the light had stripped her of any disguise, and her feet refused to leave the ground that they had fought with every neuron to occupy.

"Okay, honey? Thank you. We will see you tomorrow at four o'clock. Four o'clock. Next, please. Quickly girls, it is getting late."

The next hopeful moved half into the circle. Hallee felt the room sway. She did what she did when she gets nervous at home. She sang softly.

And the she sang loudly.

Her voice reverberated through the seats, echoed off the ceiling and absorbed the attention of all that heard her. Even the conspirators stopped their gossiping. The song rang into the hearts of all. It wasn't a child singing, it was a melodious release, a wave pulling them up with its rise. Hallee sang alone in the light, for over a minute before anyone took a breath. Then Chelsea's mother turned to Ms. Zellwood, the drama teacher, and hissed through clenched teeth.

"You had better not even think of casting her. My Chelsea…"

"…is a good singer."

"...is the smart choice for that role. That other girl doesn't even belong here, does she? I mean isn't she one of those transfer students from Carver?"

The judges' heads tilted a few degrees as their bodies leaned forward in unison. They were not judging an audition, they were observing a phenomenon. The notes flew throughout the theater and met up with the grace of butterflies dancing in synchronicity on a gentle breeze before evaporating, only to be replaced by prettier, more melodious notes. This little girl could sing better than anyone they had ever heard before. She had no music, yet her voice harmonized with the room. Chelsea's mother, her voice unsteady, attacked Ms. Zellwood again.

"And besides, I hate to tell you-but Annie is not black."

Ms. Zellwood continued to protest as Hallee's voice became the room, and the room became her voice. There was nothing else. Chelsea's mother yanked Zellwood's arm.

"Did you hear me, Zellwood? I am the one funding this play. I would listen to me if I were you. Annie is a red-haired orphan, you got it? Annie is not black!"

Ms. Zellwood, without taking her eyes off of Hallee McDaniel, spoke in a matter of fact voice that effectively terminated the talentless reign of Chelsea and her mother's despotic Fine Arts Network.

"She is now."

Two Black Women

The tea pot screamed that the stove had done its job well. Louise Keystone, hearing the high-pitched protest, walked on unsteady legs into the kitchen. A roach scurried across the floor. Mrs. Keystone could not stand the pain of quick movement so she let the roach pass for the second time in an hour. Her friend of thirty years, Maybelle Brown, was coming over to discuss the busing situation at The White School. Both of their granddaughters had been selected in the lottery. The girls loved the school, but had to ride the bus for an hour and a half in the morning and longer than that at night.

Both girls had been good students while at Carver Middle School and had looked forward, since way back in August, to attending The White School - known for its high test scores, well-behaved students, a stellar sports program, and the most well-funded fine arts pro-gram in the county. The girls wanted to get into a real chorus and a real play. Not the foolish mockup they had endured at Carver. So they were ecstatic when they were chosen. But now the busing situation had worn them down. The granddaughters just could not under-stand why they gave the worst bus on the lot to the group that had to travel the farthest. It was always breaking down. Louise knew the answer that question. As did her momma and her momma before that. But the children wanted to be a part of the Fine Arts program so Louise held her tongue.

The chorus, band, orchestra, and drama department at The White School were funded by the Fine Arts Network, or FAN. They were rumored to have raised eighty thousand dollars last year. They put on Broadway style productions in professional costumes. Over two dozen costumes. Rented from a real costume company. They hired carpenters to build the sets. They charged ten dollars per ticket and the shows sold out in one week. Last year they performed Willy Wonka and the Chocolate Factory. That was one of Louise's favorite. The production received rave reviews in the Charlotte newspaper. Over a dozen of The White School children went on to Northside Performing Arts School each year. Carver Middle School was a difference story.

Their granddaughters love singing, dancing, and just performing in general. Although both had petitioned to attend Northside Performing Arts School, neither one got in. Nobody from Carver Middle School had been admitted to Northside as far as anyone could remember. Carver had no orchestra. Their band was a ragtag assemblage of thirty students besieged with donated instruments. The tuba could only play two tubes. The third was broke. They had no dance class. Chorus was full. Everyone signed up for chorus. The teacher, Mrs. Bigelow, who had been teaching at the school for thirty-two years, put on a fine show in her day; but that day had passed. Ol' Lady Bigelow's hearing was going; her ability to move around the classroom had been diminished and what was once a vibrant Holiday evening program was relegated to a few Gospel songs the afternoon before Christmas vacation. Then there was the drama club.

The teacher, a young black male named Rick Fosse, did what he could with his budget. Actually, there was no budget. Last year, through cake sales and car washes, they raised almost one hundred and nineteen dollars and forty seven cents. "Almost" because most of the money had been taken from the jar before it made it back to school. They charged a dollar per ticket but only the parents and some friends of the cast attended. Fosse gave away more tickets than he sold and only thirty seats had bodies in them. This year he was trying to raise money to buy The Wiz.

Louise tenderly picked up the teapot and poured the steaming water into two white ceramic cups. She pulled two Lipton tea bags from a cracked Tupperware container. The roach stopped just before the closet to see what Louise was doing. She spied him out of the corner of her eye. In her day that roach would have been dead already. Her friend Maybelle Brown would be here any minute and she wanted to get right down to discussing The White School. Louise had to use the toilet before Maybelle got there and entered the small bathroom adjacent to the kitchen. The toilet dripped continuously but she had no money to fix it, nor did she know, or trust anyone that she would let in her house. She heard the front screen door open as she sat there helpless on the toilet. She opened the heavily painted bathroom door and called to her friend.

"I'm in the can. Come on in."

Maybelle Brown had kept in shape over the years. She was a believer in exercise and good nutrition. Some called her a fanatic. She constantly faulted black people for their diet as "a causative factor in their poor health" and other words like that. Whenever a news report would complain that black people had a higher incidence of heart disease, diabetes, high blood pressure, cancer, obesity, or whatever - Maybelle she would tell anyone that would listen it was because they did not eat right, nor did they exercise enough.

It was not because they were black.

Maybelle still turned heads at forty four years old. She was eight years younger than Louise, but they had hit if off right from the start. They met at one of the young black male funerals that punctuated the nineties, neither could remember which one. And Maybelle, like her granddaughter, loved to dance.

"Oh, honey I caught you. I was waiting on the porch until you went into the can."

"Girl you just cannot let me be. Bothering someone at their most vulnerable moment."

The toilet flushed, the sink ran, and after a long minute Louise emerged. Maybelle was already sitting at the table dipping her teabag in the hot water. The other cup had been placed right next to her. Maybelle smiled and waved her hand.

"Sit down, girl. I made you some tea."

The pair laughed at this ironic twist. They would tease each other as they had for years. It was their communication system.

"That funny. I thought I had made you tea."

"You thought? That's the first sign of old age. Your mind is the first to go."

"Girl, now I know you lying. My mind wasn't the first to go. My ankles done went ten years ago, my backs been gone since Clinton, and my titties..."

"Oh please, please. Please do not make me think about what two children, fifty some years, and that nasty beast called gravity has done to your titties. I just know I won't be able to drink my tea."

The pair chuckled as Louise lowered herself into her seat. They dipped their tea bags in unison, squeezing the bag against the side of the cup with a spoon; both added too much sugar, and then balanced it with a squeeze of fresh lemon. They were just starting to sip when someone beeped their horn outside the house.

"I thought you didn't turn your red light on until dark?"

"Please, you know my red light been burned out since the Vietnam War. That must be someone who seen your skinny ass shaking down the street."

"That were someone for me, they would not be honking their horns, they would be in here on they knees begging for some."

Louise looked through her picture window.

"Maybe it 's a honky honking."

"Maybe they be lost."

"Or maybe they finally found you. Them white boys like that coffee skin."

"Girlfriend, please. You know what they say about them white boys."

The car pulled away as the old friends laughed. It could have been any of a dozen of their "ex-es". They had many adventures, and many secrets, between them. Both had sown their wild oats in their day. Neither one could judge the other because of their youthful indiscretions. They knew how things were; kids today were no better, or no worse, than when they were kids. The times were different. When they were teenagers a white boy was a novelty. An interracial couple stayed hidden in those days. And it was rare. White society frowned upon it as much as the black community. Her soul sisters did not want some blonde haired blue-eyed white bitch 'stanking' up their neighborhood and taking what few good men were left. Today, the young ones did not know such boundaries. The last two generations of African-Americans, actually make it the last three or four, had worked so hard to be equal to the whites that the line between races had been erased. Young people today would sense the looks if they dated a white boy. But not much was said a besides "you're dating a white boy." There were many biracial kids running around the neighborhood. But it wasn't from the pretty blue-eyed blondes; it was an invasion of overweight white trash picking up the unemployed, no account bums that no one wanted anyway.

On rare occasion you could see a good-looking black man with a good-looking white woman. But most times it was some fat girl named Michelle yelling at her mulatto children, while trying to talk and act like she was black. That was most of what you saw in the neighborhood.

"Girl, these kids have got it so..."

"... easy?"

"... hard. Maybe I shouldn't say that. I guess it's just different for them. They don't have the rules that we had when we were coming up."

"That's because we fought to get rid of those rules."

"I don't think it was us - as much as it was our grandparents back in the fifties and sixties. They the ones who took to the streets. Got bit by the dogs, knocked on their asses by the water hose."

"I remember the night you took to the streets."

"And you was right behind me."

"Girlfriend, if you felt that that was me behind you, he must not had too much."

They both laughed hysterically.

"I do hope there are no children in this house listening to this nasty recall of your wicked days."

"My wicked days is just beginning…"

"And I feel that we could talk about the old days all afternoon. Back when I bounced around on my feet."

"I do remember one time at ol' Charley Higgins' house that you were bouncing around; but your feet were in the air."

Louise laughed so hard that her knee kicked the shaky table. It's flimsy wood caused both cups of tea to spill. Maybelle got up and pulled a cloth from the faucet. Louise grimaced in pain and held her knee.

"Sit down girl. I'll wipe up my mess later."

Louise's eyes welled up with tears. Maybelle knew that she was prone to mood swings. Laughing one minute and like this the next. It might be her reaction to the cheap generic medication she was on. Maybelle patted her on the shoulder and Louise let loose.

"How can I go to that school and stop racism when I can't even wipe up my own table?"

"You ain't alone here, sister. There are plenty of us that are fixin' to go down there."

"Oh? Is that a fact? And in whose car are we going to go? Mine ain't registered, and neither is yours. Joe Wilson will talk a good game but he's drunk by eleven thirty every day. Who else? Annabel Jenkins? Her fat ass will take up the whole backseat."

"Okay, okay. I'll go down."

"And say what? And say what? That our granddaughters don't feel comfortable around rich white kids? That the forty mile bus ride both ways is tiring the kids out? That we don't have the money to dress our grandchildren in designer clothes? Or that our kids did not get enough education at the Negro school to understand what the teacher be talking about during class?"

Maybelle patted Louise's shoulder. Louise turned her face away and wept. Maybelle looked out the plate glass window. Maybe Louise was right. It wasn't like the sixties when the entire community was starving and they took to the streets because they had nowhere else to go - and nothing to lose. Welfare and Social Security had given them just enough to buy cheap food and bottom shelf liquor. Some even had enough left over for bag of marijuana. Satellite television could be bought on the government money and if anyone had a part-time job, or even a real job, they had the premium channels.

So the great Civil Rights uprising had been put down with a fistful of dollars. The government paid off the rebels. Only a few old fools would still stand on the corner and pontificate. (But that was usually a Saturday night after too much Thunderbird.) If Maybelle and Louise went to the school, The White School, all that would be seen now is a couple of middle-aged black women trying to blame their problems on someone else. Louise laid her head on her arms and cried harder. Through heaving sobs she attempted to let out her pain and feelings of helplessness.

"It's just... that…there is... nothing... nothing we can do. We just poor black women..."

Louise reached for the towel that Maybelle had used to blot up the tea. Avoiding the brown wet spot she dabbed her eyes; then blew her nose loudly. Maybelle wrinkled her brow in concern and took the towel from Louise.

"Why did you take my crying towel?"

"You blew so loudly I just wanted to see if your brains had come out."

Louise, runny nose and bloodshot eyes, grabbed her side and laughed heartily. Maybelle with a look of mock disgust gave her the towel back. Louise returned the towel to her mucous filled nose and watery eyes while laughing out loud.

"You know, I really don't think there is anything a fat middle-aged black woman can do about them unfair bus rides."

Maybelle's eyes lit up. She drew in a breath to speak but could not. She waved her hand in front of her mouth; her fingers extended the way she had done since she was twelve years old when something excited her. She walked back and forth quickly in the small kitchen. At one point she bumped into the stove. Louise twisted her head, then her whole body, to follow her friend. Maybelle alternated between waving her hand with outstretched fingers in front of her mouth and pointing at Louise. Her eyes looked like two full moons against a dark coffee colored sky. She stopped and pointed at Louise .

"Say it again. Say... that... again. Say it again."

"What?"

"Say it again. Just say it again."

Maybelle pointed as if Louise had turned into the Holy Spirit himself. Then, Louise's eyes widened. She put both hands on the table and pushed herself up despite the excruciating pain in her back. Now standing, her knees shook like a ten foot stack of wooden blocks in the wind. But that did not stop her. She raised a sausage shaped finger and pointed it at Maybelle.

"What can a fat middle-aged black woman do about an unfair bus ride?"

Maybelle stole the words and said them herself as if to make them legitimate.

"What can a fat middle-aged black woman do about an unfair bus ride?"

Maybelle ran over to hug her friend and they almost fell. Maybelle steadied Louise and the pair laughed like children. They laughed like black people had laughed for centuries. And repeated the phrase over, and over until finally Maybelle finally said something different.

"I will show you what a fat middle-aged black woman can do about an unfair bus situation."

Just then the car had returned and was honking its horn gain. This time the car appeared to have stopped.

"I am going to tell your honky lover to hit the road. I will be right back. I am in no mood for white people right now."

Maybelle strode to the door meaningfully. She flung open the door and bounded down the steps. Less than thirty seconds later, the door that had barely closed flew open. Maybelle had returned. She was waving her hand in front of her mouth again.

"That was Joe Wilson. He has quit drinking…"

"Again?"

"He says he hasn't had a drink all week."

"Girlfriend, it's only Tuesday."

"Anyway, he looks pretty sober and he wants to drive us down to the school board to protest. C'mon now, Louise. We gots to go!"

On unsteady legs, her back screaming out in pain, Louise followed behind her friend to Joe Wilson's car, with Maybelle yelling all the way.

"What can a fat black woman do about an unfair busing situation?"

Tonischia

The street was empty except for the morning drunks that pulled their collar against the cold wind. Tonischia Davenport, basketball held close, walked past them, sidestepped their outstretched hands, and followed the street up to Martin Luther King Boulevard. She took a right at the intersection onto Mission Street. There you could see the results of generations of segregation, economic slavery and the general raw deal that blacks had been given for the last two hundred years. These houses, all ninety three of them built side by side on Mission and Savannah streets, were constructed in the early 1900's by then sitting Mayor of Charlotte, Jeremiah Porter. Porter had decided to solve "the nigger problem" by relocating the black sharecroppers to one area and declaring their old land county property. Porter purchased the land, (albeit illegally, with his rich cohorts' money) and built three room shacks that the black sharecroppers could rent from his associates. There was a small yard in the back; enough room for a few chickens and maybe a goat. Actually, there were over one hundred and fifty such small houses originally built. But when the Interstate Highway needed a route through Charlotte no one thought twice about displacing the colored folk on the West side of Savannah

Street. Tonischia's grandmother still talks about the day, which fell on her seventh birthday, when the bulldozers came and crushed her house. Every Thanksgiving she would tell the story, and each Thanksgiving, after her third glass of port wine, Grandma would cry at the cruelty of bulldozing a little girl's house on her birthday.

Tonischia bounced her basketball between the cracks on the sidewalk. She stopped and looked around at the only place she had ever lived. She was thinking of leaving her neighborhood, her friends, her school and her coach because she had been offered one of the positions at The White School. Everyone else was fighting to get in there and she really did not want to go. The deserted Community Center made her pace quicken. She liked this time of day. She could shoot baskets without having to talk to anyone. It was her home away from home ever since she could remember.

Back in the eighties when the white people started to act like they cared about blacks, they built a Community Center with outside basketball courts and an inside gymnasium. In the nineties they added a pool (mostly to keep the blacks out of the pool on Main Street which was right next to a white neighborhood) and an outside basketball court. The overt racism of the last one hundred years, the segregated schools, the 'Whites Only' drinking fountains, and the back of the bus seating, had all been replaced with Community Centers and gyms and pools to keep blacks separated from whites. And it worked. Why would anyone want to walk across a six lane interstate highway to swim when there was a pretty decent pool right outside of the Community Center? Good is the enemy of great. "White people know what they is doing," Grandma used to say.

But the size of her house, her neighborhood, the drunks, or the punks on the corner was not on Tonischia's mind today. She could not decide whether or not she should go to The White School. That Community Center that the white people built to keep blacks in their neighborhood had given Tonischia an escape, and an outlet, from and for her pain. It had allowed her to focus her energies on basketball. Every time her father had come home drunk looking to hurt someone, or feel their body, Tonischia would slip out the window to the Community Center. It was open until midnight on weekends. She would have to weave through the old men drinking Mad Dog 20/20, and listen to the cat calls of the younger men as they smoked weed and drank Colt 45, but it was easy to do because the Community Center was well lit and there were good people and security guards just inside the gate. On some hot summer nights they would leave the pool open until ten, but mostly it closed at six. By eight o'clock the older boys had finished playing and drifted, one by one, out beyond the gates to smoke weed and drink alcohol. This left Tonischia's crowd, a bunch of black kids old enough to go out after dinner, but too young to drink with the other two groups. This is where she learned about basketball. At first, when she was only ten years old, it would be, 'Sit down little nigger, you'se too small.' So she would have to go to the outside courts and shoot at the basket with the rusty chain netting and the bent rims. The light from inside would hardly help, so Tonischia developed a sense about where the center of the basket was, she shot for middle of the shadow. She loved the sound of the steel chain net when she 'swished' one. One day, just after her eleventh birthday, her father came home after dinner and he was drunker than usual. He slapped Tonischia for leaving a mess in the kitchen, and then he started getting real touchy with her mother.

"Tonischia, child, go on and play down at the Community Center, I will pick up your dishes."

Tonischia left and, her anger fueled by the confused feelings she carried from home, walked onto the inside court. When one of the older boys told her to get off and go play outside, Tonischia, standing a little behind the foul line, took a shot with the worn out ball she had. All net.

"Shee-it. Let the little girl play if she can shoot like that."

From that day on, Tonischia played with the boys. Her dad's drinking, and her escapes out the window, came more frequently. Most nights, when she returned, he would be slumped in a chair, or passed out on the couch.

Although Tonischia could shoot and dribble and steal the ball, it was Jimmy Childs that taught her the game of basketball. He approached her one day at the Community Center. Told her she had potential and should try out for the team at Carver. He showed her the strategy, how to full court press, when to pick another player, how to break away. Everyone called Jimmy Childs "Coach". Coach was a good man. He had gone on to college and played basketball for Duke. He took Duke to the state championship two years in a row. Then, in his senior year, he got into a car accident during Christmas break. Both knees were shattered. He was hit by a drunk driver, a white drunk driver. Actually it was the white wife of a big shot attorney drunk driver. Childs got a settlement, paid off his momma's bills and bought himself a house on Savannah Street. He finished his senior year from a wheelchair, but he graduated. The next year he was hired as a history teacher at Carver Middle School. Of course he coached basketball. He had moved to crutches by this time. When he met Tonischia he had his trademark cane. It was a stick that came from a tree that had been felled by a drunk driver. Coach carved it himself Coach told the students that God had sent him this stick and that it had magical powers. Whenever the team would get behind, Coach would rub the stick against his knees. It was obvious by the look on his face that it caused him pain, so it inspired many a team to reach deep and give it all they had. Since Coach Jimmy Childs had come to Carver seven years ago, they had been to the district championship six times, and won the title the last four years in a row. Tonischia Davenport, like the rest of the kids at Carver, saw Coach Jimmy Childs as their hero. He didn't drink, he smiled all the time, never complained about his knees and he was involved in the Community Center. And more kids had gone to college in the last seven years than had gone for the last fifty previous combined. Coach Childs believed in education. And that was Tonischia's dilemma.

After winning the district championship last year, Tonischia was featured in the newspaper as a sixth grade sensation. Everyone in the neighborhood knew her. One day she got a letter in the mail. The mail was a source of sour looks from her mother before this day. Her momma smiled and handed her a letter from the basketball coach at East Edgewood Middle School.

The White School.

He invited Tonischia to the summer basketball camp at East Edgewood Middle. Coach Childs encouraged her to go. All of a sudden The White School had an opening for Tonischia. A few of her friends had made the lottery and gone to The White School last year, and everybody's momma wanted them to go there to get an education. The other schools in the area were almost the same as Carver, but East Edgewood, The White School, was known for having everything – a great drama program, excellent sports, and the highest grades of any school in the county.

But the students that had been there brought back tales of racism and unfair treatment. They had to wake up before dark and drive for an hour just to get to school. The bus broke down a lot and one day the neighborhood kids didn't get home from the White School until seven o'clock. Tonischia remembered seeing the bus as she was shooting baskets at the Community Center. And then there was loyalty. Coach Childs had taught her everything. She knew where she stood with him. This new coach seemed nice, but he wasn't Jimmy Childs.

The decision was made by her momma and that was the end of it. Tonischia was on her way to The White School and there wasn't anything she could do about it.

Black Beacon

He pushed through the curtain that afforded him a modicum of privacy and walked out of his small bedroom, the former sewing room. The smell of bacon cleared his mind for a moment. The small stove sat and offered him its bounty. He grabbed a piece of burnt bacon and reached for the small glass of orange juice. He remembered what he was complaining about as the cold liquid slid into his stomach.

"Quanesha, you knows the teachers there are racists, and them rich kids are all racist. Why you making me do this?"

Rasheem's aunt was in her late twenties. Her weight, and consistent bad luck over the years, betrayed her youth. She was usually taken for late thirties. She took Rasheem in for a weekend last year, just after New Year's Eve. He was still living with her as she checked her Thanksgiving food list.

"I don't have time for this right now. We having to bring some covered plate to Grandma's house for Thanksgiving. Anyway, it only two days this week. You get off on Wednesday for Thanksgiving. I checked it on the school calendar."

"That's even more reason for me to stay home. We be watching movies all day. White people movies like Braveheart or The Patriot. We don't ever watch no black movies like Glory."

"Your momma wanted you to go there. You know she gonna be at Grandma's on Thursday."

"Who cares what my momma do? I sho' don't."

"Stop that, Rasheem. She had to go out there for that job. She…"

"…be home as soon as she can. Yeah, I don't believe that anymore."

"Alright. Listen, I know the people at that school are racists, they learn it from their parents..."

"It ain't just the kids. Everybody at that school is racist, the teachers, the secretaries, the secretaries always be saying stuff under their stank breath. C'mon Auntie, you gotta let me go back to Carver wid my homies."

"Don't get yourself riled up. You ain't going back to no failing ass, can't make its minimum standards, run down full of drugs Carver Middle School. So get on the bus. I sees it coming around MLK Avenue right now."

Rasheem snatched up his backpack, bounded down the stairs two at a time, pushed past the door and sprinted across the street. Seconds later he was on his bus. He found his seat in the rear and plopped down. It was the usual raucous ride. The noise relaxed him and he put on the IPod he had found at the Community Center last summer.

The bus pulled in, late as usual and they got yelled at by Ms. Gray to be quiet. Everyone hated when Ms.

Gray had cafeteria duty because she looked for something to complain about. Sherise whispered 'kiss my black ass' and everyone laughed. Then Ms. Gray called Mr. Bridges and everyone settled down when he came out of the office. Breakfast pizza, chocolate milk, Michaela smiling at him, and the fat cafeteria ladies telling all the niggers to hurry up. He dazed through breakfast. The late bell rang but Bridges told them to keep eating. Ms. Gray had walked to the door before the bell even stopped. The white kids disappeared, other teachers shut their doors, and the cafeteria women shook their heads and talked about the black kids.

They had distributed the black kids up, put three or four per class. But oddly enough, when the bell rang most of the students still in the hallway were black. The handful of Carver kids that were in class would be sharpening their pencil, or walking around the class. Operant conditioning. That's how they were trained at Carver Middle School. In contrast, all the white kids would be in their seats, with their books open ready to begin working. Operant conditioning. That's how they were trained at East Edgewood Middle School. Mrs. Taschenberger would address the class as soon as the bell stopped.

One time Rasheem was in his seat before the bell rang. It felt weird to him.

The principal said to ignore bad behavior and it would go away. The students in the hall, everyday late for class for three weeks. It wasn't going away. Not only that, when they came in the class, and caused a huge disruption. After breakfast, Rasheem met Susan, one of the friendlier white kids in the hall. Rasheem and Susan came running in to the classroom laughing and smiling, as it were fun time.

"Please take your seats quietly."

Ms. Taschenberger looked around. Diversity training(all eight hours of it) had told her to try and correct a white student before she pointed the finger at a black student. However no one was acting up at this time. A couple of her best students were whispering, but that was most likely about the assignment. She looked at Rhasheem.

"Rasheem, you should be in your seat."

"What about her?"

"She had permission."

Susan sat down quickly. Rasheem mocked her hurried walk and plopped down in his seat. Rasheem looked around the class and realized everyone, except for him and Susan, was sitting at their desk. Most had already finished the warm up assignment. Others were well into it. He flipped his notebook to a blank page, (as a matter of fact, all he had in his notebook was blank pages and random sketches). He found a page that had no drawings, and penciled in today's date. Then he dropped his pencil.

"Rasheem, do you mind copying the assignment please?"

Rasheem knocked his books off the desk as he stood up. They slammed so loudly on the polished tile floor that two students flinched.

"I'm so sick of this place. I hate this school. All you do is pick on people. A nigger can't do nothin' around here. If you black, you get yelled at. The white kids get away with everything. She didn't have no permission."

"Rasheem, I am not yelling at you. I'm simply asking you to the copy the assignment. This has nothing to do with..."

Rasheem picked up the pencil and walked over to the pencil sharpener. He bumped into a student, causing her pencil to scribble across the notebook. The student raised her hand with a pleading look on her face.

"Mrs. Taschenberger, please."

"Mrs. Taschenberger, please." Rasheem mocked her.

"Rasheem, leave her alone."

Mrs. Taschenberger bit her lip. *Always correct a white student before you point the finger at a black student.*

In the meantime Rasheem, still out of his seat, loudly sharpened his pencil. The pencil had been sharpened so intensively that when Rasheem finally pulled it out it had an almost microscopic point on the end. Mrs. Taschenberger opened her mouth to correct Rasheem, thought better of it, and then took her place at the front of the class. Rasheem, done with the pencil sharpener, walked up the center aisle right at Mrs. Taschenberger. The class held its breath for it appeared that he was about to confront her physically. He looked right at her as he stepped loudly and quickly. About one foot from her face Rasheem turned down the aisle to his seat. He actually had to backtrack to get to his chair. But the message had been sent. Mrs. Taschenberger closed her eyes and tried to regain her composure. She was a small woman, about five foot six. She was not an athletic specimen, nor a physical one. Her heart had raced as Rasheem walked up the aisle. Her palms had moistened. When she opened her mouth and addressed the class a dry squeaky sound emitted and Rasheem laughed, and then put his head down. His body rocked all over the place, as if he were having some sort of epileptic fit. Tears welled up in Mrs. Taschenberger's eyes. Finally Chad Brunt, a football player had had enough.

"Never do that again." Chad turned his head and then whispered "frigging nigger". Everyone, including Mrs. Taschenberger, heard him.

"What? What did you say to me?" Rasheem turned the pencil forward, and squeezed it in his closed hand. "What the fuck did you say, bitch?"

Two other tall male students stood up, they both spoke at the same time.

"You heard him. He said 'frigging nigger'. Heck, I heard him way over here."

"He said – 'Never do that again, you frigging nigger.' I heard him too."

There stood a triangle of the biggest boys in class. Chad Brunt, all six feet of him, stood between Rasheem and the door. Chad seized the moment.

"Why don't you go back to the dump that you came from?" The others, braver now in numbers, chimed in.

"Yeah, garbage isn't supposed to leave the dump."

"This is a good school, we don't want you here. And you don't scare us with that thug shit anymore. It's all a big act."

Rasheem gripped his pencil and his eyes darted to each of the three boys, one after the other. Then a fourth boy stood up. Rasheem, in his deepest voice, spoke loudly and deliberately as he approached the door. He stood in the doorway and turned to the class.

"All I did was sharpen my pencil. That other girl didn't have no permission. Everybody else be late, but black people get yelled at. What about them calling me a nigger? That's life. Right? Right?" Rasheem exited the class.

"Class, I am sorry. Boys, sit down. Please. Let's get on with our lesson."

Her hand shook as she picked up the electric pen for the Smart Board. It was obvious how shaken she was. Chad Brunt fumed.

The boys sat down and the class scribbled in silence. They could hear Rasheem yelling as he progressed down the hallway. Mrs. Taschenberger, still teaching, walked to her classroom phone and dialed the front office. She informed them that Rasheem McNeil had just let just let loose a slew of profanity and stormed out of the classroom.

In the front office. Sandy, the front office secretary, called security. She turned to the head secretary, who was perched at her desk like a gargoyle.

"You know, I'm still not used to having security at this school. I know it's been a couple of months, but Jeesh. Security? At East Edgewood Middle School?"

Security found Rasheem and he promenaded the defiant young man into the discipline office. Rhasheem stopped dead in the middle of the office. Betty looked away and Sandy returned to her computer, reading emails that she had already seen. Rhasheem wanted an outlet for his frustration. Bridges appeared in the office.

"I want to call home. Let me out of here or I will fuckin' explode."

Security turned back and Bridges waved him off.

"Come on to my office. We can figure it out from there."

After an initial hesitation, Rhasheem followed the older man. Security hung around by the entrance to the office. Rhasheem continued his discourse as he fell in behind the only person that had shown any concern of his plight at all.

"Man, all these teachers be racist. The white kids doing the same thing I did but who gets sent out? It's a black kid all the time."

Bridges turned into his office. He pointed to the chair and Rhasheem sank into it.

"So Ms. Taschenberger was trying to start the class and you were just sitting there and she sent you out?"

Rhasheem said nothing.

"Or could it be that Ms. Taschenberger was trying to start this particular class, and then you come bopping in late, harassed a student, walked up like you were going to hit her and then use the "F" word. Then you made a huge disruption as you left."

Rhasheem slid down in the chair.

"She also said that she felt physically intimidated by you, as did a few of her students."

"They called me the "N" word and she didn't say nothing."

"I will check into that, and believe me, that will not be tolerated. But first I have to deal with this situation. Who is at home?"

Bridges dialed the number that Rhasheem told him. He looked through Rhasheem's heavy discipline folder. This was the fourth number that had been written on the folder. The other three were crossed out, a comment next to each – Out of Service. When the person at the other end finally answered, Bridges asked for the parents of Rhasheem McNeil. The response was brief.

"They ain't here."

Then the phone went dead. Bridges dialed the number again. This time the person picked up the phone and yelled.

"What are you? Deaf? I done said they ain't here. Who is this?"

This is Mr. Bridges, I am the Assistant Principal at East Edgewood Middle School. We need someone to come and pick up Rhasheem McNeil."

"East Edgewood Middle School? Oh, you mean The White School?"

"No, ma'am. I mean East Edgewood Middle School. Is there someone authorized to pick up Rhasheem McNeil from school? He is being sent home for disrupting class."

"You're giving him exactly what he wants. He hates that school. He didn't even want to go today. They hardly ever sent him home from Carver, they dealt with the students."

"Ms. McNeil, we treat all off the…"

Bridges did not have a chance to finish before Rhasheem's Aunt Quanisha went into her well practiced speech. She spent five uninterrupted minutes detailing how Rhasheem wasn't comfortable at The White School, she gave instances how the white teachers made him comfortable, and how her nephew felt like the white people were always looking at him. She knew, as did a lot of other people from her neighborhood, that the parents at that school were racists, and the kids were racists- but she expected the teachers to be fair. Bridges attempted to intervene.

"I understand your concern. I can assure you…"

She went on another tirade before Bridges could finish. Rhasheem slouched even more and Bridges waved for him to sit up. He did.

"Ms. McNeil. I understand that. But Rhasheem used the "F" word in class. I would appreciate it, and I believe he would too, if you can pick him up. He doesn't…"

"Mr. Bridges, I am not his mother. I am his aunt. I am doing the best I can do. It's just hard. Kids are so, so frustrating."

Bridges was silent. He knew from experience that the next person who spoke would have to capitulate. The silence caused Rhasheem to sit up straight. Finally, voice came over the phone.

"I will be there in twenty minutes."

Thirty minutes later, Rhasheem was leaving the parking lot with his aunt. The bell rang signifying the beginning of second period. Students mingled and milled about until the warning bell, and then they rushed to class. A minute later, Ms. Taschenberger addressed her second period class.

"Good morning. Let's get started on our warm-up."

Elijah slipped into the class and looked around. A few students were at the teacher's desk. A little blond girl that never spoke was at the pencil sharpener. Joey Bonatto was picking up a notebook from Stephanie Millis. For once he wasn't the only one not in his seat when the late bell rang. Elijah was about to breathe a sigh of relief –until he saw Ms. Taschenberger looking right at him. Ms. Taschenberger asked one student that was sitting sideways to please place his legs under the desk. *Always correct a white student before you point the finger at a black student.* Then she turned to Elijah.

"Elijah, you're late for my class.

"What about all these people?"

"They had permission."

Incident in the Locker Room

He put his briefcase down. There sat two discipline folders on his desk. One was new and thin, the other about half an inch thick with various papers folded into. This thick one had seen action. When a student committed an infraction, broke a school rule, and was subsequently written up, a discipline folder was started. The referral was placed on the left of the folder; two special holes were made with the double punch. The holes were impaled by the clasps where a written record was attached of all correspondence. He closed his eyes and inhaled the aroma of fresh-brewed coffee.

Bridges picked up the lighter folder, removing it from under the worn corner of the one where, although the name was obscured by the multitude of papers, he knew belonged to Madison Watson. No one else at East Edgewood had accumulated such a file. Madison was a weekly visitor to Mr. Bridges. Whether she was in trouble or not. The lighter folder in his hand piqued his interest. Handwritten on the upper left corner, in female cursive, was the name Tonischia Davenport. Bridges shook his head.

Two folders together, both female, meant only one thing. Cat fight. At least that's what the kids called it.

Two girls fought each other to the delight of the rest of the student body. When Bridges was at Martin Luther King Middle, he broke up three of these a day. The African-American girls just could not seem to get along. They always had some crisis. At MLK the policy was to let the pugilists settle down, and if the fight had not been that bad, and the girls would agree to let it drop, they could go back to class. That was not the case at East Edgewood Middle. Fights at East Edgewood, although rare, were dealt with by sending everyone involved home for ten days. Principal Shirley Rubenstein abhorred fighting. In the twelve years of her tenure, she could count the number of fights on one hand. Rich white kids did not fight, they sniped. Shirley Rubenstein had no policy on sniping, bullying or verbal harassment. But if you fought at her school, you went home for two weeks – maybe.

Bridges heart sank. If this was a fight it was between Madison and some new student from Carver. Madison most likely started it, Bridges knew that. Madison may not be the star student, but she was Queen Bee of East Edgewood Middle School. Only a new kid would confront Madison. The other student, Tonischia Davenport, sounded familiar. Bridges couldn't place her. He hesitated to open the folder. Bridges cocked his head and took in the welcome aroma of fresh-brewed coffee anew.

"I hope you had a good time on your day off."

Sandy placed a cup of coffee on his desk. It was her oversized mug, which said "Who Invented Mondays?" on the outside. Sandy only brought Bridges coffee when something was amiss. Especially when it involved the Principal and one of her decisions.

"Thanks." Bridges took a long sip. Sandy made great coffee; she knew to let it sit long enough so that it would not be too hot, or too cold. The coffee was always just right. Like Sandy. She always wanted everything to be perfect.

"I see you read what happened yesterday." Bridges shook his head just before he took another sip from the huge mug. He tasted a long gulp, spilling some on his shirt.

"Jeesh."

Sandy turned and left. Bridges reached for the Kleenex that always stayed on the corner of his desk. He was rubbing his chest when Sandy came back.

"Stop. Stop! Move your hand." Sandy rubbed the stain with a little piece of foamy sponge. Then she stepped back and smiled.

"This is why it is a good idea to always wear white. You can bleach off the stains. My mother disagrees, but I think white shirts are much easier to clean. There, it's gone. Do you want me to get you a bib?"

"Funny. What is that sponge thing?"

"Magic sponge, bought it at the Dollar Mart. So what do you think?"

"It looks good…"

"No, silly, I mean about the fight."

It *was* a fight. Bridges smiled. He thought once that he may have been doing this job too long, now he felt that he was doing it just long enough.

"I had a feeling it was a fight. Who's Tonischia Davenport?"

"That new girl from Carver. The basketball player that Coach Roth just had to have. He begged Shirley to let her transfer. Remember?"

"Oh yeah, yeah, okay. Well, that puts her out for ten days. And Madison too."

Sandy's silence bade him to turn her way. When he did he saw that she had that look on her face.

"No...she didn't. Tell me she didn't."

"She did. And not only did she, she wants you to call Tonischia's parents and explain the situation." Bridges sat down on one of the two student chairs. Sandy took the opportunity to sit at Bridges desk. She mocked him.

"So how long have you had this problem? Maybe we could refer you to our guidance department. They are very good; they drink a lot less than the guidance counselors at the other schools. I could..."

"Funny. But Madison Watson? Why not Madison? Rubenstein can't stand her. She tried to get rid of her last year with that Chronic Disruptor clause."

Sandy looked at the doorway. Bridges slowly turned. There in the frame stood all five foot four inches of Principal Shirley Rubenstein.

"Ms. Gabrielle, have you been promoted?"

Sandy tiptoed from the room, edging her body toward the opening where Shirley Rubenstein had planted herself. Rubenstein shifted just enough to let Sandy squirm past.

"Mr. Bridges, may I see you in my office?"

As the pair of administrators rounded the corner en route to the principals' office, Bridges bumped into Sandy Gabrielle. Sandy had been standing at the door jamb in an effort to hear what was being said. Rubenstein opened her mouth to address Sandy's eavesdropping when the phone rang. Sandy spun on her heels and half ran to her desk.

"There's the phone. Gotta go."

Bridges and Principal Rubenstein strode in step on the new forest green carpet. Bridges entered the principal's office and stepped in front of a chair, Rubenstein walked past him and sat at her desk. She had her seat raised unnaturally higher than the others and she looked like a judge at the bench behind the massive, elevated desk. She motioned for Bridges to shut the door.

"First off, I do not appreciate you questioning my decisions with the front office secretaries."

"But I…"

"Quiet. And second, I expect you to support all of my decisions. If you have a question as to something I did, feel free to ask me – not Sandy Gabrielle. Clear?"

"Yes, ma'am." Bridges thought of the huge mug of coffee sitting on his desk. He thought that he should ask if he could go and retrieve it under the guise of getting the referrals, then decided against it. The bell would ring any second and he could grab a mouthful on his way to the buses.

"I am not sure if I filled out the whole referral. Did you fill out the rest?"

"To tell you the truth, I did not even get a chance to read either one. Sandy …"

"Then why were you discussing them?"

"I had just walked in…"

"Here is what I need you to do. Call Tonischia…what's her name- Daxonville?"

"Davenport."

"Right. Call her parents and let them know that she has been suspended from school for ten days for fighting. Remind them of the Pineville Community Center. Okay?"

The Pineville Community Center ran a program for students that had been suspended from school. They even had tutors. They took every suspended student except for those that were suspended for bringing a weapon to school. There was no bus service; the parents had to transport their child. They had to be there at eight a.m. and leave at three p.m. The only problem was that the Pineville Community Center was right in the middle of East Edgewood Country Acres. It was a good twenty five miles from Carver Middle School. The parents of suspended students from Carver that could drive their children to the Center had to be at work by seven, or could not get off until four-or had no car. Pineville Community Center was run by the rich wives of the power brokers that lived there. Whereas the rare white student from East Edgewood, and the other white schools in the area, could easily get to the Center, it was basically inaccessible to the black kids from Carver. The Center, which billed itself as serving the entire county, served the two white high schools, the three white middle schools and the four white elementary schools in the area. They averaged from five to seven students a day. They took care of their own, and the county had agreed to not count the suspension as an absence. Bridges assumed that Tonischia would most likely not benefit from the program. Besides, of the few students that were sent home for misbehavior from Pineville Community Centers' wonderful program, somewhere just shy of one hundred percent of them were black transfer students. Tonischia's grandmother was right. White people knew what they were doing.

"I will let them know about the Pineville Community Center. I think transportation will be a ..."

"That is not our concern. We did not ask her to attack Madison Watson."

"She attacked Madison Watson?"

"Uh, yes. According to the witnesses in the locker room at the time..."

Bridges tuned her out. If he could tell the difference from his butt to his braincase, he had learned one thing in school discipline-student witnesses are notoriously unreliable. They see, and say, what benefits them and their friends. Most did not see anything, they just want to get out of class and have someone listen to them as they exaggerate, embellish or outright lie about the situation. Bridges had completed hundreds of investigations and his policy, developed through experience, was to take no action based on student witness reports. Even if they were accurate, some would go home and realize, or their parents realized, that their testimony had gotten a classmate suspended. They would then come back and recant their statement. There was nothing you could do. One of the most administratively embarrassing things you could do was to revoke a suspension. It caused parents to lose faith in your decision. They would always call downtown and the pencil pushers down there would tell you to get your ducks in a row. No, Bridges knew better. He had not suspended anyone in years based upon student witnesses. This one was going to be difficult. Bridges wondered how his coffee was doing.

"…Mr. Bridges? Did you hear me?" Bridges returned to the present. Just as he was about to speak, the bell rang. In Pavlovian fashion he stood. He had not noticed before but now he smelled the pine potpourri in his bosses' office.

"Yes, ma'am. I am on my way."

"To where?"

"Buses."

"I want you to talk to Tonischia's parents, explain what she did, that she has a ten day out of school suspension - and that she is no longer eligible to play basketball at East Edgewood."

Bridges nodded. He knew the eligibility rule. It was one of the main reasons the sports teams at East Edgewood had recurring losing seasons. If an athlete was suspended they were off the team. He walked out of the office.

He thought it best to talk to Coach Roth before calling Tonischia's parents. Both men knew that once old Shirley had made up her mind it could not be changed.

Tonischia Davenport was off the team.

Storebought Gangsta

"Five hunnerd. I needs to pay my crew. Serious."

"No. A hundred dollars."

"Screw you, three hunnerd or go talk to one of them scrub neck niggers behind me. Serious."

Reggie held three fingers up and pushed them to within inches of the man's face.

"Three hunnerd and you gets the job done, you never hears from me again, and I will personally break his knees for free. Serious."

The man drew in a mocking breath, and blinked. He tried to feign fear. But he was full of fear so it looked more real than he had hoped. Then his heart pulsed ahead. This was going to happen. Finally get rid of Ken Montel, the man that wrecked his family. His wife would take him back now. She would come to her senses. He felt like a giddy child on the night before his birthday.

"Deal. I will pay you when the job is finished."

"Pay me after the job is done? No, no, that ain't how it works. How do I know you won't just disappear? Or run to the cops? In the end it always be black against white. You crackers always stick together. You just throw the nigger to the cops and you don't have to pay nothing. No, fuck that. I want it all in my pocket first. Serious."

"How do I know you won't run to the cops? Half up front. The rest on delivery. SERee-fuckin-US! Deal?" The man remembered his father, a New Jersey cop telling him that you could always get away with a crime if you blamed it on a black kid. *Little man, there's plenty of cops out there just looking for a reason to rid the streets of niggers. If you give 'em a reason you did a good deed for this country.*

"Half? Tell ya what. Write me a…a check. Yeah, yeah, gimme a check. That way if'n ya don't come back I go to the cops and sell yo' ass out. And the rest in cash. Serious."

The man thought about walking away. To heck with this. But the thought of Reggie pounding Montel's face into the floor was too tempting. He returned to his truck and retrieved his check book. *There's no way this dumb nigger will go to the cops and turn himself in. I'll give him a good genuine check, made of solid rubber.* He filled out the check and handed it to Reggie.

"The rest?"

The man reached into his back pocket and yanked out his wallet. His body half turned, the man then twisted his shoulder to block Reggie as he counted out one hundred and forty dollars. All he had was twenties. Reggie knew the man had more money than he was showing. (What Reggie did not know was that the man had gone to the bank this morning and attempted to withdraw five hundred dollars. The clerk grimaced and shook her head. The teller handed the man a ticket that said he had two hundred and thirteen dollars in his account. The man withdrew two hundred. It was part of the post separation support. His wife controlled the money until the next hearing.) Spinning back to face Reggie he held out the money. The man slid the other sixty dollars into his other hand. Ten was going to gas (if he ever made it inside the store) and he would need the rest for traveling money.

"Here's one-forty. I am going to..."

"Cheat the nigger. Why it is that white mother-fuckers always be trying to cheat a nigger? Serious."

"...go inside to pay for gas. I will give you the other ten when I come out." The man kept the creased bills in his hand and tottered into the store, weak from his interaction with Reggie.

"Get a nigger a cup of coffee. Serious." Reggie realized that the door had blocked his request. "Fuckin' white people. Dey is all the same. Serious." A few minutes later the man emerged and handed Reggie the cash.

"Count it so you don't say I cheated you." *You fucking nigger.*

Reggie shuffled through the worn bills. "Awright, it's all here. And I gots this check. Serious. Where is dat old bitch-ass faggot motherfucker? What did he do to you? Serious."

"He had an affair with my wife. Here's his picture."

The man produced a small picture of Ken Montel. He handed to Reggie.

"He looks black. Serious."

"That's what everyone says. No, he's Hispanic. Believe me."

The two men, each blinded by their desperation, shook hands. Reggie slipped the check and the picture into his top pocket. *I oughta cash this first*. Reggie thought about how he was going to spend his money; the man wondered how he was going to duck Reggie for the rest of his life.

"I will meet you right here at…what time is it now?

"Do I look like Big Ben? 'Bout two thirty. Serious."

"School is still in session. Don't go in now. Wait until about half past four and everyone will be gone-it's the day before Thanksgiving break. It should be fairly dark by then. Do you know where the school is?"

"Yeah, it's in the rich white section. I goes there all the time. For tea and crumpets. Serious."

"Whatever you say. Okay, just go to the sixth grade wing. Right behind the gym. You can't miss it. Montel will be there. Promise. Maybe you should wear masks or something, huh?"

"Shee-it. When I am done his Latino ass ain't gonna remember nothing. Serious."

"Whatever... Okay, I will meet you here at six o'clock. You'll get the rest then, and I got the check back."

Reggie was wordless for a few long seconds. *God, the man be looking evil.*

"Awright. Where you stay? Serious."

"What?"

"Where is you crib? I ain't..."

"I live in Charlotte, near uh, Pineville."

Reggie knew he was lying. The man wrung his hands.

"Now are you going to get this guy or what? Or are you going to wait until he goes home and eats his dinner? Get your crew together. I know he stays late. All you have to do is show up at the sixth grade wing. Montel will be alone. Hey, how are you going to get past the cops in East Edgewood?"

"I know a back way. They'll never see me. Okay? Serious."

"Yeah, that's great. But just show up; with your crew and find Montel. You don't have a problem with him being Hispanic? I mean he actually looks like he's black, but he is Spanish. Seriously."

He looked at the man, eyebrows raised.

"For three hundred dollars I would beat up my own mother. If I could ever find the bitch. Serious."

"Right. What time is it?"

"I axed you once already-do I look like Big Fuckin' Ben? You know-you look familiar. Did you coach? Serious." Reggie's Grandma eased into his thoughts. *When the devil comes to tempt you, you may think it in your mind by the look in his eye. But you will know it in your soul by the wonder of his promises and the darkness of his desires.* He shook her out.

"How long will it take you to get ya crew together?" The man's attempt to mimic black dialect was pathetic. Reggie laughed.

"What? Oh, hey you talking to Reggie Powell, my man. You gots a cell phone? Serious."

The man withdrew his phone. He hesitated. He had never thought he would be in the situation where he was even talking to a black hoodlum, never mind lending him a cell phone. He tried to sound tough.

"Make it quick."

Reggie snatched the phone and walked down the sidewalk away from the man. He told the deep voice on the other end to show up with a crew.

"Can you be at the sto' in half hour, Germaine? Who you bringin'? Serious."

Reggie listened and nodded as Germaine listed the guys he will bring with him. Reggie protested against one recruit.

"No, fuck him. He's a big mouth. That nigger can't keep quiet. Leave his black ass home wid his momma. Or wid your momma. It don't matter to me. Just don't bring that lip flapping nigger to my Latino ass kicking party. Who else you got? Serious." Reggie bobbed his head up and down. Germaine's voice sounded like a bee trapped in a tin can from where the man stood, straining to hear. Reggie whispered into the phone.

"Twenty bucks. Each nigger." He grimaced and repeated himself. "Each nigg-ah. For real. Serious."

Reggie snapped the phone shut and flipped it to the man. The man bobbled it before it fell to the ground. He picked it up and checked it for damage.

"It's a done deal. Don't even think of fucking me over. Or that little scratch on you phone will be the least of your problems. Serious."

"Wouldn't think of it."

"I be trying to go get him after fo-thirty. My crew should show up by fo'. We... me and you motherfucker, meet here at six chimes. Serious."

"I'm going to run home. I'll be back by six bells."

"You better be here. Serious."

Reggie stood in front of the Quik King, glad handing the other blacks, as the man walked to his car which was the only refuge he had left after the court hearing last week. The man filled his tank, and jumped into the driver's seat. He circled back and gave Reggie the thumbs up. Then the man smiled a smile that sent chills down Reggie's spine. Reggie winced and furrowed his brow.

"Serious." *When the devil comes to tempt you, you may think it in your mind by the look in his eye. But you will know it in your soul by the wonder of his promises and the darkness of his desires.* Reggie heard his grandma's voice trail off into the whispering wind.

Pulling into the road the man looked back to see Reggie still standing in front of the convenience store, gripping his crotch and staring off into the distance. The man shook his head as he drove off.

"Stupid nigger."

Reggie thought about his stroke of luck. Today Reggie Powell got paid three hundred bucks to slap around some Spanish bastard that was banging this guy's wife. On the brutal streets of Charlotte's West

End a man's next meal depended on what he had in his pocket. Right now, Reggie Powell's next meal looked like a buffet.

"Serious."

Twenty minutes later Reggie's "crew" appeared. They were crammed into a brown Hyandai with a spare tire doughnut on the right front tire. The wheel looked comical as the grungy car rolled up full of young, black men. The exterior was covered in a misty sheen of oxidation. Reggie looked at the broken headlight as the car menacingly approached him at high speed. For a split second Reggie thought of jumping to the side. But he dare not show weakness, he learned that in street kindergarten. Weak leaders don't last. Reggie barely flinched as the car screeched to a halt less than six inches from his baggie pants. His "crew" escaped the confines of the car.

"You almost hit me, nigger. Serious."

"Settle down, blood. Here da boys that want to assist you in your mission to eradicate Latino wetbacks in our lifetime…"

"C'mere, Germaine, let me fill ya in on the sitchaation." Reggie motioned to Germaine and the two walked away while Reggie explained what the man had told him. When he finished they turned and walked back to the crew.

"You all know the Reggie, don'tcha?

"What up."

"Word."

"Awwright."

"S'up."

One young man did not show homage. Reggie had never seen this one before; plus this stranger was too clean, too domesticated. New clothes, hair just right. Not a spot on his white hooded sweatshirt. Reggie attacked.

"Nigger, you look like a narc. As a matter of fact you would embarrass the po-lice if you were a narc. You be lookin' so much like a narc you can't be one! Serious."

The young man looked at the other street boys. His face, ashen with fear, betrayed his feelings. Germaine intervened sheepishly.

"That's my sister's keyid. He awright, Reggie, he...

"Are you... talking to me?" The clean, well dressed black youth gulped involuntarily after he spoke.

"Nigger, do I look like I talking to anyone else? Of course I am talking to your store-bought, clean-ass underwear, everyday momma tell-him-to-wash-his-face, nigger ass. Is you a narc? Or do you need a slap in your head to help you remember? Serious." Reggie stepped toward the young man. Reggie's frame blocked the sunlight and the young man's face fell into Reggie's shadow. The clean young man averted his eyes, looking down as he tried to hold his ground against this larger, street wise thug.

"Or is you just a Storebought Gangsta? Yeah, that's what you is, a motherfucking Storebought Gangsta." Reggie shifted his stance and smiled. "Well, well, well, we got us a Storebought Gangsta. Well, c'mon Storebought we gonna see what you got. Ever kill a motherfucker before?" Reggie's yellowed teeth were only inches from the nose of well-dressed young man. He zeroed in on the young man like a hawk to a crippled field mouse. Suddenly Reggie stepped back and laughed. "Wait, wait, wait. I got it. He a virgin. Boys, we got us a virgin here. I mean not only a virgin to kicking ass, but a virgin period. You ever had no pussy, didja little nigger? Serious."

"I, uh, of course. I get all kinds of pussy, uh, all the time."

"Your momma's hand jobs don't count. Serious." The group laughed. Someone spoke up.

"Reggie, I don't mean to interrupt when you're calling a nigger out, but don't knock his momma. She sure enough do give a good hand job!" Germaine was infuriated at this insult to his sister. He tried to speak but Reggie stepped in front of him. Germaine kicked at the ground. Storebought reached into his pocket and Germaine shook his head. Finally Reggie farted. The tension broke and Germaine moved back, waving his hand in front of his face. Reggie smiled.

"Damn, Reggie." The whole group laughed at the gaseous eruption. Reggie put his arm around the Storebought Gangsta and paraded him in front of the group.

"Alright, dry dick. You can come and plays wid da big boys. You better not leave us and run home. Besides, if you go home early you might walk in on your momma and some mofo' squealing like two pigs in shit. Serious." The group guffawed and moved toward the car with Reggie. Reggie closed his arm around the young man's neck as he dragged him to the car.

"Germaine, I knows that you done brought the ackahol. Please do not tell this nigger that you did not bring the ackahol. Serious."

Germaine reached into the car, produced a heavy brown bag, and smiled.

"Nigger, do you think I would show up to a 'Kick Beaner's Ass' party without a couple of sixes of Colt 45? Do you really fuckin' think this motherfuckin' nigger would show up to a ..."

"Shut up, nigger. Give the juice to the Storebought Gangsta. Let's see if he's too good to drink wid us. Serious." Reggie passed a can of beer to Storebought. The young man hesitated, looked at the other young men, popped the top and swallowed a huge mouthful. After slurping down almost a fourth of the can he lowered the can and gasped for breath.

"Sheeit. The little nigger can drink."

Germaine slid into the driver's seat and started the car. The rest of the group returned to the car, each opening a can of beer. Reggie moved into the front seat while the others forced their bodies into the back.

"Nigger, you need to get a bigger car. Serious."

The group drove off, drinking the beer and intermittently pushing each other for what little space the confined interior offered. It was not the room, but elevation in the peck order that was being sought.

"Reggie, which way we going?"

"East Edgewood. Serious." Germaine hit the brakes pushing everyone forward, beer spilling onto the back seat and carpet. Reggie hit his hand on the dash.

"What the fuck, nigger? Serious."

"Are you serious?"

"Serious."

"You want me to take this car load of niggers out to East Edgewood? Nigger, why not just shoot them now."

"I ain't got a gun." Germaine glanced at his cousin in the rear view mirror. The Storebought Gangsta reached into his pocket and fingered the .380 semi automatic that Germaine had given him "just in case". Germaine slightly shook his head. The crew pushed each other and protested.

"Germaine, you dint say nothin' about no East Edgewood. Shee-it."

"Them redneck cops shoot niggers for target practice out there."

"I heard they hung a nigger from a tree just for walking down the street."

"Shee-it. They ain't nuthin' but a bunch of chicken ass rich white..."

"...nigger hating racists. You done said so yourself, Reggie. Fuck that. I ain't going."

"Listen, we ride in, we ain't going through the center of Rich White City. I knows a way so we can goes up da back road, ain't no one gonna even see us. If they do we give up the Store Bought nigger." The group laughed nervously.

The young man in the clean clothes spoke without thinking. "Shit, we'll give you up."

Reggie turned around from the front seat and slapped Storebought across the face. No one moved as Reggie glared at the young man. He slapped him again, hard; the back hand knuckle to cheek strike was heard, and felt, by everyone in the car.

"Don't question me, nigger. Don't you ever talk to me, you Oreo cookie piece of shit." Still glaring, Reggie turned back around and plunked down in his seat with force, shaking the car. "Anyone else want to act like a pussy? Serious."

"No, we cool, Reggie. We cool."

"C'mon Reggie, that's my sister's kid. He don't mean nothing. He's just a Storebought Gangsta." Germaine's disparaging remark brought a chuckle to the group, slightly bending the tension.

"Well, he better not fuck this deal up. Serious." There was a short silence while the crew looked around and then out of the vehicle windows. "And I forgot to tell you niggers, there's some white hot-assed teacher at the school that wants to try some Charlotte Black Snake for dinner. Maybe this little Storebought Virgin Gangsta will finally get his dusty dick wet. Serious." The group laughed and pushed each other; jockeying for shoulder room as the car picked up speed and headed into East Edgewood. The group hooted.

"Let's go fuck up a Salsa stepper."

"I'm in, nigger."

"That's what I'm talking about."

"Yeah, he will head back to Mexico tomorrow. Serious."

The car rolled and Germaine drove closer to East Edgewood, Reggie directing him where to go. It was a twisted trail behind houses, a detour through the back of the mall, and then into a tree lined street. The young men in the back looked wide eyed at the height of the houses. They looked intently at the landscaping, expecting to see armed guards riding around on golf carts. There were none. Images of lynchings they had seen in library books filled their minds. Black men with ropes around their necks, tied to trees, their bodies battered, while white people stood next to the body, posing with their children. They were entering East Edgewood, a mystical forest of houses bigger than their apartment buildings.

"This place is strange. It give me da cheels."

"I heard they hung a nigger just a little north of here." Storebought opened his mouth, and then drew a breath.

"They cut his dick off." Reggie turned around but remained seated.

"For real, back in the fifties. They cut his dick off. Then his testicles."

"Nigger, please. And how just the fucks do you know that?" The group, their own thoughts fading to distant mist, turned to Storebought.

"I did a report on it in seventh grade. His name was Claude Neal. They said he…"

"Wait, wait, wait. A book report? Nigger puhleeze don't be sitting here talking about – you did a book report on some lynched ass nigger in English class. Serious." The group held silent for a second and then broke into cat calls and hilarity, slapping each other's hands and shaking their heads.

"It was Social Studies class." Everyone froze at this intrusion into Reggie's rebuke. Reggie had since faced the front of the car. Without turning around, he allowed Storebought to continue.

"Go ahead; tell these dumb ass niggers what they don't know. Serious. Maybe it will piss 'em off and they'll stop whining." Everyone angled to Storebought. Germaine looked in the rear view mirror, his brow furrowed in concern.

"It was in 1953. Just north of here they lynched a brother named Claude Neal. He was tortured for hours by over one hundred people. They kept slashing at him with knives. And not just the men. Little kids, wives, everyone was cutting little gashes into him. Some of them chopped off his fingers, and then his toes, and kept them for souvenirs. They used red hot irons to burn him all over his body. Here's the messed up part. They would tie a rope around his neck, pull him up a tree and let him choke. Almost to death. Then they would let him down and torture him all over again. This went on for twelve hours. After they got tired of hearing him scream and beg, they hooked him to a bumper, and dragged him behind a car for ten miles. When they stopped in front of a mob of people, everyone in the mob used knives and sharpened sticks to stick into his body. People kicked him, rode over him in their cars, jumped up and down on his dusty dead body.

Finally, even though he was dead, they hung him in the courthouse square and left him there, naked for four days. People came by in the thousands and took pictures. White people are sick."

Storebought looked at the group. They were staring at him with their mouths open. Even Reggie, who had pushed his back square against the window, had his mouth agape.

"Fuckin' white racist bastards."

The group rode silently as they looked at the large trimmed oak trees, wondering which branch could hold a rope. The fear dissipated when Reggie spoke.

"No, left here. Left, dummy! Jeesh. Yeah, now pull in there. Follow that service road to the end. The end, nigger." Reggie probed the back seat with his eyes. "That hot new white teacher might be teaching us niggers a few lessons on fucking her ass silly. Serious."

The group laughed and a few boys rubbed their crotches gangland style. Germaine lit up a joint and passed it to Reggie. The group took turns hitting the home rolled marijuana cigarette in their assigned peck order. Storebought took a hit and coughed. They laughed and hooted. Storebought hacked uncontrollably while they passed the burning joint to each other. Reggie took the last toke and swallowed the still burning remnants. The group was silently absorbing their high until Germaine returned them to reality.

"Nigger, that is good shit!" Stoned, the group now snickered the way a group of young men under the influence of tetrahydrocannabinol snickered. The drug bonded them. Except for Storebought.

The clean clothed, educated young man recently nicknamed Storebought had finally stopped coughing. He sat trapped in this car with these stoned street thugs. He realized how different he was. Besides not being stoned, Storebought lived in a white neighborhood. He went to predominantly white schools all his life. He only came to this because he was visiting his cousin and heard that they were going off to beat up some Hispanic guy. Germaine had said this before and all they ended up doing was driving around and yelling at girls until the police pulled them over. Then everyone went home. He had never met Reggie Powell before. And now he wished that he never had. His stomach, queasy from the beer, was telling him to run; his mind was flatly informing him that he could not leave the group. There was no way out. The boy next to him pulled out a wooden club with a rawhide string tied at the bottom. The boy sought Reggie's favor.

"Yo, Reggie, I took this off a white guy. He called it a 'nigger stick'. So why did a white ass bitch have it?" The group howled with laughter as the car slowed. The sign to the school stood out amongst the bushes. Germaine turned into the deserted school parking lot. He followed Reggie's silent motions and pulled around behind the gym. An embossed brass sign proclaimed that they were in front of the sixth grade wing. Germaine cruised past the sixth grade wing and parked behind the dumpster near the cafeteria.

"Shee-it, I'll show you a nigger stick. Serious." Reggie raised his hips in the front seat and faked an attempt to pull down his zipper. The group wailed, flipped the door handles, and fell out of the car. Beer cans clattered in the silent parking lot. The acrid smell of marijuana hung in the still air.

The deserted campus brought a nostalgic sense of foreboding to Reggie. In his short educational career he had no good memories from school. Reggie looked at the door to the office. He did not know Montel but he knew of him. The guy, like most Spics, probably had it coming. His grandmother appeared in his stoned mind's eye. *You can tell…* He barked at his crew effectively drowning out her voice.

"Shut your dumb ass nigger faces up. This ain't no joke. You are all gonna get paid for this shit depending on how well you perform this duty. We calls this performance pay. The more you fuck up this faggot wetback, I means you personally, the mores dead presidents you gets. Got it? Serious."

"But Germaine said we would get…"

"Nigger, I know you ain't questioning me. Are you questioning me, motherfucker?" The group lowered their eyes. A few absently kicked at the small rocks at their feet.

"No, man, I'm cool." Germaine shrugged and stepped forward. Reggie cut him off.

"Y'all will get your twenty pieces of silver." The young man in the clean clothes tried to show enthusiasm and spoke up.

"Let's go and get it done." His voice cracked and the group chuckled. Reggie raised his hand and the young man flinched, snapping up his elbow to avert the blow.

"Shut up, Storebought, you got a learning disability or something? I say when you go. Goofy ass bitch. Serious." After stepping away for a moment, fighting his grandmother's attempt to emerge from the shadows of his mind, Reggie turned to the group.

"Let's go. Serious."

Ken Montel locked his classroom door and walked briskly toward his car. Debbie was going to spend the evening and he wanted his apartment to be just perfect. The halls were dark and empty. By four o'clock the afternoon before the Thanksgiving break hardly a soul remained. All but one of the custodians knocked off early, he just stayed back to lock up. This year the school board had saved the Wednesday before Thanksgiving as a snow makeup day. Since no snow had touched Charlotte this year, Thanksgiving break had begun on Tuesday. As he opened the door to the sixth grade wing Ken heard a car door slam.

Ken Montel had not been with Debbie for a night alone since they began dating. He smiled and his facial muscles felt strange as if he had not used them all day, common for a sixth grade teacher. Still smiling he strode down the sidewalk and slid behind the steering wheel of his car. As he left the parking lot Ken noticed a dusty brown Hyundai parked behind the eighth grade wing. He slowed to a stop. *Should I check this out?* He put the car in neutral and engaged the parking brake. *No, not tonight. It's probably one of the custodian's kids coming to borrow money for gas or something.* He smiled and took his left foot off the brake and returned it to the gas pedal. Ken rolled down the window and breathed in the fresh air. His mind drifted to a night with Debbie. The brown car left his field of vision as he pulled forward. *Yeah, that's just someone visiting the custodian.* He tightened his grip on the steering wheel and turned out of the parking lot. This was going to be a great break from school.

In his rear view mirror, unseen by the smiling Ken Montel, a gang of black kids jumped out of a dusty brown Hyundai. Ken Montel turned onto the main road and headed home.

Just as he was swallowing his third Tylenol in an hour, Coach Roth thought he heard a car door slam. Funny, he thought everyone was gone. He was waiting for his son to pick him up, so he had hung back. His foot fell from the desk, his body swung trancelike of the swivel chair and he floated out of his glass walled office. He opened the gym door and looked behind the cafeteria; all he could see was a dusty brown car. Then all four doors opened and it poured out hoodlums.

Black hoodlums.

He shut the door and reached for his walkie-talkie. It was dead. He jogged back to his office in the manner of old men that were once young and in shape. He could hear them all around the brown car, kicking beer cans and loudly talking. He looked back when they tried the gym door. Off balance he stumbled downward until his shoulder slammed into the brick wall next to the mats. Full force, his shoulder absorbed the full impact of his momentum. Reaching over with his good arm, Coach Roth realized that he had dislocated his shoulder. He staggered from the pain. He pushed hard against his distorted arm and the shoulder popped back into place. The pain subsided, giving him a euphoric feeling of relief. Leaving through the girls' locker room on the other side of the gym, Coach Roth strode quickly toward the front office, rubbing his shoulder along the way. He had hoped to find Bridges, or a phone that worked. He was spied by Germaine as he shuffled up the walk.

"Yo, Reggie, company."

"Can I help you guys?" Coach Bob Roth held his shoulder with one hand.

"This must be one of the bitch ass racists himself."

"Yeah, he look like one. Serious." The group walked slowly until they formed a half circle around Roth.

"So you like to lynch niggers out here. Well, how's about when you is outnumbered. It's payback time, you racist fuck." With that statement hanging in the air, Germaine grabbed the "nigger stick" from the other gang member. Germaine swung at Roth, yet the seasoned coach quickly ducked away from the arc of the stick. Stepping into Germaine's back swing; Roth slammed across Germaine's back with his good arm, sending him careening over the well trimmed bushes. Roth threw a punch at the next crew member that came forward, hitting him squarely in the face. The man's nose erupted into blood as he buried his face in his hands.

"Augh! Shit! God damn! He broke my fuckin' nose." The man shrieked like a schoolgirl as he fell onto the ground, blood dripping through his fingers onto his pants. Like a bad Kung Fu movie, the next crew member moved forward from Coach's left. He half-turned to his left to face the man. Coach Roth swung into the air and missed. From Roth's blindside Reggie caught the defender off balance and kicked him behind the knee. The big coach stumbled forward and the crew member from his left nailed him in the eye with a roundhouse punch.

"There you go, white boy. How's my fist taste?" Roth's face snapped away from the force of the blow and he stumbled backwards into Germaine.

"I got the motherfucker now." Germaine pushed Coach Roth forward. Reggie jumped over the stumbling coach, grabbed the "nigger stick" from Germaine, raised it up above his head, hesitated, and then brought it down across the older man's back. Coach Roth crumpled to the sidewalk. Storebought grabbed the older man's arm as he approached the crawling body of the once mighty Coach Bob Roth. Storebought wrapped his arms around Roth's body, picking him up. For a minute it looked like he was trying to help the old coach. Then blood dropped onto Storebought's clean white hoodie and he let go of his heavy package. Germaine nodded at his nephew.

"One at a time, right Reggie?"

"Fuck just beating his ass, this bitch is gonna die."

Roth tried to get up. He was on all fours when Germaine kicked him in the stomach. Roth wheezed as the wind was knocked out of him. *I have to get up or I am going to die*. On his knees, Coach reached out to lift himself up. Reggie stepped on his fingers. The clubbed edge of the stick cracked hard on the gray haired man's skull, cleanly opening a three inch gash across his forehead. Blood trickled into his eyes. He rallied his remaining strength and grabbed Germaine's foot, pulling him off balance. Reggie kicked out and caught the coach on the shoulder. The one that he had just separated. Agony returned to Roth's shoulder and he lost his grip of Germaine. Roth had his keys in between his fingers. He held out his open hands, and then he swung weakly at Reggie, barely thumping his chest.

"umph…oh, like that hurt…you gonna die." Reggie looked down and saw blood form where the jagged end of Roth's keys had pierced his skin.

"This is a new shirt, bitch."

The crew member with the broken nose picked up a cantaloupe sized landscape boulder from the flower bed next to him and threw it at Coach - missing completely and hitting Reggie in the hip. The man rushed up to Reggie as the rock clunked onto the sidewalk and rolled to a stop.

"Sorry man. I meant to hit the racist."

"Ow, bitch-ass, what the fuck?" Reggie pushed the man back and yelled. "Look out!" It was too late. Coach Roth was behind him. As the pain seared through his shoulder, Bob Roth swung his key fist across the side of the crew members head, sending him into Reggie. Germaine hit Roth on his wounded shoulder with the "nigger stick" and the old man's knees buckled. Germaine moved to the front of the man on his knees and swung the "nigger stick" across his face. Coach Bob Roth, one of the most victorious coaches in East Edgewood history, fell back against his ankles, which twisted up under him as he lay half on the sidewalk and half in the flower bed just outside the office door. Reggie stepped toward the coach's motionless body. With one foot on either side of the staid man, Reggie opened his pocket knife. Storebought cried out.

"No!"

Reggie ignored him and grabbed a handful of gray hair, twisting the older man's face up to look at Reggie. Semi-conscious, with all of his remaining strength, Coach Roth rose to a kneeling position as Reggie stuck the knife under the coach's throat.

"How 'bout I just cuts him real quick." Reggie smiled at Storebought as he faked cutting across Coach Roth's throat. Storebought's arms fell when he saw that Reggie did not cut the old man's throat. *Okay, they are not going to kill this guy.* Storebought saw Reggie's face as it went dark. Reggie drove the knife into Roth's shoulder. His battered shoulder. In a delirium from the pain, Coach Roth twisted to the side as he felt the icy hot pain of the three inch metal pocketknife tear through his deltoid. Reggie grabbed him by the back of the neck and slit his left cheek. Bob Roth felt the sharp steel blade cross his face and sluggishly reached up to push away the pain. Reggie then jabbed his victim in the back, the burning pain stiffening the man's body. Reggie pulled the knife out deliberately and stabbed again; a few inches lower. Entranced with what he was doing, Reggie barely saw Storebought coming toward him. But he did. He stepped to the side and the younger, clean cut man slipped on the grass and fell past him.

"Storebought, you fuckin…" Reggie's tongue hung still when he looked at Storebought. The silver pistol in his hand was pointed right at Reggie.

"You said we were going to beat up some Spanish guy and then leave, Germaine. You didn't say anything about killing, or knifing, or anything else. I am not going to jail for this. Move away from that man, Reggie, you have done enough to him. I do not want to shoot you."

Reggie had recovered from the initial shock. His street "smarts" grabbed hands with his innate survival instincts and spoke.

"Chicken shit, Storebought Gangsta motherfucker. Put that gun down… no, better 'n that…give it here. Serious."

"No."

"Serious." Reggie stepped back and angled his body to see both Storebought and the moaning man on the ground. "Bitch, give me dat gun. Now, motherfucker!" Reggie's booming voice caused Storebought's hand to flinch.

"No. I will shoot you if you come near me. I know the law. I am an accessory to murder if you kill him. So…no… I will not give you this gun. You need to get your crew and leave." Roth stirred.

"Shut up bitch. Storebought, gimme that fuckin' gun. Germaine take that gun from you little Storebought nigger nephew. Ser-eee-US!" Germaine stepped toward Storebought and Storebought fired a shot over his head. At the sound of the bullet Reggie rushed Storebought with his knife above his head. Storebought turned quickly away from Reggie, assumed a crouching position and fired into Reggie's chest. Reggie landed full force on Storebought, knocking the gun out of his hand. While the crew looked on dazed, Germaine's long arms reached for the gun, pulling it out of the grass. He stood, pushing the moaning old man back with his foot; and then looked at Reggie who was lying facedown, one arm twisted behind his back at an obscene angle.

"Yo, Reg? Reggie? Yo, man I gots the gun. Reggie?" Germaine motioned to the other crew members with the pistol. "Turn him over. Yo, Reggie, you okay?" The two crew members approached Reggie like adolescent apes approaching a sleeping silverback. They unhurriedly turned him over and revealed a circular red stain in the middle of Reggie's chest. Reggie's eyes were open and fixed.

Reggie was dead.

"Goddamn, Kevin! You killed my boy Reggie. I gonna kill your ass." Germaine shot at his nephew, missed completely, but froze Storebought in his tracks. The bullet smashed through the bottom window of office door, blowing it out. Storebought stared at Germaine. The others spoke.

"Nigger, is you crazy? Shoot his ass. The motherfucker just killed Reggie…"

"He's my sister's kid." Germaine raised both hands to his head and turned in a circle. "Oh, fuck, what we gonna do. What the fuck is we gonna do now?"

"We gots to get out of here. It look like the white motherfucker is almost dead, if'n he ain't he will be soon from what Reggie done did to him." The crew member turned to Storebought.

"This bitch is gonna rat us out like a mother-fucker, Germaine. You know dat, Germaine. He gotta go, Germaine. He gotta go... hey, man lookout!" Before Germaine could react, Storebought stole up from behind him and pulled the gun from his hand in one swift motion.

"No one is going to die. Germaine, I will shoot these two jerks, and then you - if you do not leave right now. I am not playing anymore. Go!"

"And how the fucks are you gonna get home? Walk through the rich section? These people will hang your ass."

"I will make it ..."

The other gang member, still bleeding from his nose, interrupted.

"Fuck it let's go, Germaine. I's getting hungry anyway, man."

Germaine pointed to the ground where Reggie lay.

"What about Reggie?"

"He dead. Reggie dead. Ain't nothing we can do for his black ass now... let's go, Germaine." The other crew member chimed in.

"Yeah, man, this shit done went bad. C'mon, let's go."

The crew member with the bloodied nose walked over to Reggie, rolled Reggie onto his stomach, and wriggled Reggie's wallet from his pocket. He took out the money that the man had given to Reggie only two hours ago. Reggie eyes were open. His mouth revealed the corn chips that still resided in his teeth.

"You won't be needin' this my man. Get that white motherfuckers wallet."

The other crew member fished the wallet out of Coach Roth's pants and pocket it. He turned to Storebought.

"Fuck you, little faggot ass nigger, I will see yo' ass again."

Storebought tightened his grip on the pistol and stuck his jaw out. The three men ran down the sidewalk. Just before he turned the corner, Germaine screamed out of the side of his neck to his nephew.

"They gonna kill you, you know that. They gonna kill your nigger ass out here. C'mon, little cousin, let's go home."

Storebought squeezed off a shot hitting the wall behind Germaine. Germaine yelped and then disappeared around the corner. Over Roth's labored breathing Storebought could hear the car doors shut, the starter motor whine until the engine caught, and the sound of tires squealing into the night. Darkness edged down upon The White School.

Storebought spun around and sprinted to the front of the school, jumped through the trimmed bushes and hurdled the decorative split rail fence. He heard the sirens when he stopped. Someone must have heard the shots. What he did not know was that the night custodian, Eric Blummer, had watched the entire ordeal while concealed behind the counter in the front office. Blummer was in the cafeteria when Reggie's crew pulled up. Waiting until the crew went around the building, the custodian ran to the front office to find Mr. Bridges office locked and empty. Eric called 911 as he sat locked in Bridges' office.

"There's a gang of niggers robbing the school."

He spoke quickly and hung up the phone. Then Eric ducked behind the counter. He could hear Roth being beaten but decided to wait for the police. One dead hero was enough.

As Storebought rounded the corner he saw two police cars pull up. Both officers emerged with their weapons drawn. Storebought skidded to a stop, and then froze.

"There's one. Lookout, he's got a gun."

Storebought ran back toward the gym. The officers ducked down for a quick second. Two other cars pulled up and the officers on foot motioned to his partner that he was going around the back of the building. He pointed for the three men to join him.

"Let's head him off around the back of the gym. Watch out, the caller said there was about a dozen of them." he whispered hoarsely.

The men left; crouching as they ran to the back of the gym. On the other side of the gym, Storebought was shaking so bad he could not think. Oh my God. What am I going to do? He hunkered down behind a small bush outside of a classroom window. He hyperventilated like a rabbit on the run from a pack of dogs. His knees shook uncontrollably. *I gotta get out of here.* He left his cover and dashed down the sidewalk, looking back to see if he had been followed. Fifteen yards from the end of the building he saw four officers in blue round the corner behind the cafeteria. *Oh damn, they went around the other way.* Storebought stopped and stared wide eyed at the police. The men in front of Storebought scrambled for strategic cover. Storebought looked at the gun in his hand, and then around the school. He was putting the gun down when movement to his right caught his eye. He spun around with the gun in front of him. The officers raised their pistols.

Storebought screamed as they opened fire.

Holly and Ivy

A smooth leg stepped out of the metallic gray Mercedes Benz. The foot, snugly nestled in the soft fleece of a slaughtered ewe, the inner dermis of the ewe, with its fleece still attached, tanned and treated to look like suede, stepped onto the recently painted yellow dividing line. Uggs. Standard issue in Holly Van Derhagen's circle of influence. Although the generic version of the same boot was cheaper, and did not require the killing and skinning of sheep; the worse poison dart that Holly could hurl is to accuse someone of wearing fake Uggs. Holly once brought the indomitable Mary Ellen Pike to watered eyes after one such clandestinely tossed dart found its mark. Mary Ellen, unschooled in the fine art of shoe spotting, truly believed that the generic version of Uggs her grandmother purchased as a Christmas gift would pass off as the real thing. She was wrong and wore only sandals since that attack. Mary Ellen, Queen Bee of the tough girls, knew better than to reply to Holly Van Derhagen. What minor status, beyond what she had gained as a fighting female, Mary Ellen enjoyed would be erased by Holly. It was better to wear nothing than fake footwear at East Edgewood. Uggs were in; fake Uggs made you an outcast. Boots that cost more than a week's salary for some of the Carver students.

The other tanned, marble smooth leg swung out, for a moment making Holly regret that she had worn a miniskirt. She took her time, although Mr. Montel was eagerly waving her across the road. Holly Van Derhagen would get there when she was ready. As usual. She stood with a heel on either side of the reflective yellow stripe and smoothed her miniskirt, purposefully looking away from the repetitive arm movements of Mr. Montel. Her mother scrutinized Mr. Montel's pupils, almost daring him to look at her daughter as she leaned over into the car to retrieve the Jan Sport backpack. Momentarily taking her eyes off of the pointing and waving black man directing traffic, Doris Van Derhagen turned to her eldest daughter.

"Good luck with your presentation dear. Your grandfather would be proud."

Her shirt, straight from Macy's, was the latest in Egyptian cotton. It was accessorized by a Midori belt and covered by a North Face jacket. "Speak clearly and look in each student's eyes for one second. Just like in summer seminar. Okay?"

"I will, mother."

Holly shut the door and waved to her friend Ivy Bergen. Ivy wore the same basic outfit as Holly except that her Uggs were a powder blue and her miniskirt tinted to match. Holly held up her 'John McCain for President' poster. Six cars behind them someone hit their horn. Holly slowly tucked her cell phone into her backpack. Mr. Montel took a step toward the stationary car just as Doris Van Derhagen pushed the gas pedal. She drove a few miles faster than the posted speed limit and her rear view mirror breezed within inches of the open armed Montel. Holly stepped in front of an on-coming van without looking. The driver hit the brakes and the van, although only traveling a few miles an hour, lurched to a stop. Holly stepped onto the curb to meet Ivy who was shaking the poster as if it were greatest discover since the Rosetta Stone.

"It's authentic! My father called the RNC and they sent it. It will go perfectly with our presentation. Did you get the birth certificate?"

"Love, do you think for one minute that my step-monster would let me down? She took it off the internet, had it clarified, digitized and it is now a full page slide on Powerpoint." Holly pulled out a small flash drive in the shape of a Maserati.

"Obama is an alien. And we can prove it."

"What about his health care proposal?"

"My father's secretary gladly worked it into the presentation, three slides just on how much it is going to cost the taxpayer."

"Mr. Desfourneaux is going to love this."

"I see an 'A' in our future."

Holly and Ivy strutted through school. One seventh grade boy dropped his books as he turned to watch them walk. They did not have to navigate through the crowd of students, everyone moved out of their way. One heavy girl, with her back to the pair, was yanked out of their way by a friend. Before the girl could pro-test she looked at Holly and Ivy and remained mute. Holly Van Derhagen and Ivy Bergen both had lockers, right next to each other and at the preferred position at the end of the hall (whereas the official policy was that all lockers were randomly assigned). After touching up their makeup the pair entered Mr. Desfourneaux's class and placed their backpacks and the poster on his desk. On the wall behind Mr. Desfourneaux's desk were typical school pictures of Lincoln and Washington. Above these pictures were eight by ten glossy photos of George Bush and Ronald Reagan. On the current events board hung the yellowed picture of former President Jimmy Carter as he stumbled while jogging. Other articles touted fiscal responsibility and the benefits of tax cuts. Holly placed her flash drive into Mr. Desfourneaux's computer. He entered the room as they were typing in his password.

"May I help you?"

"We have it thanks."

"I believe we are going first, correct?"

Mr. Desfourneaux slid his hands off of his hips. Holly and Ivy, the two most arrogant examples of an overindulged child that he had ever seen were his two top students, whether he liked it or not. However, Holly's father had allowed Mr. Desfourneaux to enter into the upper circles of Republicans that he could only dream of in his younger years. Last year he met with all three Bushes at a fundraiser for John McCain. Holly Van Derhagen and Ivy Bergen were going first today.

"Sure, since you are already, uh, ready."

Holly gave him a look that a man of his stature would only see in the movies. Ivy breezed by him, her perfume a faint wisp, yet ostensibly odiferous. Mr. Desfourneaux glanced surreptitiously at her clicking heels. Holly approached him from behind. Desfourneaux flinched.

"Where can I put this?"

She shoved Ivy's McCain poster less than a foot from Desfourneaux's face. He thought for a moment of the family tree of the child in front of him.

"How about on my desk? You could prop it with my tape dispenser."

She handed the poster to him and he positioned it on his desk, covering his papers and almost knocking over his coffee. Holly nodded.

"That's good right there."

Ivy had turned on the overhead projector and the blue light became brighter as the computer loaded the program. The projector, which usually had the morning assignment on it, read clearly what was about to take place. Within a few minutes the early bell rang and the students filed into the classroom. Everyone looked at the John McCain poster that had taken over Desfourneaux's desk.

A gang of four undersized white boys straggled in and each stole a fleeting look at Holly's miniskirt. Each was lost in their own sordid thoughts, the thoughts that a budding teenage boy thinks when girls as beautiful as Holly Van Derhagen wear skimpy clothing. She would have been more at home in a Parisian nightclub than a middle school in Charlotte, North Carolina. Ivy had dressed similarly, but the difference in body shape, and morph, had made her look less elegant and more like a prostitute. Mary Ellen Pike entered just as the bell rang and sank into her seat.

Everyone was aware of the projector, which usually had the morning assignment on it, and knew clearly what was about to take place.

THE END OF AMERICA
By Holly Van Derhagen and Ivy Bergen

Just after the Pledge of Allegiance, Holly Van Derhagen and Ivy Bergen, totally disregarding Mr. Desfourneaux's attempt to take attendance, took center stage and began their presentation.

"Thank you very much for attending today. My associate, Ms. Ivy Bergen and I have researched for many weeks and have prepared a treatise to save our country, or at least our way of life, for future generations. Ms. Bergen?"

"Thank you, Ms. Van Derhagen. My assignment in this groundbreaking research was to determine if Barack Obama, the Democratic nominee for President, is legally qualified to run for President. As you know, the President must be born in the United States…"

Holly and Ivy, buoyed their subject with the expressions that they had learned in years of acting school, phrases they had heard their parents say at fundraisers, and stopped just short of making any statement that was overtly racist. The five students of African American heritage shifted and looked down during the majority of the presentation. Holly made special effort not to look at any of them. All had a scowl on their face – except for Patricia Ferguson. At the conclusion Mr. Desfourneaux clapped his hands and stood up.

"Any questions?"

No one had ever dared to approach, never mind question, Holly Van Derhagen or Ivy Bergen. They would get an "A" on their project, as always, and Mr. Desfourneaux would tell them how wonderful they were and talk up to them like a schoolboy.

"Then if there are no questions…"

"Anyone that don't vote for Obama is a racist."

Sherise Davis, fresh back from a three day suspension had broken the silence. Holly rolled her eyes, Ivy looked at Mr. Desfourneaux.

"Don't you roll your eyes at me, bitch. I'll slap the black off you."

Holly pulled her chin to her neck, and made her most practiced face- that of disgust.

"That doesn't even make sense…"

Desfourneaux saw his possible future pass before his eyes. He walked between Sherise and Holly.

"Sherise, if you have something to add to the discussion you will do so in a civil manner. We are not on the street here. We will follow Robert's Rules of Order for this discussion…

Sherise sat back. She remembered what her mother screamed about getting suspended again. She held her tongue.

"Now, according to Robert's Rules, do you have something to add?

"Robert who? Both of them miniskirt ho's is racist. That's…"

Before Sherise could finish her statement, Holly snapped back.

"Talk about racist? You're only voting for Obama because he's black. You don't know anything about him. Do you know what his plan for Medicare is going to be? His stand on welfare? What direction he is going to take with the war in Iraq? Afghanistan? Every word my Ivy and I spoke is based on fact. You - and all the rest of the blacks that are voting for him because he is black – you're the real racists. I mean the man was not even born in America."

Sherise restrained herself. She had nothing to say. Holly was right. Obama's specific plans for America, the running of the country, the military, and the war – none of it had been spoken of in Sherise's neighborhood. That Obama was black was the only issue. The skin color issue, and that some white racist would probably shoot him. Sherise had nothing to say about the facts that Holly and Ivy were presenting. It could be all made up as far as she was concerned – but yet Sherise could not intellectually comment on any of it. Sherise knew that the white kids would laugh behind her repetitive back if she accused the two rich white girls of racism again. The alienation she experienced because she was from Carver would be multiplied and worse, personified. Sherise wanted to scream. She wanted to slap Holly. That's how it was done at her last school if someone embarrassed you. You slapped them. Sherise grabbed the book on the corner of her desk. She visualized throwing the book right into the straight white teeth of Holly Van Derhagen. That would wipe the smug look off her face. Then Sherise thought of her Momma. She was out of excuses at home-and she would most likely be sent back to Carver. The anger of her mother was dwarfed by the disappointment her grandmother would heap on her if Sherise was thrown out of The White School. The class held its breath. Sherise lifted the book and stood beside her desk. Mr. Desfourneaux stepped back, closer to Holly. Even the students that normally zoned out during class were watching. Dustin Blackstone thought that any fight between Sherise and Holly would result in the compromise of Holly's miniskirt. His pulse quickened when he fantasized about the miniskirt clad Ivy Bergen jumping into the fray. Dustin smiled. *This is gonna be great!* The tense seconds of the standoff hung time on the wall. No one moved. Then suddenly a voice entered the stillness from the rear of the room. It was Patricia Ferguson, the African American (as she liked to be called) girl that was raised on an Army base in Germany.

"Barak Obama is not the only Presidential candidate that has had questions raised about his place of birth."

Holly cocked her head, looked at Mr. Desfourneaux, and then scurried to a safe area behind his desk. Ivy followed. In an attempt to instill some normalcy for the remaining forty minutes of his class, Desfourneaux unconvincingly took on the role of inquisitive teacher.

"Is that so, Patricia? Who were the others?"

Sherise, still clutching the book, mumbled as she sat down.

"If it ain't the Oreo cookie."

"Well, I heard about Obama's birth certificate on the news and I decided to do a little research of my own – and yes, I just heard you, Sherise. Anyhow they were quite a few that were questioned."

Holly and Sherise's mouth dropped open at the same time. Desfourneaux stepped to the center of the classroom as he saw Patricia take out what appeared to be a few pages full of notes.

"Thank you, Patricia. I am sure there were others. And that is a discussion I would love to have. But we have other presentations scheduled for today. Let's continue with …"

"I apologize for interrupting you Mr. Desfourneaux, but Holly asked if anyone had questions on her topic, didn't she?"

Desfourneaux turned to Holly and Ivy, both safely barricaded behind the McCain poster and Desfourneaux's solid oak desk. He weakly asked Holly if she would like to entertain a question.

"Yes, of course."

Patricia picked up her notebook.

"Coincidentally, my presentation is on Presidential candidates that were not born in America, and how the Twelfth Amendment to the Constitution is applied."

Patricia glanced down at her shoes, then at Sherise. Sherise's balled hands loosened from fists, her red eyes blinked. Sherise smirked at Mr. Desfourneaux, then turned her ire to Holly Van Derhagen. Sherise sat back when Patricia spoke.

"Do you mind if I go next, Mr. Desfourneaux?"

Mr. Desfourneaux was confused. He knew he should send Sherise to the office, but did not know if he could explain how a racial discussion got out of hand. He was pretty sure that he would not be able to convince Mr. Goodman why Sherise should be suspended on her first day back. In addition, he thought of the response from Holly's father. He half pointed to Patricia, a look of disbelief on his face. Sherise turned away and sucked her upper palate with her tongue making a "tchut" sound.

"He ain't gonna let you go."

The class held their breath again. Would someone truly challenge the duo of Holly and Ivy. Is that what Patricia was doing? Or was she going to reinforce their point – after all she did seem to agree with the white side of things.

"Mr. Desfourneaux? May I go next? I think I could make a good connection with a few counterpoints, maybe even introduce an alternate view."

Desfourneaux looked at Holly as she faintly moved her head from side to side. Her eyebrows angled down as she sensed that Desfourneaux was about to concede to Patricia.

"Mr. Desfourneaux? I believe that there is an order to the presentations. Am I correct?"

Desfourneaux nodded his head like a bobble headed dog in the back of a car window. He stepped to his desk, whispered "thanks" to Holly loud enough for the students in the first row to hear, and retrieved the list of students that were to give presentations. He ran his finger down the list, posturing submissively to Holly while she stood with her hands on her hips. Ivy remained strategically behind Holly and did not remove her peripheral vision from the movements of Sherise. Mr. Desfourneaux leaned close to Holly and showed her the next name on the list his demeanor gaining her approval. Holly muffled a laugh. Mr. Desfourneaux moved confidently to the front of the class.

"Mary Ellen Pike. Are you ready, Mary Ellen?"

"No. I left my stuff at home."

"Dustin?"

"In accordance with Robert's Rules of Order, I yield the floor to Patricia Ferguson."

"Uh, this is class; we are not abiding by Robert's Rules…"

Sherise jumped up.

"See? See? That's what I been saying. There's a different rule for whites than there is for blacks. White people always be changing the rules."

"Sit down please Sherise or you will be asked to leave the classroom."

After an obligatory stance of ego appeasing defiance, Sherise slid back into her seat. Before she did she shot a pleading look at Patricia. Patricia spoke.

" I am afraid that I must agree with Sherise. Are we going by Robert's Rules or not?"

"Fine we will use Robert's Rules. However, if you yield you can only yield to the next speaker, which is…" He ran his finger down the list. "…Elijah."

Elijah looked at his folder. He had done his report on the early years of Barack Obama. His was hand drawn pictures, colored with Sharpie markers that had bled through the paper. He had used a stack of multi-colored paper that his mother had picked up at the Dollar Store. He sat in his room and plagiarized what he could from a book he had checked out two days ago from the library. He only had four pages and would be done in a few minutes. After the presentation that just happened, with its miniskirts and real campaign posters and high definition pictures, he would look like an idiot with shabby paper he recycled from his Martin Luther King project. Plus he had become stimulated while watching Holly and Ivy wiggle back and forth in their miniskirts. He was not going to stand up for any reason.

"I give the floor to the next speaker in the house."

Desfourneaux frowned and slid his finger to the next name, which he had already scanned when he picked up the paper.

"Patricia, you have the floor."

Patricia stood up while Sherise raised her hand to high fiver her as she walked past. With the hand blocking her path, Patricia had no polite social choice but to high five this girl (who just minutes before had called her an Oreo cookie) in order to pass to the front of the class. She smiled and the other African American students sat up.

"Mr. Desfourneaux, can someone hold my posters?"

Elijah and Sherise scrambled to the front of the class, Patricia looked to Desfourneaux for approval and he nodded. Elijah held one side of the poster and Sherise held the other. It was a three foot high hand written copy of the twelfth amendment. Desfourneaux was impressed.

"Did you make that, Patricia?"

"Yes sir. I soaked it in tea to give it the antiqued look, but I wrote the rest myself."

"You have the floor."

"Many people have been trying to prove that Barack Obama was not born in America. Can I see a show of hands of people that believe it is important for someone to be born in America as a condition of running for President?"

The initial hesitation was like a flame to a pile of hay after Holly raised her hand. Sherise raised hers and waved it into the air. Within half a minute the entire class had their hand high in the air, including Mr. Desfourneaux.

"So it appears it is unanimous." Patricia ceremoniously raised her hand. "I also agree with the Twelfth Amendment. Throughout history the subject of adherence to the Twelfth Amendment has become an issue, never a major issue, but an issue nonetheless."

Patricia explained how Chester A. Arthur was accused of being born in Canada, how the first eight Presidents from Washington to Jackson were actually British citizens. She explained how Barry Goldwater's birth in Arizona (which was not yet a state at the time) raised a minor stir during the 1964 election. Patricia hesitated and looked down. The uncomfortable silence left may wondering if she was overcome with emotion or finished with the presentation. Desfourneaux stood up, relieved that Patricia had veered off the controversial topic of Obama's birthplace, and opened it up into a history of the Twelfth Amendment.

"Thank you Patricia, that was energetic and very informative."

"You're welcome, Mr. Desfourneaux. However, I have not finished yet. Next poster please."

Elijah and Sherise tussled over the next poster, trying to put the first poster at the back and finally dropping all three on the ground. They picked them up and pushed the second one to the front. Patricia's foresight, and knowledge of human nature, was apparent in poster number two. Patricia read aloud as she pointed to each word.

"Should a man that is suspected of foreign birth, and refuses to show his birth certificate, be allowed to run for President of the United States?"

The agreement throughout the crowd signaled Holly to speak up. Patricia, the black girl who acted and spoke white, had polarized the group more than Holly and Ivy.

"I for one do not believe that anyone born outside of the United States, regardless of the Twelfth Amendment, should be even allowed to run for President."

"So you believe that anyone born outside of the United States, regardless of the Twelfth Amendment, should not be allowed to run for President? Regardless of who the candidate is?"

"Yes."

"Even if he is a sitting United States Senator?"

"Yes."

Desfourneaux looked at Holly. He knew where Patricia was going.

He knew.

"Next poster, please."

With practiced dexterity and synchronous motion, Elijah and Sherise dropped the second poster to reveal the third. The room erupted into a cacophony of denials and questions of surprise.

"Do you still feel that anyone born outside of the United States should not be eligible for President?"

John McCain was born on August 3, 1934 in the country of Panama. McCain has steadfastly refused to produce a birth certificate despite requests from all of the major news networks. Patricia put her hands on her hips and spoke loudly.

"Any questions? Holly? Ivy? Mr. Desfourneaux?"

Politics as Usual

Three tired black girls stood at the locked door, their arms full with rolled-up posters. The trio had worked late into the night to finish these sacred scrolls. Signs that proved that one of them was a candidate, just like the rich white kids whose posters had been printed professionally. Now here they stood, the three of them, looking through the green glass of the locked doors. A teacher walked by, they knocked loudly and the teacher half turned but did not break stride. At East Edgewood students were not supposed to enter the building before the first bell rang.

"Look, there's Holly Van Derhagen and that other girl putting up posters."

Sherise, whose eyes were half closed until this point, eagerly pointed to two white students taping their posters up in the hall. She had arrived late to May May's house last night. May May's father started drinking around nine thirty so she tried to hurry the other kids up. May May could usually gauge his behavior by the number of beer cans on the table, and would shuffle her friends out before he got ugly. Last night that time was eleven o'clock. But that was all right because it was late anyway. Her friends Sherise and Hallee headed out the door just after her father cursed the racists at The White School.

"They're going to get all of the good places." Hallee said disappointedly.

"How did they get in?" Sherise queried.

May May knocked hard on the door. The head secretary, a short woman who the kids nicknamed 'The Midge", stomped out from around her desk. She barked through the glass.

"No one is allowed into the school before the first bell."

May May pointed beyond the secretaries' shoulder.

"What about them? How do they get into the building?"

The secretary did not even bother to turn around, never mind answer May May's question. Instead she threatened all three with a week's lunch detention if they even touched the door again. May May pleaded through the glass.

"But I am running for Student Council President."

The secretary shook her head no and stomped, with dwarf like movements, back to her desk. The two girls inside turned down a hallway with their stack of identical cardboard signs. A teacher walked by them and smiled. May May shoulders dropped and Sherise grabbed her arm.

"Girl, don't give up yet."

Hallee touched May May on the shoulder.

"That's right. I learned last year that black people couldn't even vote until the sixties. So, we shall overcome."

The three girls laughed at her rendition of Martin Luther King. May May stood straighter and forced a grin at her friends.

"You know, you right. I may not win, but at least they could let me put my signs up."

As the girls waited a few white students gathered a safe distance behind them. No one talked to the three girls. Finally a kid they called Skinny the Guinea jumped out of a faded blue minivan with a broken rear view mirror. He strode up to them.

"Youse missed the bus too?"

"Youse? No, Sherise momma drove us. We here early to put up signs. May May be running for Student Council President. You better vote for her."

"Oh, I will. I'll tell everybody to vote for you. I have a lot of friends. I'm Dustin…

"Skinny the Guinea. We know who you is."

The girls laughed and inched away from the young man with the eager smile. He relegated himself to the empty space between the white kids and the three black girls. Sherise said that he was from their neighborhood but he told everyone he was Italian. Dustin looked down and kicked at a small rock. May May thought he might be able to bring in some votes and she waved him over.

"Skinny, I mean Dustin; can you talk to some your friends? Can you spread the word to vote for May May?"

Dustin did not want to tell them that he had no friends. As a matter fact they were the first girls that had talked to him since he came to The White School.

Although he was in eighth grade, one teacher, on the first day of school directed him towards the sixth-grade hallway. Dustin walked down there and ended up being late to his first class. Dustin would do anything, for anyone, at any time as long as they were nice to him.

"I got all sorts of friends. You may not be aware now - but that's the case. Dustin Blackstone is your new campaign manager. You may have well just won the election."

May May cocked her head cynically. Sherise whispered something about Skinny the Guinea and the trio laughed obnoxiously. All three turned their backs to the door as they stepped toward Dustin. None of them could see that their opponents had returned and were stapling signs to the wall in front of the office. The sound of the staple gun turned their heads. Holly Van Derhagen, looking exactly as she did on the huge poster, smiled smugly at them and then whirled on her heels. Her aide, Ivy Bergen waved. The pair disappeared down the hall. May May told Sherise and Hallee that as soon as the bell rang they would run in and hang the posters right next to Holly's. The crowd behind them had tripled as the time for the bell appproached. Mr. Montel waved cars along and the line was now backed up to the main street. At East Edgewood, most of the car riders showed up at the same time. A horn beeped as Skinny approached his new trio of friends. The crowd of students jostled him forward, May May said something to him but it was drowned out by the bell. After the custodian opened the door all three girls ran into the hallway. They were stopped by Mrs. Taschenberger as the crowd flowed past them.

"Go back and walk, girls."

They were dumbfounded and stood their ground like rocks in a stream. One student's backpack hit Sherise and she dropped one of the posters. She reached down as a chubby kid stepped on it, crushing the rolled up poster.

"Hey watch it, you idiot."

"Excuse me, young lady. But that is not how we talk to each other at East Edgewood Middle school. I want you to apologize to that student."

"Why? He squashed on my poster."

May May reached down to pick up the poster. Another of the rushing wave brushed her hip and sent her forward. Her posters flew as her arms stretched out to break her fall. By this time they were in the middle of about thirty students. The posters that they had worked so hard on about the student bodies, among their legs, and were kicked or crushed by the careless students. May May screamed out.

"Stop!"

"That is it. The three of you to the office right now."

As the first wave subsided the trio picked up the rolled placard; Sherise had full possession of hers, and tried to roll the creases out as Ms. Taschenberger marched the three girls to the front office. The short secretary peered over the top of her glasses. Eyebrows raised in acknowledgment, she shook her head and made a clucking sound.

"Those are the same three were trying to kick in the door a few minutes ago. I could not even answer the phones they were so loud. What else did they do?"

"Pushing and shoving. This one pretended to fall down and then screamed like a banshee. This one here was shoving our students. I tried to explain to them that this may have been the way they acted at Carver Middle, but it is not the way we act at East Edgewood."

"Someone pushed *me*. They knocked my posters all over the floor."

"What about the kid that knocked me down?"

Taschenberger and the midget secretary gave each other a knowing look.

"Can we go now?"

"I will tell you when, and if, you can go anywhere."

"I think the three of them should sit here and explain their rude behavior to Mr. Bridges when he gets in from bus duty."

"All I wanted to do was to put my signs up. We ain't causing no problems. I'm running for student council. I'm not a bad student."

"Student Council? I don't think Student Council needs any President who pushes our students and screams at their classmates. You just sit right there, young lady."

May May could not stop the tears from filling in her eyes. Sherise and Hallee were furious. They knew they had better follow Ms. Taschenberger's orders because she had a reputation of writing up and suspending black kids. May May knew that she had better follow the rules. One of the first things that May May did was to find out what the requirements were to run for Student Council President. If she were suspended she would not be eligible. Taschenberger and the midget secretary stood talking with their hands over their mouth. Taschenberger rolled her eyes, laughed and then walked away. The midget secretary spoke rudely without looking up.

"The three of you can go to class. Ms. Taschenberger has informed me that she is writing all three of you up on a discipline referral."

Sherise jumped from her seat like a rubber band snapping back to its original position. She flung off her backpack and rushed toward the secretary.

"We didn't do nothing."

May May walked over and tried to pull her friend back to the bench. When she put her hands on Sherise's arms from behind Sherise instinctively swung around and her elbow struck Hallee in the face. Hallee's nose immediately sprewed blood. The midget secretary screamed.

"Stop! Stop it. Someone help me! The black girls are fighting."

The midget secretary snatched up her radio. She pushed the button so hard the radio flew from her hand and landed in the trash can. May May reached down to pick it up and she banged heads hard with the midget secretary who was reaching into the can at the same time. The midget secretary looked up at her, then her eyes crossed and she fell back in her seat. She mumbled, incoherent at first, but then May May look at her in horror as she heard with the shrinking secretary was saying.

"She hit me. That black girl hit me."

Ms. Taschenberger heard the screaming and returned to the front office. She walked in to see the midget secretary, broken glasses on the desk in front of her, turning sheet white splayed out in her chair. She saw Hallee with blood running through her fingers and onto her shirt. And she saw May May standing there with a walkie-talkie in her hand. Taschenberger frantically called for security. Hearing the noise, a crowd of students had gathered, and looked through the office window.

Though the crowd most could not see anything but commotion; but they knew there had been some sort of altercation. They gathered and watched like students had done for the last one hundred years. The midget secretary continued to playact and holler as if she were going to meet her maker. May May left the office and ran through the hall to find paper towels. As she pushed through the door, the heavy steel edge hit a sixth-grader that was watching the spectacle. The corner of the door crushed his slip and was stopped by his tooth. The tooth cracked, the lip split wide, and a white fragment in a river of blood flowed down his chin. Two other sixth graders screamed. The little boy bent over keeping his head jutted out from his shoes and jacket and spit blood and more tooth fragments onto the floor. May May put her hand to her mouth.

"I am so sorry. Wait, I will bring some paper towels."

May May continued to the girls bathroom. As she neared the intersection where the entrance from the buses met the cafeteria she heard a strange sound on the radio, which was still in her hand.

"Two of them were fighting. One is sitting here with a bloody nose. The one that hit me ran out of the door, smashed a white student in the mouth and kept going. She is running toward the buses."

May May heard this and wanted to protest. *That's not what happened.* This could not be the real world. In the quickness of the events that just transpired a deep voice from behind did not seem real either. It appeared that everything was a bad dream. But what she heard, accompanied by the jingling of keys in his pocket, was Mr. Bridges radio. He had heard a muffled cry for help over his walkie while at the buses and was calling her name. He knew it was the front office secretary by her voice. In his years with her he knew that not only could she make a bad situation worse, she could make a situation out of nothing at all. One teacher once described the secretary as causing more problems than she solved.

Bridges had found that terminology to be correct. He slowed from a run when he saw May May. He had spoken to her before, but it was not anything to do with her behavior. *She wanted to get on one of the clubs or something. Student Council, that was it. This is the girl that had asked him two weeks ago about Student Council.* Although Bridges dealt with dozens of students each day some seemed to stand out while others faded into the herd. He had wondered that throughout this entire administrative career. Why did some students get seen and heard every day, and others attend the school for years and no one know their names? That always puzzled Bridges. That rule did not apply to the students from Carver Middle School however.

Every teacher, every student, and just about everyone on the school volunteer list knew the names of the kids from Carver Middle. Bridges slowed to a brisk walk. He had better use a stern, command voice.

"Young lady. Hey. Hey…slow down. Hold on a second."

Bridges thought about making one of his jokes. He had found it effective, and as much as he tried to not treat anyone differently, jokes seem to work better with the kids from Carver. A raised voice in a stern manner stopped an East Edgewood kid dead in his tracks. But that did not seem to have an effect on the Carver kids. Although they initially would hesitate at the sound of a male voice, within a few seconds they would react in one of two ways. Run or argue. May May stopped. So much for generalities.

"One of my friends is bleeding and I need to get some paper towels. And there is a white kid bleeding too."

She held up her finger and continued in the direction of the bathroom as if her dire circumstances gave her a free pass.

"Stop, come over here. Who is bleeding?"

"Hallee. Hallee McDaniel, my friend. We tried to come in early and put up election posters and they wouldn't let us in. They let the white kids in. And that short little midget lady, at the front desk, the one that everybody hates, started yelling at us just because we wanted to hang our posters. But she let the white girls in and they get put up their posters at all the good spots. And then Sherise accidently hit Hallee, and I bumped heads with the midget lady when she dropped her walkie-talkie…"

"Wait a second. Hold the press. Slow down a second. Go get those paper towels and meet me back in the office."

Bridges hustled toward the front office. He could hear the little head secretary calling for help on his radio. By the time he got to the front office the crowd was a mob

"To class. Everyone to class. There will be no late passes. Move. Now!"

As he raised his voice the crowd scattered. The kids walked by talking about how they saw everything. A couple of seventh grade discussed how the student spitting up blood almost got some on their new boots. Others said there was another kid in the office bleeding too. Another student swore he saw one of the black girls head butt Ms. Petty, the little secretary. His friends agreed excitedly. Bridges opened the door slowly. When he walked into the office it looked like an emergency room triage center.

One girl was bleeding and using a sweatshirt from the lost and found box to stop the hemorrhage. Her blood was on the floor, her shirt, and in isolated spots, diminishing in color on the sweatshirt. She was crying. Ms. Petty (the midget secretary), in Bridges estimation, was overacting. It would not be the first time. She was the most aware, dazed person that he had ever seen. She pathetically triedd to make her eyes look unfocused and roll in her head, but yet they tracked Bridges' every move.

"Ms. Petty? Ms. Petty? Betty, are you okay?"

He bent at the knees and put his hand on the desk to steady himself. He was now at her eye level and she avoided his eyes as she struggled to appear dazed.

"What happened"

"They started fighting... and then one hit me."

"That's a lie!"

Bridges turned to Sherise, before he could speak she blurted out her defense.

"That's a damned lie! Nobody was fighting. I elbowed Hallee by accident. Her nose always bleeds. And then I don't know what happened, May May tried to help that midget lady and the next thing I knew she be saying May May hit her. No one touched her."

The midget secretary sat up straight at this and had fallen out of character. Her dazed and confused eyes focused on the accusation of falsehood.

"They started first thing this morning. Banging on my door. It sounded like they were trying to kick it in. When I tried to correct them they started back talking me. When, finally, Ms. Taschenberger intervened they became rude and insubordinate. She is going to write them all up."

Bridges stood in between Betty Petty and the two black girls. He knew they did not have a chance, and he knew any chance they did have would be skewered as the midget secretary refined her story all morning. One thing was true about Betty Petty, she caused more problems than she solved. Suddenly the office door flew outward and May May strode into the room with a comically large amount of paper towels. It looked like a brown floral bouquet arranged haphazardly. If not for the look of fear upon her face she could have been going to the custodial ball, her corsage in front of her. She went to Hallee and handed her all of paper towels. The young man that was bleeding in the hallway looked up.

"Mind if I have a few of those?"

As if on cue, Ms. Taschenberger entered and looked at the scene; the midget secretary in the rolling chair returning her hand to her forehead, Hallee McDaniel replacing the bloodied sweat shirt with brown paper towels, and this kid with blood pouring from his mouth begging through his split lip. Taschenberger had had enough.

"What have you people done? Mr. Bridges, something must be done about the way these kids act. Everyday it's something – screaming in the hall, pushing in the lunch line, enough already! Now they're in here fighting, assaulting the staff... I have three referrals right here. These three gave Ms. Petty backtalk and were rude and insubordinate to her. God knows what they did to this young man. I just hope you don't try to find some excuse for them this time."

Taschenberger slammed the three discipline referrals on the desk. Betty Petty, in her attempt to appear dazed, did not see it coming and jumped to her feet.

Bridges glared at her. *She causes more problems than she solves.*

Bridges heart sank when he understood that Taschenberger was involved. Two of the most shrill, talkative and unreasonable people in the school on three Carver students. Bridges knew one thing. This probably did not happen the way the Betty Petty and Mary Taschenberger said it did. Not that they both were lying blatantly to get the students in trouble. It was that their fears, their fear of black students, filtered the experience into a mind that was primed to interpret that black people were bad. Everything that Taschenberger and the midget secretary would write down did happen. It happened in their minds. Bridges job, which he had fine-tuned over the years, was to piece together what really happened and subtract the teachers prejudice and clouded perceptions from the equation. He learned that in his first year on the job over a decade ago.

"Thank you, Ms. Taschenberger. I will investigate the situation."

Taschenberger had her hand on the door handle as it half opened. She stood there for a few seconds, turned halfway, and then continued out the door. The midget secretary stood on wobbly legs, theatrically holding onto the desk for support.

"There is nothing to investigate. These girls were rude, disruptive and started hitting each other right in front of me. This one hit me in the head as I was correcting her; somehow I did not even see how she did it. But she did."

"I do not hit you in the head. I bumped your head. We was both trying to get the walkie-talkie out the garbage can."

"Whatever. And God knows why they attacked this poor young man. Are you okay?"

She turned before the youth could answer.

"Mr. Bridges, this has got to stop. These Carver children have turned this school inside out. What do we tell this young man's parents? Oh goodness, is your tooth chipped?"

Bridges passed out student statement papers to each one. The young man with a broken tooth sat in the nurse's office awaiting his parents. Hallee's nose stopped bleeding, but she had already called her mother to come and get her. May May sat in Bridges office, trying to explain to him the bizarre chain of events.

"It all happened so fast. I did not mean to hit the boy with the door, and Sherise didn't really hit Hallee hard. Plus, it was an accident. They done been friends since kindergarten. We all friends, wasn't no one fighting. We was all at my house until late last night. We was making posters to put up. See?"

May May held up and unrolled one of her posters. It was done in crayon and outlined in magic marker. Bridges thought of the printed that he had seen in the hallway. Those were two foot by three foot with a large picture in the middle. They were professionally printed, most likely at Staples, probably at about twenty dollars apiece. He looked at the child in front of him as her face changed. She was done defending herself. She turned the unrolled poster so she could see it. It was creased from where the students had stepped on it; dust from the floor had accentuated the crease. And along the top where it said 'Vote for' there were drops of blood. Bridges watched May May as her lip began to tremble. Her eyebrows furrowed in anger and her defensive posture arose slowly. Her eyes, staring blankly at the poster, filled with tears. Finally, one drop left and traveled the void from the corner of her eye to the carpet. There it joined all of the other tears that had fallen in this room. She collapsed back in her seat, defeated.

"We don't have a chance here, do we?'"

Bridges leaned forward.

"I'm not sure what..."

"Us. The black kids. No one wants here."

She stared at him with tear-occluded eyes, boldly, defiantly, but ultimately helpless. The tears trickled down her face and landed on her worn jeans causing dark circles on the faded material. She wiped her eyes with bare hands, drying them on her jeans. The tears flowed, and she cried. Then, suddenly her voice changed into the angry, helpless squeal of person that had no hope.

"You know it's true. Everyone says that you ain't a racist. That you treat black folks okay. But you know we don't have a chance. We not here to hurt anybody. We just..."

Her emotions overcame her like a rogue wave, interrupting her breathing, and her posture. She jerked her knees to her chest in the fetal position and sobbed loudly. Bridges felt it in his soul. *This child is in pain.* This was no act to get out of trouble. Teachers and midget secretaries rarely saw this side of the situation. They only saw the child they had backed into a corner. They only saw the child trying to maintain some dignity in front of their friends. They had nowhere to turn in this office. And the kind eyes of the heavy balding man allowed them release.

"May May, can you tell me what happened?"

Sobbing uncontrollably, May May moved her legs back to the floor. She wiped her eyes again and again with extended fingers. She hyperventilated spasmodically. *This child is hurt.*

"I just... I just... wanted to put up… my signs. My momma was all excited… about me running for Student Council. I knew I wouldn't win. But momma, momma… she said..."

She let out a wail that came from generations past. A wail of pain and hopelessness so basal, so guttural that it made Bridges flinch. It was a long, sobbing cry. Entrenched in her psyche, the cry began silently last summer when May May knew she was going to The White School. The cry held back as May May hoped she would fit in. She dreamed that she would have some white friends, and that everyone would treat her like one of them. It came from the months since when even the teachers didn't hide their disappointment at the black students from Carver. The cry came from the embarrassment that May May felt when the black kids were acting ghetto and she wished they would just stop because she really, really wanted to get accepted. Not as a black student, but as a person. Just another teenage girl hoping to fit in to her new school and make some friends, maybe even be in the popular crowd and have sleepovers, and talk about boys and eat popcorn and laugh. Like she saw in the movies. She wanted to be one of them, not just as another black kid from Carver; but what her mother said all the time, that people should take you for you. Not lump you in with all the blacks that were acting the fool and cutting up. May May wailed again. Her pain shook the seasoned Assistant Principal. He had seen dozens, no hundreds, of students cry in his office over the years. But he never *felt* one cry before. May May was letting it out. Bridges thought of how the first slave must have felt when she was whipped on her bare back, he wondered if she screamed as long as May May was crying. He thought of how the whip had subjected an entire race for generations. The whip was gone but the damage was done. Even after slavery was over he knew blacks lived in hopelessness and fear. Cheated out of land as sharecroppers. Lynchings. Racial slurs constantly in the air. Burned out of their homes. But even today it continued; blacks were continuously reminded that they had lower scores than white students. Whipped into submission with test scores. He wondered if this had been inherited genetically by May May, or had racism slipped into the twenty-first century while everyone was busy worrying about terrorist attacks? Her powerlessness, her bitter disappointment of not being good enough, echoed from her soul. Bridges held back-he had nothing to say. He believed May May, knew that the midget secretary disliked the Carver kids and would provoke them. But what could he do? Except try to listen and make some changes.

The thought had pursued May May, after staying up most of the night and coloring posters, that she was just another nigger from Carver. But she evaded it. Denied it when she saw the other posters had been printed by a professional. Dodged it when the midget secretary denied her entry into the school. But it had caught up to her now. Here in Mr. Bridges office, the deep biological anguish that comes with the understanding of what the word nigger really meant. How long had thirteen year old African American girls screamed against injustice?

The balding man's eyes filled. Not enough to run, but enough to touch the brim of eyelids. No one had ever cried so long and so hard before. Some used crocodile tears to persuade him. Or anger. The child before him was not trying to persuade him. She had never been in trouble before. May May always had a smile on her face when Bridges saw her in the hall, or the cafeteria. He opened his desk drawer and pulled out a box of Kleenex. He took one and handed the box to May May. She took it without looking up, wiped her eyes, and then she breathed in moaning sobs. Breathing in long breaths she deliberately composed herself and then sat up. Her breath settled a little, just enough to speak.

"That's what…happened. That short little secretary would … not let us in. But I know …she let them white girls in. I just know she did."

"Did you see her let the other girls in?"

She folded her arms and set back.

"No, she too good for that. White people never let you see what they be doing. Especially when it comes to keeping us out."

"May May, I don't think that…"

"Mr. Bridges, I hope I don't sound rude, but am I getting suspended or not? Because if I get suspended I'm not eligible to run for Student Council. I wasn't going to win anyway- but it would've made my momma real proud to see me try."

Bridges grabbed the hastily written discipline referral and put it in the newly made folder that said 'Sumaya Webster' on the flap. He closed the folder delibeately.

"Not today. I need more time to investigate. It may have been an accident but you broke a kid's tooth today."

He leaned back and looked at May May.

"When's the election?"

"Wednesday."

"Well, I need a few days to investigate this very complex situation. And with my workload, I really can't get to this until at least Thursday. So, uh let me interview witnesses, and uh, take statements, talk to parents - and I'll get back to you by Friday."

May May smiled through reddened eyes and smeared eyeliner. She tenderly gathered up her ruined posters. She tried to smooth out the wrinkles. They remained.

"Do I need a late pass to class?"

"Eventually, yes. Right now you need to put up your posters. Come back when you're finished and I will sign your late pass. Do you need some tape?"

Ken Montel

The sun permeated the thin membrane of Ken's eyelid. Like a handful of sand thrown into his eyes it was scattered and blinding. *Now I know how vampires feel.* He twisted away from the brilliant light and his elbow hit human flesh. Next to him in his bed was a female form. Her face revealed smeared makeup; her dark roots supported chemically desiccated blond hair. The night came back to him. The empty feeling he always felt after a night of hard drinking settled in on him. As usual - the panic. Did he do anything stupid? Ken rose from the bed like a zombie and dragged his numb, hollow body to the window. Opening the curtain, he squinted through the pervasive sunlight. His car was there. It was too bright to see clearly, but he tried to see if there were and new dents or broken headlights . He drew back when he spied Mrs. Abersham walking her dainty Pomeranian in the bleached daylight.

"I hope I never get that drunk", he said in reference to bedding down with the old woman.

The sound of his voice caused the blond head to move. She turned over as the sliding sheet revealed her. She jogged a fuzzy, dream world memory in Ken.

She spilled her drink on him at the bar. It was a different kind of icebreaker but Ken exploited it. He had no problem picking up one of the jungle fever curious white women that frequented his bar. Ken did his best to be cute, funny, and harmless-so she sat down with him. Four drinks later she went home with him. Ken did not mind the wedding band. Most of the women he found here either wore one, or had just taken it off leaving a band of tell tale white skin. At one point during the night she had asked him if he knew who she was. With his luck she was probably a Kennedy or something. He doesn't remember carrying her over the threshold, but she did. Nor did he recall dropping her on his bed, falling across her and passing out. She lay awake for awhile, contemplated rushing home and dodging her husband's questions. But she had had enough -she wanted out of the marriage. This was as good a night as any for her. He turned from the window and looked at her, almost quizzically.

"Debbie. Debbie Granger? You told me I was the most beautiful girl you had ever met. Last night. Remember?"

"Funny. I just didn't realize how much we drank."

"How much *you* drank."

She got up from the bed and stepped over a scattering of Ken's clothes and shoes and into the small bathroom. Ken looked at her in the way a hunter looks at a prize deer on the hill. *God, she was beautiful.* The lights of the night club, her smiling face as she danced had come back to him. Her perfect figure under a tight leather miniskirt and loose blouse. Ken felt like the time when he was in fifth grade and he had stolen a bicycle. He wanted it but he was afraid to ride it around for fear of getting caught. Who was this lady?

The toilet flushed and she emerged from his bathroom. He was enamored by her. But like the bike, she was somebody else's property.

"Feel like some breakfast?"

"I can't. I have to get home."

"Married?"

"Not for much longer."

"You live around here?"

"You don't know me, do you?"

"You look familiar."

Ken did not know what else to say. He knew that he had to stop drinking and picking up these white women. He always felt bad for them afterwards. Except this time. This one was a real beauty.

"Familiar? I guess I should. You are my daughter's Social Studies teacher."

Rap, Sports and Tech Nines

It was sickening. These fat, ugly white teachers trying to act like all we know is rap, sports and street guns like the Tech Nine. They point their electric pens at their Smartboards and project their lessons into the impressionable minds of captive adolescents. Those who protest are punished. Accepting their dogma is the only way to survive. No problem. That's the way education has been since the first cave man blew some paint on his cave wall and tried to show the rest of the clan how important his message was to the tribe.

What really bothers me about these white teachers is that they have the audacity to say that they will also accept essays about rap, or sports heroes or street gangs. They look right at the black kids, like me, when they amend their white assignment to accommodate what they think are the black interests. It is almost expected that we write something about these stereotyped topics. The funny thing is these teachers don't know anything about rap sports, or tech nines. Well, then again, neither do I.

I have five tattoos. I have three on my back, an eagle and a puma one each arm, and two on my neck. The one I have on my neck, it say "Onslo". That is based on my granddaddy's farm in just west of Charlotte. He was a sharecropper. Just so the white people don't think I am just another ignorant nigger from Carver Middle let me enlighten you about sharecropping. Sharecropping was not a new social institution peculiar to the newly freed Negro. Sharecropping had a long history, centuries before my granddaddy inherited his grandfather's farm. His father inherited it from his father, who was a slave. Now let me see if I got this right. That means my great-great grandfather was born a slave. But I did the math on that and it didn't add up. I didn't have to compose a rap, or a story on a sports figure, or tell how a Tech Nine helps the Crips beat the Bloods in South L.A. (which I have never visited if you must know.) Anyway, oddly enough, the system of sharecropping started hundreds of years before the Civil War and there were a lot of traditional systems.

The Italians had mezzadria, the French people had metagaye and the Spanish had mediero- all forms of the sharecropper method. Even the Muslim terrorists had muqasat, which they still use to this day. That is when they ain't bombing something. This will comprise most of my report. I know the teachers are going to prejudge my report and expect me to say how tough life was for my forebears. I won't give them the satisfaction. It is going to be heavy on history and fact. Only towards the end will I introduce my heritage of sharecropping, and how we came to live on the farm we inhabit today.

Well, sorry I got off on a tangent about my report. I just always feel that I have to prove myself intellectually. More than ever since I enrolled at The White School. I read a lot of books in Carver Middle. My father, and my mother, made sure of that. Yes, it is my natural father. That would shock a lot of people. You see most of the kids, the white kids I mean, think all of us live in housing projects with our single mothers, or better yet -our grandmothers. Sorry to disappoint you but I live with my mother and father. Natural by birth. I have a brother who has the same parents as I do. We go on family trips, summer trips out of state but local weekend ones too. We spend time at the library. And yeah, we live in the black neighborhood. Well, just outside of it actually. On my grandfather's farm. It's not in Alabama, it's in Charlotte. It was a cotton farm when my great-great-great-grandfather worked it. Then it changed into tobacco production during the 1930's and 1940's. My grandfather made a lot of money from it. But he would always say how broke he was. Oh, by the way, I was just kidding about the tattoos. I don't have any. My mother would never allow it. Kind of like those white parents that watch over their kids that everyone is so familiar with. Some black people do that too.

Well, I guess I said that about the tattoos because I get tired of white people expecting us all to be the same, and act the same, and care about the same stuff. I don't like rap music. I could give two shakes of a fat rat's ass about what Michael Jordan is doing right now. And, to tell the truth, I don't even know what a Tech Nine looks like, I mean I could probably pick one out from a pile, but that's it. That's why it is so frustrating when white teachers tell us to do a rap, or write about Michael Jordan or other stereotypical topics. And a lot of my friends do it. My friend Ke'Shawn has turned in the same report about Michael Jordan every year since the sixth grade. He changes a few things, like the date, and a few other facts, prints up a fresh copy and turns it in. He gets an "A" every year. Black people, as well as whites, keep the stereotype alive. At least that's what my dad says. He says sometimes blacks can be their own worst enemy by acting the way white people expect them to act. So when I decided to do my English essay on sharecropping I am sure all my teachers thought that 'now there's an educated young black man.' But he is still limited to black topics. Well, if you only see the old Uncle Tom pictures of the guys after they come in from the fields, then you will also see the stereotypical sharecropper. But we have pictures of four generations of my ancestors in their Sunday clothes too. Some were taken of them reading books on the porch. They don't show those pictures in the history books. Dad says not to worry about it- the stereotypes, I mean. Just be yourself and get what you want from the world. That's what he taught me. So let me tell you a little about my essay, and I bet my teacher gives me an "A" just because I'm black.

My grandfather changed his main crop from cotton to tobacco around the 1930's. I guess cotton was too hard to pick, or it wasn't selling very well. Dad says it is good to rotate your crops so that you don't exhaust the nutrients. Different crops require different nutrients. Anyhow, Grandpa also had chickens and both kinds of cows, dairy and meat. He fed his seven children and actually put two of them through college with the money from his crops. My dad was one of them. He has a bachelor's degree in horticulture. He met my mother in college. She didn't graduate – and not because she was black. She had to go back and forth in a beat up car and finally got tired of it. Just like some white people. And no, she did not get pregnant with me until they were married for two years. Sorry to keep disappointing you. So they got married and my dad went to work on the farm - back to work would be a better way to say it because he worked there all through high school and then summers in college. With his knowledge, and Grandpa's faith in him, my father started growing grape vines. A few at first, then a couple of acres. Finally, just before my Grandpa died they had decided to turn the farm into a vineyard. Now it is a winery. My mother runs the store and dad figures out the acidity of the grapes and all that scientific stuff. We do quite well, Dad just bought a new truck and we are planning a trip to Washington, D.C. this summer. We stayed in New York City last year for a week. Right there in Times Square. We saw The Lion King and Cats. Those are two Broadway plays that do not involve rap, sports figures or Tech Nines. (But I guess one is about Africa and the other about the ghetto.)

So you can see how I am bitter at the way the white teachers treat us. I am sorry I called them fat white and ugly. My mom would be disappointed in me for using that type of language. I apologize. But I wish people would just let you be yourself instead of labeling you and sticking you into a group that maybe you don't even like. Nobody wants to be stereotyped, but I might be just a little more sensitive than most.

I don't like rap, I don't really follow sports, and have never even seen a Tech Nine. My name is Kevin Johnson and I plan to go to college to study horticulture. After that I plan on working with my Dad on our winery. I think North Carolina is going to be the next Sonoma Valley. Oh, by the way, I have been to Sonoma Valley. We went when I was seven years old. Dad wanted to see how they grew their vines. He spent every day talking to the growers and taking notes and pictures. He even ate dinner with the pickers. He always says that he learns more from "where the rubber meets the road." Mom and I and my little brother took day trips and even went to Disney. (I liked the one in Florida a little better.) We steered clear of L.A. though. Too much crime. You know with all of those blacks running the streets shooting off Tech Nines and robbing everyone.

So I had better get going, I have to start typing my report on the history of sharecropping and how it has helped my family. I hope to shock my English teacher with my succinct use of the language, interesting facts, and a story line that embodies the benefits of sharecropping.

Even if it gets me a lower grade.

The Pistol

Rob Granger sat amidst the boxes in the cluttered studio apartment, head at an odd angle, absorbing the uneven drone of the highway. A large truck rumbled past less than a stone's throw from his rusting steel bed. The hazy window vibrated in its loose wooden frame as a large truck thundered down the road. Rob could not decide if the persistent odor in the room was exhaust from the highway-or the enduring stench of the previous tenants. Robotically, he lifted the heavy revolver and inserted it into his mouth; resting the barrel on his bottom teeth. Placing his thumb on the trigger, he looked down the length of the barrel, a spontaneous tear progressing down his ashen cheek. Rob drew a breath, closed his eyes and then slowly squeezed the trigger.

He couldn't do it.

As he withdrew the gun from his mouth the top sight connected with his front teeth. The heavy, metallic clacking of the blued metal against his tooth enamel awakened him from his depressed state. Rob reflexively cried real tears, wondering when everything went so wrong. Why did this happen? He had a beautiful house in a great neighborhood. Everything was great until the black students were allowed into the school. The revolver hung loosely in his sweaty hand, threatening to fall. Inadvertently, and unknown to Rob Granger, the barrel was pointed at his heart.

His thoughts oscillated from the unremitting misery of the last year to his beautiful daughters. Pain and guilt muddied his parental pride. Feeling good about his children made him cascade into the vortex of darkness. He had "lost them" in the divorce. A divorce caused by that new black teacher. All Rob Granger could do now was visit them as an outsider. Wednesdays, and every other weekend. He was shamed at how defenseless he was as his empowered wife stripped him of his family, his house, and his money. All done mercilessly - right in front of his two magnificent daughters. He tried to stop her; but the law (and her black lawyer) gave him no options. After his first month in exile his daughters stopped looking him in the eye. Their previously pleading eyes had faded to furtive glances, then no eye contact at all. Both girls. He was no longer their sovereign one; how could they believe in him when he was the one that left them? They begged him not to move out, but the threat of a restraining order kept him packing. His wife had made it clear. She was going to divorce him, one way or another. She would make his life miserable (more miserable?) if he did not cooperate in his own demise. Sort of like politely holding still for the executioner's axe.

He tried to keep it together for months, to keep his family intact, give her anything she wanted. He slept in the spare room on the old couch. She could come and go as she pleased -no questions asked. The end became irrevocable the night she went out with friends and did not come home until the next morning. She spoke and the words went through him, "It is over. I want you out of my life; I… I am in love with someone else. I'm sorry… but it is the first time I have been happy in years. I haven't… I haven't loved you for a long time. I'm sorry…Please don't make this more difficult. The sooner you move out the faster we can get on with our lives."

Yeah, the faster she can get on with her life.

The words echoed in his mind as he boxed his belongings and moved out. Like a bad rash the words lay down with him every night, greeted him every morning. They hovered at his side while he was at work, irritatingly pinching his thoughts if he ignored them even for a second. One day he looked in the mirror and he saw the face of a forty-one year old balding man with gray hair. He was no longer sexually attractive. He was used and unwanted. Rob and Deb Granger and their two daughters, the Grangers from down the street, were no more.

Rob always thought that he would grow old with his wife. That he would be like his grandfather sitting in the rocking chair telling stories to the grandchildren, handing out financial advice to his daughters and their husbands. While his wife, retaining her beauty into old age, shuffled around the kitchen baking cakes and cookies for Sunday's dinner (was today Sunday?). He thought the ravages of old age would dignify and solidify their relationship. Now the ravages of old age only solidified his place alone in the world. Isolated without a family forever.

All because of a black teacher hired to teach black student that should never have been there in the first place.

Rob had been dethroned and deported, banished and condemned to a life of humiliation. It was like it was written on his forehead as he walked through the mall, in his gait when he jogged. He was unwanted. His sentence was simple - Rob Granger was to die a lonely old man with no family. His beloved Debbie read the verdict without remorse or expression. He still did not know his offense for such a harsh judgment. Criminal mediocrity? Felony sexual monotony? Practicing daily routine without a license? Accepting that his daughter had a black teacher at the White School? Excessive liberalism is what his father would call it. Regardless, Robert Granger was found guilty of numerous unnamed offenses by his wife and the courts agreed.

He blindly saw it coming. The coldness over the last few months, her lack of interest in sex (with him, anyway), and the disdainful way that she talked to him. He breathed in optimistically each morning despite the averted forecast of nightly rejection. He arose each day hopeful that today would reignite what once was; fell asleep emotionally wounded, and sexually frustrated, each night.

He first sensed the inevitable the time her phone rang and she left the room to talk. One day she came home with a different cell phone (even though she said she hated cell phones). She joined a gym. And a tanning salon. His sexual attempts were snubbed in inverse proportion to how attractive she was becoming. The better she looked the more he tried. It had been months… The chastity had a strange effect on him. He desired her all the time; knowing that his chances were becoming slimmer each day. "I need some space," was the excuse of the week. Then she asked for "some time apart". She spent one weekend with her friends; came home even more distant than when she left. Debbie's inability to look him in the eye was overcompensated by her extra affection to their girls.

The weekends apart brought the discussion closer to a trial separation (so they both could think things over). He cautiously agreed- maybe a trial separation would give them a break. Some time alone. You know, the kids are a handful, and keeping the house is a tough job. Maybe she would even miss him. He almost talked himself into it; but his gut feeling was that it was a one way street. Until finally he had no choice. He found a seedy apartment with a cheerless landlord. When he returned to his house he found that Debbie had gutted the picture albums, kept every picture that did not have him in it. His pictures were thrown into a box. Even then he still had hope. Called her daily. Tried to keep it simple; about the kids. How was she doing? I'll cut the grass Saturday. I miss you, remember when…? Click.

It wasn't long before he heard the outrage that the new black teacher at school was dating one of the parents. At first he did not connect the two. In retrospect he felt like a fool. The nights out, volunteering at school, the phone calls. In the end it all made sense. He had never felt so much pain. Then it became worse. It was her daughter's teacher. And he was black.

The pistol fell into his lap.

His thoughts were interrupted when he looked down at the revolver. He reached between his pasty white legs to pick it up. Debbie and Ken. What a cute interracial couple… Then his dark thoughts took over again.

Each Wednesday was torment; picking up the kids, trying to make a happy face and be buoyant while the kids had scowls and asked repeatedly why he couldn't come home. He would try the movies, arcades, go-kart rides. None of the transient artificial fun could replace the permanent authenticity of a true family. His older daughter got caught skipping school. The girls hated Ken (Ken?). He was rude to them, ignored them, always touching mommy…

He recalled last Wednesday when he was trying to chide his oldest daughter for failing a Social Studies test. She replied, "Why can't you just come back home, Daddy? Please? We will be good. We won't argue. I swear. Please come home, Ken scares us." Her eyes. Eyes that he had not looked into in weeks, pleaded to him in a way that only an estranged parent could feel. The emotions were imprinted on his genes; wrought about through thousands of years of caring for children, putting them first so they would survive. So that the human race would survive.

Race?

It was basal to not let your family be taken by another tribe. These ancient feelings were intertwined with his own emotional need to be their savior, their leading man once again. Like the time they woke up scared from the thunder, or when the puppy ran away, and he went into the night to find him. The look on their faces when he returned with Patches, little arms reaching out for the fuzzy bundle of canine energy. Daddy, you found her! He knew he would never see that look again. Part of what he was feeling was instinctual parental protection; most of what he was feeling was the emotional loss of his children. He strained to keep from asking them if Ken spent the night, he tried to…. His thoughts left him.

He was in his apartment and a loaded pistol was in his hand. He did not remember picking it up. He put the gun against his temple. To hell with it, I have nothing to live for. Twenty years of double birthdays for each daughter; one with mom and her black boyfriend (new husband?); one with dad in his pathetic apartment. To hell with it.

He placed his thumb on the trigger. All he had to do to end his agony was squeeze the trigger a fraction of an inch. He visualized the traveling bullet. The gunpowder would explode pushing the copper jacketed lead into the twisted lands and grooves of the barrel. The bullet would turn three times before it exploded through the open hole at the end of the gun. The escaping gunpowder would singe his skin as the bullet popped a tight hole through his skull, built up a cone shaped compression of his brain cells and nerve synapsis inside his skull, and blast out of the back of his head spraying the wall with shattered bone and bloody bits of brain and gooey matter.

His mind wandered. How long would it be before they found him? Who would it be? The neighbor just walking by? What a mess he would leave. He wondered if his wife was making love at this precise moment. He felt his loins stir and he hated them for it. Was she looking at Ken Montel the way she used to look at him when he was inside her? Was her nude body gyrating… His eyes filled with tears. He couldn't even look at another woman. They scared him. He was a prisoner of war and had been beaten severely by the enemy. He identified with his captors. But only one, his wife. Ex-wife. Debbie Granger. The tears flowed. The revolver leaned heavily against his head.

He was never going to be married to her again. Never wake up early with her on Christmas and make love before the kids awoke; never skinny dip in the pool. She was probably swimming nude with Ken – right this minute. The warm water flowing over her silky skin. Then back to their bed to make love again. He whimpered. And then an emotionally forced vacuity, the emptiness of a man that has suffered too much pain. He felt the revolver's weight against sliding down his cheekbone. He raised it to his temple. It was his only hope now. The notion that she would hear about his death and feel nothing nauseated him. A minor inconvenience as she gets on with her life. A voice in his head screamed.

PULL THE TRIGGER! NOW!

His hand flinched. He would never see his daughters again. The emotional pain of his suicide would reduce him to a blur in their minds. His influence on them would fade to a wisp of a childhood memory, the anger and resentment would overshadow the good memories. They would bear life long scars, he had read the research. (He actually tried to get Debbie to read it but she refused.) They would be prone to drug use, to teenage pregnancy, to lifelong issues with relationships. He looked at the revolver. It was now a part of him. Inseparable. It was all that remained. All he had left. He was committed from the first minute he thought about blowing his brains out. All that was left was to consummate the relationship by pulling the trigger. He sobbed like a child as his tears fell. Soon it would be over and the pain would stop.

The revolver was solid steel. Blued carbon alloyed with iron that held rounded cones of lead that looked up at him like little nuclear missiles awaiting the countdown. Each one wanted a chance to explode through the barrel; to cause a cone shaped evacuation in his skull. He closed his eyes, squeezing out tears. The tears ran down his face and landed on his hands. He lost his grip on the pistol. His thumb slid off the trigger but he caught the metal guard (which kept the gun from falling to the floor). He angrily seized the gun. He summoned the courage to pull the trigger. He cried bitterly as gravity once again lowered the gun from his weakened hand. The pistol fell to the floor.

"Oh God, please help me…"

He picked up the gun from the worn burgundy carpet, placed it in his lap and buried his face in his hands. His elbows dug into his thighs and it hurt. The gun awaited in his lap. He looked around the room. Maybe he should shower; he didn't want to make the coroner wince.

He saw the headline, "Smelly Loser Commits Suicide". He smiled, and then laughed aloud at the foolish thought. His laughter faded to a resigned sigh and then his face contorted into crying position and then relaxed. He unexpectedly laughed again through the flowing tears. Then pain washed away his laughter. He exhaled, a deep life releasing breath from his soul.

He thought of her, with him. Ken Montel. Where were his children while his wife was making love? Did the girls know what they were doing? Could they hear? He looked at the gun waiting so patiently in his lap. It would only take a second and his anguish would end. He remembered someone had once said that suicide was a permanent solution to a temporary problem. That saying didn't apply to him. His divorce was a permanent problem and he needed a permanent solution. The thought of her, with him, was too excruciating to bear, to encompassing to forget. It awoke with him, traveled with him to work, ate lunch with him, and tortured him into a fitful sleep each night. How could she be so callous? This wasn't some high school romance. They were a family, a mother and a father with children. Now she was....

He remembered seeing her last week. She had lost weight, bought new clothes; she looked good, sexy and confident. When she looked at him he felt ugly and weak. She glowed. He felt a strange mix of sexual yearning, jealousy and submissiveness when he saw her. She spoke to him as if he were the garbage man's cock-eyed apprentice. Making sure he knew that she would be out all night, to keep the girls with him. She must be looking forward to an all nighter with lover boy.

Her black lover boy.

He awoke sporadically most of that night, each time thinking what she was doing at that exact moment. Was she lying naked next to him? He felt shame for thinking like that in the same room as the girls. He remembered how he looked at them in the darkness. He was so powerless, so much of a failure. He had been emasculated in front of his children, his friends, and his family. The whispers of his wife with a black man were ear splitting. The stares in the restaurants as everyone knew what the white woman was doing with the black guy. Rob was sure she told all of her friends what a good lover her new boyfriend was, that the rumors were true. He had not been with anyone else since he married to her. He had not had sex since months before the separation. Had not even… To hell with it.

He snatched up the revolver.

It felt heavier than before. The beaten man visualized pulling the trigger as he placed the barrel against his temple. Once you see it in your mind it becomes reality. That is what his dad always said. The cold metal touched bluntly where his hairline met his skin. A voice of rage, reacting from the tearing in two of his heart screamed "Do it". He forced his eyes shut and placed his finger on the trigger. "DO IT!" He whimpered at the assault despite his emotional pain. Tears surged like summer rain down a worn tin wall.

He was going to kill himself today. That was one thing he was sure of. He could not face his daughters anymore; nor absorb the pain of their lives. He could not suffer the scorn of his wife (actually ex-wife) any longer. He would be dead soon and all of his pain would end. He hoped it would go quickly.

Deliberately, he sat down and decided calmly to get it over with. He wasn't going to bounce back this time. The destruction of his family would haunt him for the rest of his life. He could never love another like he loved her. Never would he dare to take a chance again. Not at his age. The haunting image of her telling him it was over would never leave him. This was it. It was over. His suffering would be released out of the back of his head in a few seconds. His essence would slowly dissipate into nothingness as his clumped brain matter slid down the wall. Through tear streaked eyes he abruptly smiled. He felt relief as he readjusted his hand on the trigger. Taking a deep breath he squeezed the last tears from his bloodshot eyes. He pressed his breath out and asked his thumb to squeeze the trigger slowly so he would not know when it was going to happen.

Slow…continuous…pressure.

He could feel the metal trigger slip against the metal seer. Tight metal slipping in increments of millionths of meters.   Metal against metal, held together by springs wrapped tightly.

And then the phone rang.

The ringer startled him and he flinched, almost jerking the trigger. The hammer of the gun was a fairy hair's breadth of tense metal from giving way. His hand shaking, he placed the revolver on the armrest. Walking past the stacks of boxes he leaned over the tattered box of family pictures and picked up the phone. He didn't say hello, just held the receiver to his ear.

"Daddy?"

Slave Language

The newly painted door to the bus loop flew open. Before it crashed against the robber stopper Mary Taschenberger snapped her head in the direction of the noise. The door slammed into the stopper with a muted thud before rebounding into the first invader. She pushed the door back and laughed. The door rotely repeated Newton's Third law for each of the dozen intruders. The cacophony of sarcastic and derisive come backs were unintelligible to Mary. She did not speak Ebonics (as she was proud of saying). To Mary's left a pair of teachers walking down the hall saw the group, froze, and looked at each other. One spun on her heels and shuffled back to their classroom. The other, Amelia Gray, walked toward Mrs. Taschenberger as the African American students burst into the cafeteria. The dark skinned students laughed raucously; pushed and guffawed at each other. The students sitting in the cafeteria took notice. Some held their hands to their mouths and whispered; others moved their backpacks in closer. All eyes were on the unruly black students. Mary Taschenberger rushed toward the mob. Amelia Gray quickly moved into Mary Taschenberger's path.

"Don't waste your time."

Mary Taschenberger looked at the mob as they jostled into the food service line. She moved her eyes to Amelia's; less than half a foot in front of her. Mary relaxed her shoulders and eased back.

"I'm not sure those kids wouldn't be better off in their own school. I mean most of them are not at all prepared. The reading scores on the pre-tests have gone down this year."

"Mary, I agree with you, about the scores I mean. But let the administration deal with them right now. Okay?"

"Who? Bridges? Yeah, right."

"Maybe Rubenstein will hear them and leave her office."

"Now I know you are fantasizing."

"You're right. But why do they have to be so darn loud? Why can't they go from point A to point B without screaming and jumping up and down like a bunch of monkeys?"

"Careful. One of those primates may hear you."

"Honestly, Amelia? I really don't care anymore. I am sick of walking on eggshells around these kids."

"Well, I see. Didn't get any last weekend?"

"Of course not. How about you?"

"Last weekend? How about last month?"

Their gelatinous bellies wiggled as the duo chuckled. They had been together at East Edgewood for the last thirteen years. Actually, they met in the front office as both were interviewed on the same day. Their similar interests, and the mutual disdain for the men they married, had bonded them from day one. Over the years both teachers were known for obtaining the highest scores in their respective subjects. Those scores were now in peril.

"Besides the way they act, I guess my chief complaint is their language. They still talk like slaves. They use that ghetto English; I can only understand them half the time."

The pair shook their heads in unison like chubby synchronous swimmers.

"Remember they called it Ebonics?" They shook their heads again. "My chief complaint is that they don't even attempt their homework."

"Oh don't stop there. Not one of that crowd has turned in their research paper. Not one."

"You are right about the language, though. I can hardly understand half of what they say."

Ms. Gray bulged up her eyes and pursed out her lips. Taschenberger playfully grasped her arm.

"I can go to da baffroom?"

Their comic relief was interrupted by the rear approach of Sumaya Webster. The kids called her May May, but neither teacher afforded her that privilege.

Both teachers looked at each other with full to bursting eyes. Sumaya cleared her throat.

"Yes, Sumaya. Can we help you?"

"I was jus' wondering if'n I can turn in my paper tomorrow and still get credit. I had to…"

"You can turn it in for half credit. It was due yesterday."

"But I…"

"Half credit. And that's the school rule. If it were up to me it would be a zero."

"But Ms. Taschenberger, I had to…"

"Never mind your excuses, Ms. Webster. I do not want to hear them. Half credit."

May May stormed away, joining her friends Kaneisha and Tonischia. They walked a few steps before the trio burst out laughing. All three looked towards Ms. Taschenberger.

"Keep laughing you little…"

"Nice. Let's be nice. If'n you say something wrong you just may be…"

Both women giggled into their hands at this mockery of May May.

"How much time before the bell, I mean 'da bell' rings?"

"Back to the slave language. My great-grandfather came over here on the S.S. Siberia from Ireland in the late eighteen eighties. Full blooded Irishman, came over here with hundreds of other Irishman, all looking for work."

A commotion in the breakfast line interrupted Ms. Taschenberger. Then there was a scream and two students started shoving each other. The cafeteria supervisor moved in between the disruptors. She sent one to the office and made the other sit down. A minute later the security guard, Kendrick Campbell, took the sitting student outside for a talk. Taschenberger and Gray could see them through the cafeteria plate glass.

"Why do they do that? I mean all they do is reinforce the stereotype. Right?

"Do what?"

"They hire some black ex-street thug to police these kids. All he does is tell them to keep acting the fool – just not when whitey is around. They are the reason nothing changes. They think only black people can teach black kids. That's racism right there."

Taschenberger tried to cross her stumpy arms over her ample bosom. She fell short and only her wrists intersected. She awkwardly held them in place. Her steel blue eyes bulged over the top of her tortoise shelled rimmed reading glasses.

"Anyway, as I was saying…"

"Sorry, that just makes me so mad. Go ahead, Mary. You were telling me about your grandfather."

"Great-grandfather."

For the next ten minutes Mary Taschenberger held the floor. Amelia Gray nodded as Mary told her the plight of her grandfather. He had come to this country with eight children and a young bride; his first wife was buried in Ireland. He left during the height of the potato famine that wiped out most of Ireland's farms.

"And, according to my Aunt Dorothy, he had this thick Irish brogue. At least that's what she told me. So everywhere he went he had to keep quiet. You know, not talk."

"I see you didn't inherit that trait."

Mary continued to tell Amelia how most places would have signs that said, "NO IRISH" and that Irish were called "White Niggers" by everyone. Amelia half listened.

"He eventually found a job as a window dresser. Back in those days that was a profession and people would come by to see the window displays of all the new clothes."

"A window dresser?"

Two black students were flicking cereal back and forth, garnering most of Amelia's attention.

"He held that job for fifty years. Retired at seventy eight, but he had told them he was sixty five. You see he came over at thirty three years old but he told everyone he was twenty. They believed him."

"Thanks, but is there a point to this story? I mean we were discussing Ebonics. Hey, over there. Look!"

One hooded figure from Carver threw a handful of cereal at another. Amelia stepped forward and pointed. Mary grabbed her hand.

"Don't waste your time. They will not do anything to him anyway. You must know that by now."

The custodian picked up the broom and long handled dust pan and swept away the mess.

"Here's my point. It is simple. My great-grandfather came to this country with a thick Irish brogue. Let's say, for arguments' sake that he was here at the same time that little mister cereal thrower's great-great grandfather was here."

"The bell rings in three minutes."

"So cereal chucker's grandfather speaks like a slave. Hoo be, habee, massuh, etc. Right?"

"Cereal chucker? I though it was..."

"Don't even think it! Anyway, my grandfather had a thick Irish brogue..."

Suddenly the bell rings and both women flinched.

"I guess my watch is off. Sorry."

Thick ankles in delicate shoes moved in agreement in the same direction. Walking together, Mary continued her story as they navigated past the students heading to class.

"…and his ancestor has the dialect of a slave. Then tell me this – why do I not speak with a brogue…"

Amelia nudged Mary's elbow arm to let a pack of black students pass. One of them was Sumaya Webster. May May. She shot both teachers a dirty look and mumbled under her breath. After they passed Amelia Gray finished her friend's story.

"…yet one hundred years later blacks still talk like slaves?"

"Good point."

"But why? Why do they act like they just got off the boat from Africa, and talk like they are out picking cotton – and yet expect us to treat them as if they were well behaved studious young ladies and gentlemen."

"That is the question, isn't it?"

Skinny the Guinea

Mr. Bridges, the Assistant Principal, just called and told me that the police were on the way to my house. I just wanted to know if my Dusty was okay, I mean I begged and screamed. Bridges would give out any information once the police were involved -except that Dustin had brought a weapon of some sort to school. It's not in Dusty's nature to hurt anybody. A weapon? What made him bring it to school? Dusty had told me things were okay at The White School.

I had hoped he would make some friends. If not, I just hope they weren't teasing him about being biracial, or you know how girls can be at that age. The poor guy has been through enough. They had no idea the tragedy we just endured. I mean he buried his father and his brother last February, both of which he adored. Dusty never had many friends in Jersey; he usually hung out with his brother. But now his brother was gone and Dusty had brought a weapon to his new school – The White School. The White School loved you if you are white, shunned you if you are black -but my son, Dustin, fit neither category.

At least in New Jersey Dusty could blend in. Maybe we should have stayed there. But we needed to get away from the tragedy, and my parents offered their condo here in East Edgewood. At first Dusty was all for it. It was nice when we got here. New neighborhood. Great weather. Dusty and I had the whole summer to explore Charlotte. We also checked out the schools. At first, we tried the black school, Carver Middle (which we were zoned for), but that bitch principal asked if Dustin was adopted I petitioned to get into The White School, East Edgewood Middle (which was actually closer to us). Were the police ever going to get here?

I had held it together until a few minutes ago. I walked into his room and his hamster was running on its little wheel thing. Then, the realization of how good things had been last year, and how bad things were now, came crashing down like a dozen baseball bats from an overhead shelf. Like a nightmare that you wake up to find out it is real. Only those that have buried a son and a husband in the same week can understand that.

After the funeral reception Dustin and I just wandered around the mall. We were like zombies just trudging along. Was that just last February? It seems like ten years ago. After we moved Dustin said he wanted a hamster. His brother, Brad, had a cute brown and fuzzy one when Dusty was little. Brad had bought all the tubes and angled connections with money from his paper route. Brad hung them from the ceiling on wires, snaked them up under his bed, and around the desk. It was kind of cool. Little Dusty would follow the hamster as it ran through the colored passageways. One day the hamster escaped and we set every kind of trap we could, even Big Brad was in on it. We had a lot of fun coming up with traps, and where he could be, and if he was watching us right now. Little Dusty's eyes would light up as Brad told stories about the hamster running through the ceiling and in the walls… that was a good memory. Yeah, that is a good memory.

Finally, after a couple of weeks I put the tubes and connectors in a box- and that's were they stayed for years. We revived the whole thing, Dusty and me, when we moved down here. That's when I bought him the hamster. He loved putting the tubes and the connectors together. He had a crazy figure eight that went under his bed and ended on the cage on his desk (actually it was Brad's desk). But that was just a Band-Aid on the real issue.

I got the news about the accident when a policeman came to the door. I was eating my favorite sandwich - tuna fish on rye (I haven't eaten one since.) and watching television. Dusty was in his room. Regular day. I guess. Then the police knocked and gave us the news. A couple of teenagers were racing and did not even slow down at the four corners. Brad and Brad Junior, we called him B. J. most likely never even saw them coming. By the time the ambulance arrived my oldest son was dead. An hour later, the only true love of my life joined his son in heaven. No one can tell me different.

Before that Dusty, Brad and B. J. were inseparable. Even in the liberal North they were somewhat outcast. When we would walk through the mall the looks would say it all. But it bonded us as a family-we never thought that we were the classic American family. But we were tight. Anyway, we were supposed to be going to see B.J. play in his basketball tournament in Camden that weekend. They were on their way home from basketball practice when it happened. In one horrible instant Dusty lost his dad and his brother - his two best friends.

I know my parents were sad for me, I truly believe that. But they were also relieved for themselves. They had made a few remarks, actually quite a few; in the beginning when I first told them Brad and I were dating. They fell apart the night Brad asked me to marry him. They did try to show some enthusiasm when the boys were born. It was perfunctory, as was their new role as grandparents. Right up until the accident. I hardly spoke to them at the funeral.

You know, I am not one of those white girls with daddy problems that gets off on black guys because they treat white women like queens. Brad was the first black guy I ever dated. He was so funny, and to tell the truth, I didn't see him as black. I loved him, not because he was black, or I had been infected with Jungle Fever, I just loved him - period. I wanted to marry him, and have children with him and spend the rest of my life with him. Like the song says, two out of three ain't bad.

Both Brad and Dusty looked Italian, or Hispanic. I wasn't embarrassed, but it made it a little easier for my boys to integrate. B. J. did okay, but Dusty never really fit in. It wasn't the racial thing, it was something else. He was different. Is that a car door?

Through the window I can see two policemen coming up the sidewalk. Here it is again. They are going to tell me if my only son is even alive. I guess Mom and Dad won't have to worry anymore about explaining away their grandchildren's skin color because I fear that I am about to be alone.

I remember speaking to Dusty just before he left for school this morning. He seemed okay. Except for the back pack thing. After I said "Good morning." Dusty zipped the backpack shut kind of quickly. It was strange so I asked him about it.

"Why are you taking a backpack today? I thought they kept a set of books at school?"

"Oh yeah, they're allowing kids to have backpacks now. I guess it's a cool thing to do.

"Oh, okay. When I was a kid, the only people that had backpacks were hikers; you would get laughed out of school if you wore a backpack. By the way, are you making any friends?"

"Mom, stop. You promised you wouldn't say anything."

"I know, but it's hard when you start a new school and then what, three months later..."

"Mom, I … please stop, okay? Will you feed my hamster for me?"

He never had many friends at the old school either, but at least he had his brother. The little guy seemed okay when he left this morning.

I wiped the tears from my eyes and moved into the front room. The police were here. They walked up the sidewalk to my parent's condo just like they did last winter in New Jersey. I am sure the news is just as bad.

Just as the cops showed up, my phone rang and it made me flinch. Who else could it be? It was my mother. She had heard about it on the news.

"Mom, can you hold on? They are at the door."

Charlene put the phone on the side of her hip and opened the door. A man, dressed well in a cheap suit, opened his badge.

"Ms. Blackstone? I'm Detective Righter. May I come in?"

"Yes. Yes, come in please. How is my son?"

The detective looked around. They did the same thing in New Jersey when they came in to tell me that my husband and oldest son were dead. Looking all around the house like I had Jimmy Hoffa stashed under the couch or something. It made me feel that I had commited a crime.

"Detective, is my son alive?"

He looked into the kitchen, and then looked back at me.

"Ms. Blackstone, there was an incident at school this morning."

I had answered the expected formalities as quickly as I could. I wanted to choke the answer out of this smug man.

"Is my son alive?"

Detective Righter pulled a pistol out of his pocket. It was B.J.'s BB gun. I had totally forgotten about it. Righter held it up in front of my face.

"Is this yours?"

I did not know how to answer. I wanted to know my rights. I did not want to do, or say, anything that may hurt Dusty (if he was still alive). But the feeling of relief started in my toes and rose up to my jaw. This just might be okay dared to enter my constricted and protected mind. My jaw and I smiled, yet I feigned ignorance like any good mother would do.

"That's a BB gun isn't it?"

"Is it yours?"

I thought for a long minute. *Of course we both know it is mine you asshole.*

"It belonged to my oldest son."

"May I speak with him?"

"No, you may not."

"I can get a warrant. I can bring him downtown if that's what it will take."

"You can't take him anywhere. And I don't care…"

"Ms. Blackstone, may I speak to your husband?"

"No, you may not. Is my son okay?"

Detective Righter moved to the front window. He nodded to the outside. I laughed when I saw my Dusty get out of the car. He was escorted by a female in regular clothing. I was jumping up and down inside, yet restrained physically by the idea that my son may be in a lot of trouble.

"Dusty!"

Constrained by the handcuffs, he ran like one of those Irish jig dancers. He bounded up the stairs with tears in his eyes.

"I am sorry Mommy. I didn't know what else to do. They would not stop picking on me."

A BB gun? Dustin was alive. That is all that mattered.

Mr. Montel's Dinner Date

Built in 1905. The brass relief sign on the wall greeted everyone that entered the restaurant. The gilded statue of Christopher Columbus stood watch over the well dressed patrons. On the few empty tables silver knives and forks were aligned perfectly on linen napkins like knights in armor. Transparent green glass pitchers of ice water stood aside the flower arrangements on each table. The picture frame covered brick walls held the history of this restaurant like a timeline. At least a dozen picture of Frank Sinatra stood among a myriad of other celebrities from Don Rickles to Sylvester Stallone. Everyone that visited Charlotte ate at Graziano's.

Tonight there was a disturbance in the bar. A black man was noisy and behaving obnoxiously. These were the three things that Marcato Graziano did not tolerate in his restaurant. Marcato's clientele included the upper echelon of Charlotte society. They did not take reservations, and Marcato had a method of keeping the riff-raff out. Undesirables, specifically blacks, would be kept in the bar while awaiting their table. That table would never come and most got the message and left quietly. Tonight that routine had been interrupted.

Marcato stared at the loud black man at the bar as he leaned sideways to the headwaiter. He whispered in the man's ear without taking his eyes off of the black man.

"Jimmy, remember the good ol' days when moolies were not even allowed in here by law- never mind sitting with the white wives of the taxpaying public."

Jimmy took a drink from his club soda and nodded, following his boss's gaze to the dark man at the bar. Jimmy had been with Marcato since the early days. Marcato hired Jimmy as a cook but found him drunk between a box of flour and the canned tomatoe shelf in the cellar. Most people would have fired him, especially since Jimmy had already drank away his house, his wife and his children. Jimmy had not touched a bottle since that day-the day when Marcato offered him a beating and a job or his walking papers. Jimmy still touches his jaw every time he thinks about that day. Jimmy, sober ever since, had repaid Marcato's loyalty to him by staying at the restaurant through eight American presidents.

"Those were the days. Everyone stayed in their place."

"Things went better then."

"At least for us."

Both men laughed and Marcato gently patted his friend of forty one years on the back. Marcato glared at the black man at the bar with the well dressed white woman. The bartender caught Marcato's eye and concurred by shaking his head.

As the bar slowly filled with happy hour patrons. Debbie Granger and Ken Montel attempted to order another drink. They were ignored. The bartender, after checking his other customers two times each, wiped his area clean, poured a glass of water for no one, and kept his back to Montel.

"Cosmopolitan and Molson Golden Ale."

While pretending to fix a soda fitting the bartender looked up to see Ken Montel standing right in front of him. Montel waved his hand in a sarcastic greeting.

"Cosmopolitan and Molson Golden Ale. Please."

Without acknowledging the man, the bartender mixed the drink, filled a frosted mug from the tap, and walked the Cosmopolitan down to Debbie, and left the beer in front of Ken's seat. Montel returned to his seat, frowned and switched the drinks. He spoke loud enough for the bartender to hear.

"He did that on purpose. It's the twenty first century and these retrofits can't stand seeing a well dressed black man out with a white woman."

The bartender hesitated, and then moved on to the heavy set bald man tapping his glass. Debbie shrugged and gulped half of her beer. Montel nestled his pink drink in front of him.

"Maybe he made a mistake."

"Mistake? Is it a mistake that I am the only black person in this place?"

"I…uh…I didn't notice. This is Marcato's. They have excellent Italian food."

"Forget it. Let's not let it ruin our night. How are the girls taking it?"

"Okay, I guess."

Ken could not hold it in.

"Racist bastards."

"Ken, please. Let's just finish our drinks and leave."

"Why? Because they don't serve niggers in here!" Debbie took another long swing of her beer, emptying the still frosted mug.

"Let's go."

"You look nervous? Is it because I am black? Are these racists getting to ya?" Montel waved his hands and leaned back almost falling off the bar stool.

"Let's just be two people out for a drink. Don't start that racism stuff. Please."

He bumped into the man behind him and the man half turned to Montel before thinking better of it to continue his conversation with the man to his left.

"No, it is because I don't want to make a scene."

"Oh, so let's stick our tail between our legs and leave? Is that what you want?"

"Stop. You know I ..."

Ken grabbed Debbie's hands, and then stared into her darting eyes. Finally, Debbie averted his gaze. The man that was bumped into half turned again, opened his mouth, and once again returned to his conversation without commenting.

"Come to Miami with me this weekend. You know you want to."

"What? Miami? My daughter is having her birthday party Saturday. Are you kidding?"

Ken finished his drink and the alcohol raised his voice a few decibels.

"I want you. I want to be with you. I want to have children with you."

"Now you lost me. No more children. No way. I have had my fill of children."

"Well, how about the rest? I sense that you want to go." Montel slid his hand under the table and stroked Debbie's leg. She jumped and then smiled flirtatiously.

"Stop. There are people watching."

"So let them."

"Come on, let's go. My ex has the kids for the night. Let's get out of here."

"I'm hungry. I have dealt with this type my whole life. They can't throw me out just because of a little dark meat."

"Stop... you're getting too loud."

"Loud!" Ken stood up and yelled straight at Marcato. "Hey, waiter. When's my table going to be ready?" Ken sat back down with a smug look on his face. "Now that's loud."

Montel threw up his hands and accidently hit the man behind him on the shoulder. The man stood, walked around the bar stool and faced Montel.

"Could you please stop hitting me? It is getting irritating."

"Well move back then. I am trying to have a conversation with this fine woman."

The man stared at Montel and, shaking his head in disgust returned to his stool.

"Yeah, that's right. Pick on the black guy."

The man stood again opened his mouth. No sound came out. A few seconds later the man leaned onto the bar and waved for his check. The bartender quizzed the man's plight with a nod of his head toward Montel.

The man paid his check and left with a wave of his hand. Debbie watched the man shook his head and threw his thumb to the bar as he approached Marcato Graziano. She became uneasy because it was obvious to her that the man was someone important. She had heard of Marcato Graziano but had no idea what he looked like. The man talked to Graziano for a minute and then left. Montel remained oblivious to the exchange and continued to spew romantic drivel to Debbie.

"So do you want to go or not? Miamim I mean."

Debbie returned to the conversation without taking her eyes off of a very upset looking Marcato Graziano.

"Yeah, right. The last time I let him…" Montel's cell phone rang. He held his hand up, quite obtrusively, in Debbie's face, effectively occluding her view of Graziano.

She protested with a withdrawal of her chin. "That was rude. Ken, I think the manager is…"

Montel repeated his hand movement more exaggeratedly and closer to Debbie's face. His now turned body brought his face in the opposite direction of his waving hand. He brushed her nose, effectively hooking her nostril. She backed up and away from his hand and released her nostril. Idly embarrassed, she motioned for another beer. The bartender looked to Graziano. Marcato Graziano shook his head and then aimed his index finger at the door. Montel put his formerly offensive hand over his free ear and spoke loudly into the cell phone.

"Yeah. I do not care. Too bad. Hey, I am surviving on a teacher's salary. Anyway, we're separated. Period.

I don't care how she gets to work." Montel snapped his phone shut and leaned forward as he slid his hand on Debbie's inner thigh, rubbing in slow circles. Her eyes flitted around the bar to see who was watching.

"Are you ready for another beer? Yo, barkeep." Montel waved and the bartender looked directly at him before turning to another customer.

"Did you see that shit? Are you... God damn...did you see that?"

"Ken, let's go. I hear this place is overpriced anyway. Let's try Appleby's."

"Screw that. Someone has to stand up to these redneck assholes."

Half the bar turned toward Montel. His voice had carried and interrupted the conversations of everyone within ten feet of him. Marcato Graziano had seen enough. He walked intently toward Montel.

"Is there a problem here?" Montel looked up at the larger man.

"Who are you?" Montel spoke defiantly to the big man with the wavy gray hair.

"I am Marcato Graziano. This is my place. Is there a problem here?"

"Oh, you de owner? Good. Yeah, there's a problem. That bartender is a friggin' racist. He doesn't serve blacks. So...if I don't get a drink here in the next ten seconds then I'm gonna slap a civil rights suit on you so fast you won't know what hit you. You think you can keep niggers out of your bar? Well, welcome to the twenty first century. By the time I am done with you in court I will own this dump."

Marcato drew in a long breath and steeled his look at Montel. Out of the corner of his eye he could see his bartender slipping through the opening at the far end of the bar. In seconds the muscled bartender stood a foot away from Montel. Debbie spoke.

"Ken, let's just go."

Marcato saw the wedding ring tan on her left hand. He had learned to read people in his decades as King of his establishment. Here was a woman, probably newly divorced, that had left her kids with the sitter so she could have a night out with darkie. The black man had no such ring. She probably shook her ass and snagged some poor banker who is living in a crap apartment while she gets the house, the kids, and ol' darkie here. Marcato looked down his nose at her. She looked away.

The two stout men stood behind the pair. Montel went into his Uncle Tom act. In an overly exaggerated Southern Negro accent he taunted his new sentinels and then downed his drink in one gulp.

"Oh, whatcha gonna do? Lynch me? Hey, some-one goes and gets da rope so's we can lynch us dis nig-ger."

"Ken, let's just go." Embarrassed, Debbie left her chair and squeezed quickly by Marcato. She headed for the door, stopping at the bar entrance with the hope that Ken was following her. He had remained in the bar.

"Civil Rights Act of 1963. That's right. That's what I am going to sue you under. I will own this shithole. Think I'll call it Rufus's Reeyibs. Fo' black folk only. Step aside, Bigfoot, this nigger is leaving."

The bartender held his ground until Marcato nodded. Marcato walked behind Montel until they got to the door. As Montel grabbed the door handle Marcato spoke loudly.

"Hey buddy, you forgot to pay your bar tab."

"Fuck you, you greasy guinea." Montel flung open the door and hit the base of the statue of Christopher Columbus. The statue tottered on its base. Jimmy grabbed the statue and steadied it. Christopher Columbus's face remained stoic. Marcato broke the silence.

"Jimmy, call the police and tell them that we just had a man walk out on his bill. Give them a description of his car and the tag number." Jimmy rushed out into the parking lot with his pad in hand. He wrote down the plate number. GBZ 73P.

When he returned Marcato was at the bar calming his guests. A round of drinks was ordered on the house.

Ten minutes later, when the police arrived, they took over a dozen statements.

Across town, Ken and Debbie pulled into Appleby's. Within fifteen minutes both Ken and Debbie had polished off three drinks each. Ken, now louder than before was approached by the manager, Mike Young. It was Mike's first week on the job.

Montel stood up and squared off with the Mike, sticking his finger in the manager's face.

"Do you have a fucking problem, sir?" Mike half smiled complacently.

"This is a family restaurant. If you cannot keep yourself under control, I will have to ask you to leave."

"Ask me to leave? Oh, I get it. I just so happens to be the only black man in the place. Let's get rid of the nigger so the nice white people can eat- is that it?"

"Sir, you are drunk. Please leave before I call the police."

"Ken, let's go."

"This place sucks anyway. Where'd you learn to cook? At McDonald's? This place is for losers."

Ken shoved the dish in front of Debbie on the floor, smashing it and causing spaghetti to fly up on the managers' pants. "Sir, will you please leave quietly. Please. This is a family restaurant."

"Yeah, the Addams Family. What are you goobers looking at? Haven't you ever seen a black man eat before? Were you expecting me to order watermelon? Huh? Stupid rednecks."

A burly man in a crisp white shirt stood up. His wife pulled his arm. His two young children, in designer dresses, looked up at Montel with big eyes.

"Oh, are you going to do something? Whatcha gonna do? Sit your dumb ass down." Montel and Debbie left the restaurant, slamming the door hard as they left. It had an old fashioned bell that rang when the door opened. The bell tumbled to the floor as the concerned patrons watched.

At the car Debbie attempted to take the keys from Ken. "Let me drive. You know that you will lose your job if you get a DUI."

"I'm fine. Any cop that pulls me over will get charged with racism. I will make it home no problem."

Debbie knew that Ken was drunk and a DUI would also bring her name in to the report. But her car was only a few miles up the road at the mall. A few miles and she would be on her way home.

In their anger, and their haste to leave, neither Montel, nor Debbie saw the Charlotte Police car, that had followed them from Graziano's, cruise behind them as they pulled onto Route 75.

Street Ball

John stood beneath the grand staircase facing his wife. She spoke in hushed whispers. He looked up at the ceiling, twenty feet over his head and noticed that it had a slight crack. His head was at enough of an angle to let her know his displeasure.

"I don't want those kids here. The neighbors don't deserve seeing a bunch of 'hoods in our yard."

"They are Jayson's friends from school."

"I know who they are. They are the ones bused in from Carver. You know they are probably casing the house. They will probably come back tonight and rob everything- or worse. Why does he feel the need to bring them here?"

"Casing the house?" He mocked her. "Oh, boys ya look like ya are casing the joint. Are ya?"

"Funny. But it won't be so funny when your new Nikon is missing."

"No one is going to steal my camera."

"How can you be so sure, Mr. Know It All?"

"Because it is locked up in the safe with my other valuables."

For a brief moment it appeared that Marana was re-treating. John leaned forward to walk past her; then she returned her attack.

"What about my jewelry? Our Ming vases? The remote control?"

"You really think they are going to steal the remote control? I thought we agreed to not teach our children to be racist?"

"They're dressed like thugs. Racism has nothing to do with it."

"Are you sure? If these kids were white would you care how they were dressed?"

"No, a thug is a thug. And I saw them teasing Ryan. Ryan has been friends with Jayson since first grade. He is a good kid. What is wrong with those kids?"

Steve walked into the open foyer. Walking around the huge cherry wood table he looked into the glassed in aviary. The Lady Gouldian finches were chasing each other around the delicate fern fronds. The small pond at the bottom gleamed with koi. To Steve the huge aviary was the most fascinating part of his brother's house. He helped stock it and keep it thriving. Steve was the one that installed the mist hosing and the timer. Through the glass of the aviary, Steve could see his brother in the hall.

"Hey, John, can I borrow a shirt? Like a T-shirt or something?"

Marana stepped out from behind the wall. She looked at Steve with pleading eyes.

"Steve, you must understand what I feel."

"I just need a shirt."

Marana slammed her dish towel on the table and disappeared into the bedroom. John threw Steve a shirt and the brothers walked outside.

The group gathered outside in front of a basketball net in the driveway. Two of Jayson's new friends from school passed the ball back and forth. It was Devon, and his older cousin, Marcus. Marcus and Devon were making sport of Ryan.

"Come get it, Ryan. Show him, Marcus - dat's right."

Ryan was unwittingly playing into a 'monkey in the middle' scenario to the amusement of the other two. Marcus bounces the ball between Ryan's legs. Devon retrieved it and hooted. He saw the older men approaching and passed the ball to Ryan, hitting him square in the chest. Ryan fumbled around after the ball. After tripping over it he picked it up and shot. The ball bounced off the front of the rim.

"Yo, Ryan, get up on your toes, man. You're getting caught flatfooted."

"Man, Ryan. You are too slow and too white..."

"Jayson. Cut the racial garbage. I don't want to hear that kind of crap while I'm playing. Let's just play."

"I'm just joking, Pops, stay calm, bro."

"Pops? Who are your friends? Give me the ball, Ryan."

"Oh, yeah, yeah. Pops, Uncle Steve, this is Mark and Devon. Devon is new to my school. He a good ball player."

"He's a, or he is a... not he a."

"Chill, Pops. It's b-ball language."

The older black youth held out his hands for the ball. John hesitated, and then passed it to him.

"Marcus. My name is Marcus."

Marcus turned quickly, sprung into the air, and flipped the ball into the air toward the basket. It sailed in an effortless arc until it slipped onto the net without touching the rim.

Jayson cheered.

"All net, bro."

Uncle Steve whispered to his brother.

"Bro?"

John looked at Jayson.

"Bro?"

"Lighten up, Pops, and let's play some hoops."

Ryan picked up the ball, dribbled and shot another pathetic rim jammer. The ball bounced right back into Ryan's face. Marcus snickered. Devon grabbed the ball.

Try it again. More arc this time. Shoot it up, not straight." Devon motioned an arc with his hands. He flipped the ball underhanded to Ryan. Ryan caught it with one hand, rubbed his nose with the other hand, then looked at his watch.

"I, uh, didn't plan on actually playing a game, Jayson. I thought we were just going to shoot around."

Marcus glanced at Devon. Devon shrugged. John motioned for the ball. Ryan released it to him, sailing past Marcus's head. John set his feet, crouched a few inches and pushed up a shot. It sailed into the center of the hoop. All net. For the next few minutes the boys took turns shooting and rebounding. After Uncle Steve threw up a shot that bounced off the rim, Jayson yanked the ball from Ryan's outstretched hands and held it.

"Alright. Okay. It's me, Uncle Steve, and Devon against Pops, Marcus, and Ryan. What's up?"

Marcus motioned for Jayson to throw him the ball. Jayson threw the ball to Marcus - hard. Marcus caught it and looked to Devon with a 'what the hell' look on his face.

"Sounds good. Are you ladies ready to play?"

The game began with Marcus missing an easy shot. Jayson grabbed the rebound and dribbled the ball back to the starting line.

"Here we go."

"Awwwright, Uncle Steve. Let's kick it."

Jayson drove to the basket and was elbowed by Marcus. The bone on hard muscle thud was felt by everyone on the driveway court.

"Wo, wo. Easy."

"Hey, this is for fun."

"Yeah, take it easy."

"Our ball."

"You calling a foul on that? Shee-it, nigger."

"Hey! None of that language."

Marcus passed the ball to Ryan. Marcus ran right at Jayson. The red on Jayson's face belied his increasing frustration.

"Awright. Here's one for you." Jayson moved to the basket and Marcus pushed him again.

"Oops. Sorry, nigger."

"Oops, my ass." Jayson threw the ball at Marcus, hitting him hard in the shoulder. The pair squared off and stared each other down. Jayson, tall for the eighth grade, stood at eye level with the older Marcus. The two sweaty muscled youths stood inches from each other. The rank breath of Marcus permeated Jayson's nostrils.

"Brush your teeth once in awhile."

"Fuck you."

"Hey, no fighting on my court. Jayson, take the ball." Steve reached down to get the ball as it rolled by him. He yelped and came up holding his finger.

"Wait. Ow. Ow. Dang. Wait. I think there is something wrong with my finger. It's jammed."

Steve held his finger in his other hand as he bent over in pain. Jayson walked over to Steve.

"Are you okay, Uncle?"

"I think it's jammed, pull it out. Pull it out!"

Jayson grabbed Steve's finger and pulled it to a simultaneous emission of rectal gas. Steve ripped a huge fart. Everyone voiced disgust. Even Marcus smiled. The tension was broken.

"I feel much better. Let's play ball."

"I can't see through the fog."

"Well, Jayson, you better get used to it. I saw what your uncle was eating."

From the crowd of ballplayers another fart ripped.

"Aw, c'mon. Jeesh. Show some class. Someone get a cork. Damn, that stinks."

"Phew."

"Even the ball is trying to get some air." John pointed to the ball as it rolled down the hill. The whole group laughed.

"Let's play ball, ladies."

"Man, my new sneakers are getting dirty."

"Candy ass."

"Let's go."

The game continued. Jayson and Marcus pushed each other in an attempt to shoot, pass or get to the basket. Marcus was tired and out of breath. Jayson beat Marcus to the basket repeatedly and Marcus compensates by roughing up Jayson; pushing him and fouling him every time. John and Steve gave disapproving looks to Marcus each time, trying to keep up the spirit of competition edged with the aura of racial difference.

"Here you go, boy."

After Jayson's team scored, Jayson threw the ball to Marcus. Marcus was not looking and the ball hitsMarcus hard on the side of the head.

"What the fuck, Bitch? Make sure a nigger is looking before you throw the ball." Marcus picked up the ball and threw it back at Jayson, hitting him in the shoulder. Jayson moved toward Marcus and squared off with him. The two are face to face again and about to fight. Devon, Ryan and the other players shake their heads and wave at the pair.

"Jayson! Cut the shit. Jayson! You know that your shoulder could pop out at any time. I do not want to see you back in surgery. Slow down!"

"Nigger, you better listen to your father."

"Marcus. This is my house. Jayson is my son. This is supposed to be a fun game. Take it easy- and quit using the "N" word."

"N" word? Ya mean nigger? Man, fuck this shit." Marcus stormed off and got into his car. He squealed his tires as he left.

"I have just one thing to say."(another fart is ripped) "Hey, it works automatically without someone having to pull my finger. It's a miracle."

Everyone laughed, and the remaining players slap hands.

"Hey, sorry about my cousin. He's from the hood-don't know better."

"Aw, don't worry about it. No problem. It's cool. No biggie."

The Wrong Number

Although he knew she would not answer the phone he wanted to call her anyway. His rational mind told him she would not pick up; there is no way she will be at the other end of the line. But his heart told him to try.

Sometimes miracles happen.

The inconsolable man reached for the bright white phone on the kitchen wall. Just as his hand touched the receiver he thought better of it and pulled away. His fingers gently rubbed his chin. With stooping shoulders he trudged to his bedroom. Better to just get on with the day as he done every day since he last saw her. Better to just be numb all day. *Time heals all wounds. Isn't that what they say?* He lay on his wrinkled bed for a few minutes before deciding to cook some eggs. The way she taught him to cook eggs.

After breakfast he cleaned up a little. Not every-thing, just a little. Living alone there wasn't much to pick up. She had taught him to keep things in order. He did. Put things back where you found them, she would always say. Cleanliness is next to Godliness. He moved into the kitchen where the telephone stood out like a light house on a cloudy beach. The glowing white case beckoned through his pain—*"Reach for me. If you dial her number you will at least hear her voice."* He stopped and just looked at the phone like a dispas-sionate neighbor watching a burglar breaking in next door. A few long minutes later, he sat down his chair and opened a book. Out of the corner of his eye he could see past the living room door and into the kitchen. The phone was still there.

Stop torturing yourself, his mind ordered.

The man flipped a few pages until he realized, although he had read the words, they had not caught. Like rubbing a piece of paper over Velcro, nothing stuck. He wandered through the next few pages and, upon reflection, could not recall a single word that he had read. He threw the book against the wall, hitting her picture, it fell and the glass shattered. Through shards of glass she gazed up at him. She was younger then. He placed his face in his hands and wept.

After cleaning up his mess and putting it in the cardboard box (like she had showed him so that the slivers wouldn't poke through the plastic bag when he took out the trash) he carried it to the bin. On the way out he looked for his keys. They were above the phone on the key ring. He walked to the cabinet. *Put one hand on the knob and the other hand the phone.* He released one and picked up the phone.

He dialed her number. The phone rang. The little buzzing sound protested twice. He waited for the message machine. Just to hear her voice at this point in time would be enough. Two more rings and the message machine would pick up. He would listen to her voice as he had done many times since he last saw her. His ritual was interrupted by a female voice.

"Hello."

"Hello?"

The man looked at the phone as if it had turned into a dead snake. He was aghast - there was someone on the other end of this line. He placed the phone down and backed away. He stared at it, waiting for it to leap up and wrap its cord around his neck like in one of those late night science fiction movies. How could she answer? *She was gone.* He could hear the soft tinny voice emanating from the white phone with a braided cord.

"Hello? Hello? Is someone there? John, is that you?"

The man stood motionless listening to the voice.

"Hello? John? John?"

He moved towards the phone. The room blurred the floor; an inconsequential counter bumped his hip. All he could see in his world was that white object less than a foot away, emitting a tiny voice, a voice of hope coming from some little holes at one end. He reached down. Seeing his own hand enter his field of view as if he were watching through a movie camera startled him. Slowly, and with great apprehension, he picked up the object.

"Hello?"

"Yes, hello. Who is this?"

"You called me. Who is *this*?"

The young man thought it sounded like her, yet the voice was a tad bellicose, more lively, rejuvenated almost. He had not felt that liveliness in her during the last few months before she left. After hope was gone, her voice fell lifeless. The man cascaded through emotions from anger to sadness, helplessness to absolute power. How could she be on the other end when he knew she was gone?

"Rob."

"Rob, who? I'm sorry I don't know anyone named Rob."

Then it hit him. He had dialed the wrong number. He had made a mistake. Relief swept over him like an ocean wave floating in off of a rocky bottom. The coldness stung his feet and he was pulled into a sea of weightlessness and ecstasy.

"Is this 704 992-6851?"

"Yes, it is as a matter fact. That is my number. My new number."

The voice sounded so much like her. But yet, the hopelessness was not there. There was an optimism embedded in her question. And there was something else, an accent or a dialect of some kind. He could not place it. *Was it Southern?*

"Who are you trying to reach?"

"Who is this?"

"John, is this you?"

"John? No, my name is Norm. I'm sorry, I'm not John."

He heard on sobbing on the other end. Before he could respond she spoke.

"John was my son. He sounds so much like you."

The man thought about hanging up the phone. Someone had taken her number. She was gone for good now. There would be no more voicemail message to listen to after the third ring. He would never hear her voice again. Near the cradle the tinny voice spoke.

"Norm, are you okay?"

It sounded less like her. This is just some cruel joke. She was playing one of her pranks. Even as a child he used to delight in watching her pull her pranks. He can remember in grade school opening up his lunch box. She had put a rubber lizard in there attached to a string. It flew out when he opened it. He smiled and snuggled the phone to his ear.

"No, I mean yes, I am okay? Who was John?"

"John is my son. He was killed in a car crash last year. He was always on me to get a phone. I never needed one. I guess I'm just old-fashioned, what they call old-school. Now I have a phone. Who were you calling?"

"My mother. She died four months ago. This was her number. I listened to the voice mail message when I missed her most."

"I can tell that you miss her a lot. You sound like you were a good son."

"Thanks. And yes, I do miss her. You sound like a good mother. You must miss him too."

"Yes. Yes, I do. Can I ask you a question?"

"Sure, go ahead."

"What do you do?"

"I'm a teacher at East Edgewood Middle School."

"The White School?"

Then it hit him. She was black, she had a slight hint of African American dialect.

"I guess you can call it that."

"You sound like you are white."

"Does that matter?"

There was a long silence as the two lonely individuals contemplated their pain and loneliness. And then he decided to allay the question.

"Can I ask your name?"

"Gladys."

"Gladys?"

"Yes, Norman?"

"Can I call you again? You know, just to talk?"

"Sure, I would like that."

"Then it doesn't matter if I am white?"

"As long as it doesn't matter that I am not."

The Revenge of Raquan Watkins

Blood trickled down the valley created by his broken nose and swollen cheek. He attempted to stand but the duct tape held fast. His wrists and his forearms were tightly secured to the arms of the chair. His ankles, which were taped to the rusting legs of the tubular metal seat, burned as the sharp edges of the tape cut into his skin. A thick ribbon of tape ran around his waist and circled the back of the chair. Under his arms a taut loop of tape circled his chest four times. Dave Bridges sat in the only chair in the room and breathed in the freshly sprayed insecticide (that barely masked the odor of wet dog). The last thing he remembered was…

He opened his eyes, one of them anyway. The other was so swollen he could not open it. The light flew through his exposed pupil and flooded his retina. It took him a minute to focus. He was in an abandoned mobile home. But why? The back door and some of the windows had been nailed shut. Someone was very serious about keeping him here today. The room was bare of furniture, save the odd box, or length of wood. Beer cans nestled in one corner under a rain stained wall. The boarded windows were covered with scraps of cardboard (except for the one above the tarnished kitchen sink which had flattened Budweiser twelve pack cartons taped over it). How did I get into an abandoned mobile home? Then the toilet flushed.

Wiping his feet as he left the bathroom was Raquan Watkins. He walked with the same brash demeanor as he had in middle school. That was ten years, and thirty pounds, ago. Raquan had put on as much weight as Bridges had.

"Damn thing still flushes."

As Raquan swaggered toward his former Assistant Principal, Dave Bridges could see that Raquan had a cut off broom stick in his hand. The round end had been wrapped with duct tape for a make shift handle. The cut off part (or what Raquan's dad called "the business end") was splintered. Watkins raised the stick and Dave leaned away from it as far as he could under the constraints of the tape. Raquan smiled as he slowly lowered the stick. He wanted the man taped to the seat to know who was in control. It's going to be a long day.

"So Mr. Wonderful, Mr. A-hole A. P...uh, sir. Remember me? Raquan leered sarcastically, inches from Bridges' brutalized face.

"Yes, Raquan. I do. I remember you."

In his clouded mind he spoke, yet only a muted sound buzzed inside his mouth. The tape on his lips allowed only a mumbling pathetic vibration of duct tape resonance. The echo of Raquan's decade old threats bounced into Bridges' head. Raquan struck Bridges across the face with his hand.

"Ten years, bitch. Ten years I done waited for this." Raquan swung the stick across Bridges' shoulders and glancing off his neck, slashed the tender flesh near his jugular. The stick flew, again and again, onto Dave's shoulders, tearing through his shirt and lacerating his skin. Dave Bridges bucked in the chair as his scream was muted by the tape.

"You like that? That's what my daddy did to me when you got me suspended. Except it was more like this, ya bastard!" Raquan rained the stick harder and faster. Restrained cries of agony ballooned the front of the tape. Raquan slammed his heel on Bridges' toes. Another stifled cry of pain. His fury building, Raquan faced Dave and kicked him mercilessly in the shins, dancing an improvised Irish jig with each kick. Each deadened howl of pain delighted Raquan as he tormented his former Assistant Principal. This inventive pain allocation continued, with pauses for verbal taunts, for the next twenty minutes. A kick, hair yanked, a slap across the ear, and the stick. Always the stick. Winded, Raquan dropped the broom handle and lit a cigarette.

"Remember the time you got me suspended me for smoking, faggot?"

As Raquan ripped the tape off Bridges' dried mouth thin slivers of skin tore off from Dave's lips and were replaced by lines of blood. His head throbbing, the welts and tears from the stick burning, Bridges spoke through heaving breaths.

"Please...Raquan ...why are you doing... what was going on ...the school... oh, please... let me go."

"I bet ya don't even remember coming here this morning, do ya?" Bridges recalled walking to his truck, lunch in hand, like he did every day. Then he woke up here.

"Yeah, I came from the side of your house, then wacked ya in the face with your own bat. Then I stuck this here chloro foam rag in your face. Your danged eye swolled up like a frickin' water balloon. How do ya like my tape job?" Raquan made a fist and punched the back of Bridges' head. "Huh, how do ya like it? My dad used to tape me to that very chair before he took this stick, this same danged stick…" Raquan whipped Bridges across the thigh. "…to me." The front door opened, flooding the room with the morning sunshine. Bridges called for help as a thin pale woman walked in. Then he stopped.

It was Darlene Dubois. Oh, God. Not her.

"Go ahead", Raquan yelled, "Nobody can hear you. They didn't hear me when I got it." Raquan bawled mockingly. "Aah. Aaagh! Help! Help! That no good Raquan Watkins is gonna beat me to death with a stick! Help!"

Darlene quickly shut the door and threw her hands up.

"Shut him up! Why'd ya let him loose? Someone's gonna hear him." She picked up one of the leftover rolls of duct tape and ripped off a foot long piece. Darlene held the tape over Bridges' lips as the older man protested.

"Please Darlene, don't…"

"Oh, you remember me? I thought you woulda just plum forgot ol' Darlene Dubois, the stupid girl in the Special Education class. Hi, Mr. Bridges." She turned to Raquan. "Jesus, what didja hit him with?"

"A baseball bat."

She moved toward Bridges again. He shook his head to avoid the tape and yelled for his life. Raquan held him by the hair while Darlene taped his mouth.

"You missed it, girl. I just gave ol' Bridges a good whuppin' wid the stick. Like this." The stick slammed square against Bridges' back. Bridges howled as Raquan skipped around to the front of Bridges. Raquan smiled in Bridges' face and then whipped his captive across the thighs. Bridges violent attempt to rock free tipped over the chair. His nose was thrust into the urine stained carpet; up close Dave noticed that the dog hairs may just outnumber the carpet fibers. Something was crawling on the rug. Were those fire ants? Raquan thrashed Bridges' left side until Darlene protested.

"Okay, Raquan...Raquan, that's enough." She felt bad for the older man as he writhed helpless on the grime matted rug. Raquan thrashed at him like an orphan breaking open a pinata. Exhausted, Raquan quit. He was out of breath again.

"I'm going to get some beer. You watch this old bastard while I'm gone."

"You cain't. I tried before I got here. They won't sell no alcohol until eleven o'clock."

"What? Oh, shut up... Damn."

Raquan went to the sink. When he turned on the water a rusty liquid sprayed onto his faded blue jeans. He jumped back to avoid the spray, tearing his pants when the zipper cover hooked the edge of a protruding nail.

"God damn it. I just got these britches." His yellowed underwear was exposed.

"Ooh, baby, now I can see everything." Darlene chuckled uneasily in an attempt to lighten Raquan's mood. She had known Raquan since they were kids. Her momma did not like blacks, she warned her to stay away from him – her momma swore that Raquan would be the death of her. Raquan glared at her.

"What the hell am I going to do now? There ain't nothing left in this frickin' house. I can't go out like this."

"What about…" Darlene looked at the middle aged heaving sack of moaning human flesh on the floor by her feet. She nodded at Dave Bridges. Raquan laughed in acknowledgment.

"Get them pants off, boy. Get 'em right off." Bridges looked up like a pathetic dog that had been run over and was awaiting the hasty death blow from the callous driver. He whined as Raquan wrenched a knife from his tight pocket. Bridges screamed frantically into the tape; red faced, he moved the chair a few inches in his desperate attempt to get away. Raquan put his foot on the chair, and in one swift motion, slid the chair into a half circle. He bent down and glared into Bridges' battered face.

"You look like the damn Elephant man. Remember that one Darlene? From the movie?"

"Yeah, you did him just like you said you would. Now cut him loose and let's go."

"Sheeit. I ain't cuttin' no one loose. I'm just getting started." Bridges shook spasmodically on the floor, frenziedly trying to get loose as the knife approached his crotch.

"Settle down old man. I ain't gonna cut ya. I just need your drawers."

Raquan cut the tape away from Bridges' pant legs, then dropped to his knees and unraveled the tape. Bridges felt endorphin relief as the blood flowed into his numbed lower legs. Raquan slid the knife between the tight tape on Bridges' thighs, with the tip pointed right at his groin, Bridges shrieked against the tape.

"Quit yer whining. I ain't gonna touch nothing up there."

Darlene laughed nervously. She was not comfortable with this whole scene. Raquan was acting like a maniac. God, she wished she had some weed. That always calmed him down. When she first agreed to help him out, like get him the chloroform from her sister's job, and be his lookout, he just seemed like he wanted to scare Bridges. Now he looked like he was…

"Darlene, do what you're good at and take his pants off."

"What? Ok, okay. Undo his shoes and take them off first."

"See? She knows exactly how to do it."

Raquan grimaced and untied the older man's shoes, yanking them off and hurling them into Bridges' face one at a time.

"C'mon Raquan, you done him enough. Let him go. He won't bother wid ya no more."

"Get his pants off right God damn now, Darlene."

Raquan picked up the stick from the corner. "I done told ya twice. Now unless you want some of this, ya better get me his drawers." Darlene undid the man's belt amid Dave's bug-eyed whimpering.

"I think he likes it. Look at his fat ass wiggling."

Darlene smiled and removed Bridges' belt, throwing it on the floor. Raquan picked it up and whipped it across Bridges' temple. Bridges whimpered in resignation, then sobbed as much as the tape would allow. Darlene pulled his pants down, grabbed the cuffs and yanked them over his ankles. She noticed that Dave's thighs had purple welts where the stick had met the skin. She threw the pants to Raquan. He pulled off his torn trousers and replaced them with Bridges' pants.

"Quit yer crying old man. Hey, these fit nice. Well lookie here- keys. And money!"

Raquan opened Bridges' wallet and whistled.

"Thirty-two bucks. Damn...Darlene. Can you watch him for a couple of hours? First, I gotta stop and get some weed from Germaine. By then it will be eleven and I can get the beer. Then...oh ho...then we'll have some fun!" He pulled Darlene close and whispered in her ear. "You are in on this too. Don't you dare let him go." Darlene exhaled despondently, and then stole a surreptitious glance at Bridges. *Raquan is going to kill him.*

The sunbeams danced through the room as Raquan left. Bridges twisted his bruised neck and looked up at Darlene. The white of his thighs striped with welts created a contrast of skin color. Purple bruises and white pasty skin. She avoided his eye. Outside, they heard Raquan peel out of the driveway in Bridges' truck, shooting gravel against the side of the house. Bridges forced a few muted protests to Darlene through the tape. Then there was a prolonged stillness as their eyes met- two to one and gazed at each other. Darlene gave in first.

"You should never have got him riled." Bridges rocked the chair, pinching his leg between the floor and the metal. Searing pain shot through his thigh. He screamed into the tape.

"What?" She threw up her hands. "What the hell do you want?"

Darlene squatted and ripped the tape off his mouth. The blood slivers returned.

"Thanks. Oh, God, please Darlene. Please. You know he's going to kill me... I have children..."

"No, he ain't. He just wants to scare ya. Ya know ya deserve it. You're the damn reason that Raquan's life's done been ruined…"

"Darlene, I'm not even an Assistant Principal at Martin Luther King Middle any more. I hated it. Suspending kids, arguing with the parents and teachers all day... I moved to another school a couple of years after you left. I have been there for years. Please, you don't know anything about me."

"Yes, I do. You're Mister Bridges the asshole Assistant Principal. Everyone was scared of..."

"That was the job! If it wasn't me it would have been someone..."

"Shut up. Just shut up." Darlene held up the tape. "Just be quiet. Stop talking. Stop dang talking!"

"Please, oh God… you know he's gonna kill me. Look at my face, Jesus…I am bleeding everywhere. I think he broke my nose. He won't turn me loose like this because he can't turn me loose like this. You know it, please Darlene let me go. Oh, c'mon…God…no!"

Darlene slapped the tape over Bridges' mouth. It stung his torn lips. He had had enough pain for one day. He yelped a muffled objection and tried to communicate to Darlene with his good eye.

Did you know my wife can't stand me? That I dilute her disdain each night with a pint of vodka? That you might be doing me a favor if you kill me? Just make it painless. Please. Did you know that I hated suspending kids? And putting up with the teacher's lies? How can you let him kill me if you don't even know me?

Five miles away, Raquan flipped the gearshift into fifth gear. He picked up speed until the truck was bouncing at every bump and gliding up at every swell in the road. He was going too fast to keep the little red truck from crossing the lane divider line as he whipped around the sharp corner just before the middle school. His forward vision was occluded by overgrown bushes and trees; Raquan could not see the gasoline tanker stopped in the road ahead. The red truck was flying along at eighty five miles an hour as it rounded the corner.

Eighty five miles an hour.

Panicking when he saw the truck in the road, Raquan slammed on the brakes. But there were only forty yards between him and the truck. He could have stopped in sixty yards, but at forty he slid under the tanker, sparks and metal flying. Everything appeared to stand still after the horrific metal on metal union.

For a second the dust looked like it was going to settle. Raquan, jammed under the tanker, raised his head a few inches. The truck, with its top twisted off and its chassis wedged under the tanker, was still. Raquan looked through bloodied eyes. Puzzled, he shook his head and inhaled misty gasoline.

Then it exploded.

Raquan's face was sheared off by the initial blast. When the tanker detonated it charcoaled everything down to the front seat of the truck. The truck's gasoline tank, oddly enough, did not erupt. The top half of the body in the truck was incinerated leaving burnt negligible flesh on blackened bone. A black cloud bellowed into the sky.

Most of the tanker's fuel burned off in the first few minutes. The fire blazed hot and fast as was the case with gasoline fires. It was fifteen minutes before the fire trucks appeared and sprayed their foam onto the twisted aluminum tanker that appeared to be giving birth to a black and red hybrid of itself. The body inside the red truck was pulled from the wreckage, bagged and transported into town - destination morgue.

Incinerated beyond recognition; all that remained were Bridges' trousers, Bridges' wallet and Raquan's shoes. These items identified Raquan's body as Dave Bridges, local Assistant Principal. There was no question. He drove that road to school each day. Rumor had it that Bridges drove fast. On this day Dave had the bad luck of running into a gasoline truck that had jackknifed on a blind curve. Done deal.

Bridges' wife was notified of the accident, the truck identified by the license plate (once the soot had been wiped off), the wallet (complete with driver's license and insurance card), and the new pants that his wife had "just bought him for his birthday". As far as his wife knew, Dave's gruesomely scorched body lay in a chilly morgue, the torso resembling burnt chicken wings that had been left too long on the grill. Charred meat. Destroyed flesh. She awoke in the middle of the night. Guilt? Or was it relief?

The mortician did not have the heart to ask her if the name "Darlene" that was tattooed above his pubic area was an ex-girlfriend. He let it go, filled out the death certificate and then signed it. Period, and thank you. He had to get home for dinner. Dave Bridges family received word throughout the night and made plans to travel from all over North Carolina to grieve for him.

Four hours after the accident there were still two people in an abandoned mobile home in an abandoned trailer park. Darlene paced the room. Raquan had been gone too long. She spoke aloud to herself and incidentally to the condemned man next to her.

"Where the hell is he?"

Bridges had loosened the reapplied tape on his leg. He knew about duct tape. It wasn't as sticky once you undid it. Raquan would have been better to use new tape. He sure had enough of it. Releasing one leg would do no good-but what else did he have? Darlene ripped the tape from Bridges' mouth. He sounded like a broken record. Unable to break through the role of teacher, he had run out of things to say.

"Please, Darlene, let me go before Raquan comes back and kills me." She remembered how she once feared this sunken man; but that was before he had lost his hair and gained so much weight. Darlene tramped to the bedroom. Raquan had a cot and a pile of tattered blankets under his worn sleeping bag. Shaking, Darlene jammed her hand in pocket and struggled to remove a handful of pills. She popped a Xanax, and some other pill Raquan said was a painkiller. She tucked her pocket back, shoved the other pills in it, and lay down.

The sun rose. Again. Bridges awoke as he had several times during the insect dominated night. Darlene emerged, tired eyed and bushy haired, from the bedroom. Bridges was still tied to the chair. No Raquan. Darlene spoke Dave's mind.

"Where is he?"

The burning in Dave's throat delayed the realization that he could barely swallow. It had been two days since he had drank anything- Raquan clubbed him before he could drink his coffee. He floated in a dehydrated delirium. The pain in his throat; and his biological knowledge told him one thing. *I must have water.* Darlene returned from the bedroom pushing a large blue cooler with her foot. A step, a push. Regroup and do it again. Bridges tried to clear his throat. He could not. And the tape did not help. She looked at him, the blue cooler and then back at Bridges.

"You must be thirsty." Dave nodded his head weakly. She reached back, opened the cooler and pulled a cold can of grape soda from the watery clear ice. She placed it on the floor by the door.

"I don't know what happened to Raquan. But I'm fixing to let ya go. But I swear I'll kill ya if ya come near me. Don't move until I am gone."

Darlene slid a kitchen knife from her back pocket(she had slept with it) and cut the tape off his wrist. As she yanked the tape from his mouth Dave released an insane laugh. Puzzled by this outburst, Darlene ran through the open door.

"Goodbye, Mr. Bridges."

Bridges struggled in the chair. He looked like a Tyrannasaurus Rex as he reached for his other arm but fell short by inches. He heard a vehicle and screamed past the tape still attached to his cheek. Yet he made only a hoarse exhalation. Water is needed to vibrate the cords; and he had none. Dry vocal cords produce no sound. His throat burned in protest. As a former science teacher he knew the consequences of dehydration. His system was shutting down. Kidneys would be first. He held back dry tears. *I refuse to die here*. Mustering his energy Dave wrestled the chair onto its back. Once again he swung his free forearm wildly. He felt the tape roll into a rope around his elbow. He made the tape, once easy tear, now into a rope that even a sharp knife would have a hard time shearing. Out of the corner of an eye he spied fire ants.

Fire ants!

The first one bit him five minutes later. And then it suddenly it felt like the whole colony was in his nose and mouth. In their ant language they relayed a simple message. We have prey. This aroused the sentient soldiers chewing on stale crumbs in the rug. Human flesh was a delicacy to these persistent insects. He blew hard through his nose and phewed ant bodies out of his mouth. Dave moved up and down, serpentine fashion, to get away as far as his drained, desiccated body would allow him. He stopped and rubbed his nose and mouth on the filthy carpet. No sooner did he feel some relief when they attacked again. He gyrated his body up and down for a second time; and once again he got away, just not as far this time. Soon they were back. Their pincers injected formic acid into his body like a hundred miniature syringes. He knew that the ants would not stop pursuing him. He had actually taught a science lesson on South American fire ants. They had colonies in the tens of thousands. They were capable of killing a cow. Through his pain Dave managed a weak smile.

Raquan Watkins would be cheated of his revenge.

In a few minutes their venom would send his body into anaphylactic shock. Inundating a dehydrated human with formic acid exacerbated the effects of the poison as each cell was pulling in as much liquid as possible. Soon, he would be unable to move away. Then they would feast. If only I had seen Raquan in my yard I could have fought like a man. Now I am going to die like a run over possum on the side of the road. Who will find my body? How long before it is found? Weeks? Months? Longer? Oh, God I am going to die. In less than an hour I will be gone. My dreams, my goals, my children's father... No more. The ants covered his face. And then the door swung open.

It was Darlene. And she still had the kitchen knife.

Darlene walked straight at Dave. He rubbed stinging ants off his face into the carpet before he looked at her. The remaining ants continued to bite. He readied himself for the hot blade, wondering how long it would take to die (and if he could possibly feel any more pain). She slid the knife under the rolled tape on his arm, cutting the rope-like structure. His arm freed, Dave pulled the tape from his mouth. He squeaked as he swung weakly at Darlene. She dropped the knife and ran out the open door again like a strange déjà vu. Bridges removed the rest of the tape. The blood flowed to the formerly restricted parts as Bridges crawled to the grape soda and clutched the metal pop top. The ants kept biting and he kept swatting them. He could not harness, nor focus, the energy to pop open the resistant metal. He pried and snapped but it refused to open. Dave stumbled to the cooler, cupped his hands and drank the cool, icy water. He alternated between drinking and splashing his face with the energizing liquid.

Shoeless, bruised, and without pants, Dave Bridges stepped outside slapping from his back and ankles at the voracious ants. He sauntered like a lame gorilla down the driveway as the sharp gravel jabbed his feet. The smooth asphalt of the road welcomed him as he headed toward town.

Bridges' relatives had driven from all over North Carolina as soon as they heard of the tragedy. Most were local but some had come from as far away as Raleigh. No one rented hotel rooms. Cheaper just to wait for someone to invite you to stay at their house. The widow was dressed in navy blue, her feelings ambivalent while she expressed shock and grief. Everyone brought a dish (as was the custom). Some of the older people had become used to funerals and the family bonding it brought. They spoke of Dave as if they saw him yesterday. Dave was a good man. He had done well in the small town known for its high unemployment. He worked in the schools for years. Stories of his dedication to family and friends worked the room. Twenty-six friends and relatives from seven to seventy-eight years old milled, or sat, around the Bridges house. They consoled the distraught widow and rubbed the shoulders of the crying children.

Then the front door opened.

Other Books by Patrick O'Cahir

The Leader of the Lost People
The Drinking Man's Guide to Women (and Divorce)

Available at
www.a-argusbooks.com
or
amazon.com
or
barnesandnoble.com
or
order at your favorite bookstore.

Made in the USA
Lexington, KY
08 June 2014